D1017380

Starlings

Starlings

AMANDA LINSMEIER

Delacorte Press

Text copyright © 2023 by Amanda Linsmeier
Jacket art copyright © 2023 by Colin Verdi

Visit us on the Web! GetUnderlined.com
Educators and librarians, for a variety of teaching tools, visit us at RHTeachersLibrarians.com

Library of Congress Cataloging-in-Publication Data
Names: Linsmeier, Amanda, author.
Title: Starlings / Amanda Linsmeier.
Description: First edition. | New York : Delacorte Press, [2023] | Audience: Ages 14+. |
Summary: When seventeen-year-old Kit visits her father's hometown for the first time following his death, she discovers not only that her family is strangely revered among the locals, but that she also has an important role in the town's future.
Identifiers: LCCN 2022037934 (print) | LCCN 2022037935 (ebook) |
ISBN 978-0-593-57233-7 (hardcover) | ISBN 978-0-593-57234-4 (library binding) |
ISBN 978-0-593-57235-1 (ebook)
Subjects: CYAC: Families—Fiction. | Secrets—Fiction. | Cities and towns—Fiction. |
Fantasy. | LCGFT: Fantasy fiction. | Novels.
Classification: LCC PZ7.1.L5645 St 2023 (print) | LCC PZ7.1.L5645 (ebook) |
DDC [Fic]—dc23

The text of this book is set in 11.5-point Adobe Caslon Pro.
Interior design by Michelle Crowe

Printed in the United States of America
10 9 8 7 6 5 4 3 2 1
First Edition

This story is, in part, about the immense love a daughter has for her parents. I couldn't have dedicated this book to anyone else but my own. Mama. Dad. I love you forever.

You are the mirror of my pride;
Your vast clouds in mourning
Are the black hearses of my dreams,
And your gleams are the reflection
Of the hell which delights my heart.

I adore you as much as the nocturnal vault,
O vase of sadness, most taciturn one,
I love you all the more because you flee from me.

—Charles Baudelaire, "The Flowers of Evil"

CHAPTER ONE

She was supposed to be dead.

That's the big lie I can't make sense of, and the closer we get to finally meeting her, the more nervous I become. I've traded a living father for a dead grandmother, and I still can't wrap my mind around it. But there's no time for that now.

We're almost there.

My mom taps her fingers on the steering wheel to an old song, our car sagging with fatigue after delivering us from Callins, North Dakota, to the big woods of northern Wisconsin, miles of trees as far as my eye can see. Naked oak and birch and maple, pines standing proud and full, a dusting of snow everywhere, the buttery-pink rays of early light streaming through them.

It's beautiful enough, but there's still a part of me that wouldn't want Hawaii, not even Florence or Cairo. There's a part that only wants *home*. Wants to burrow under my bed-covers and escape reality in sleep. Sometimes I want to sleep forever so I don't have to remember.

Swallowing the loss, I reach over and trace the papers tucked inside the door. A touchstone. The opening line to my dad's last book, one he never finished:

We went into the sapphire water with our pockets stuffed full of jewels.

It's embarrassing how often I say it to myself. In my head, out loud, under my breath. A good-luck charm, a mantra. An underlying question that might haunt me forever.

Why did you leave us?

And for the last couple of weeks, another thing I can't stop wondering:

Why did you lie?

Sick of the snowy landscape whirring by, I lean my head back and close my eyes, thinking of stolen gems, and two ill-fated lovers on a ship, and a pirate's rough laugh, and all the ways my dad brightened my world. My throat swells with the kind of pain that burns—sadness or rage, I sometimes can't tell which.

My thoughts take me to places I don't want to go, so I give up on thinking and open my novel to the page I dog-eared, glancing up to see a road sign.

ROSEMONT 10 MILES

"We're close." My mom's tone is light, but her shoulders are drawn up; she's escaping into herself. Anxiety is her shadow. I do what I can to help ease it, including trying never to add to it. The drive was difficult on her, but she only let me take over for a few hours. Despite the smile pulling at her lips, when she looks at me, sadness is tucked away in her gaze. I have her memorized: those eyes—the hazel of her irises, black pupils flowering in the centers—those high cheekbones, the blue floral tattoo winding up her forearm, her great laugh.

I hate that the pain in her eyes is familiar now. Resentment tugs at me. I return to the page, try concentrating on the fae lurking inside the story.

"How's the book?" she asks.

"Really good," I murmur. And it *is*. I just keep having to read the same lines over and over. Nothing is connecting in my mind. I won't be able to relax until we arrive.

God, what will she be like?

"Seems like it's taking you forever," my mom says, interrupting my thoughts.

"You could've bought your own. . . ." I flip the page; the words swim.

"Why would we need two copies?" she asks. "Isn't the best part of having the same reading taste that we can share books? We can't share shoes, you know."

"Well, you got skis for feet," I answer.

"Ohh, *hilarious*."

I snort, shut my book, trading reading for nothing.

"You okay?" Her worry pulls my attention.

I measure the expression in her eyes. Her pitched brows. Wish I'd kept reading, or at least pretended. "Yeah. I'm just nervous. You know."

"I know." She gives me a gentle smile as she turns onto a dark ribbon of a road. "She seems cool. I think we'll like her."

We pass underneath a canopy of trees politely inclining their heads above us, and drive toward a large, weathered wooden sign:

WELCOME TO ROSEMONT!

HOME OF THE ETERNAL ROSES.

ESTABLISHED 1781

POPULATION 2,089

We cross the town line as the morning light casts itself upon the sign. It's so perfectly charming, I'm surprised that shit doesn't sparkle. I face forward just as something runs in front of the car—a blur of an animal—a fox.

A cry. My mom swinging her arm against my chest instinctively, a seat belt of herself, as if I weren't already wearing one. The brakes scream as the car swerves nearly off the wet road.

I wait for the beat of my heart to settle as it dawns on me, we're fine. We're fine.

I stare out the windshield, watch the fox dart away, blow out a breath. "Shit."

Mom drops her arm and doesn't correct my language. My parents always told me there were a lot worse words than curses: slurs, things that hurt people, ways you could make someone feel less than. Those were the ones I was taught never to say.

"We're okay," she reassures me, even as her hands shake.

"We didn't hit it; it got away." We both hate seeing animals killed, bloody bodies strewn along the pavement after meeting their unlucky fates with vehicles.

"It just rattled me." Her breath comes out low and slow—one of her tricks. Sometimes it helps.

"I know we're close, but can we get out for a minute?" I don't wait for her to agree. My legs are aching; I need to move my body, and I know she'll follow. It will calm her. I slip on my shoes, and she trails me out of the car, rubbing her bare arms.

We checked out of a motel super early, only a couple of hours ago, but we both stretch when we step onto the road. She shrugs her coat on over an original Nirvana tee—she has a deep and unending love for Kurt Cobain—while I hold my phone high, trying to catch a signal. Could I will the service to be less shitty? It's been on roam for the last thirty minutes. But apparently it's part of the charm, that Rosemont feels like another time entirely.

I stick my phone into my pocket and observe our surroundings.

Even with my mom having semi-prepared me, and a cursory Google search, I didn't expect the outskirts of town to be so empty of anything but trees. They surround us, and to our right the woods are thicker, wilder, vast and unending. I'm following the line of tall trees up to the brightening sky when something catches my eye: a cloud of birds.

My mouth goes slack as they start to chatter, because of all the things . . . it had to be this?

"Mom." I point out the birds in flight, voice strained. "Starlings."

Our namesake. But even more. We watch the flock move,

growing louder, swooping in formation across the watercolor sky, diving here and there. Our eyes connect, and I can tell that her heart is pierced like mine; I know what she's thinking of, what we're both remembering now: that hot day in August. The starlings didn't dance in the air then. They perched in the branches and cried.

Our skin sticky under those black dresses, our clammy hands squeezed together, and the starlings—dozens, hundreds, maybe thousands, crying in the trees, mourning when I couldn't.

Breaking the memory, my mom steps closer to me, whispers, "A murmuration."

This is the third noteworthy time I've seen starlings. The first, when I was seven—then it was beautiful, strange. The second time at the funeral, just four months ago. And now. But in this moment, it only leaves a sick feeling in the pit of my stomach. We watch the birds until they drift out of sight. Silently we look at each other, return to the car. I click my seat belt into place. Why them? Why now?

"At least the fox is okay." Her smile is wobbly as she turns the key in the ignition, then pauses. "I think it was a fox anyway. You good?"

No! I'd like to scream. *No, no, no. I'm not good. I'll never be good again.*

I nod. "I'm fine. Let's go."

As she drives, I fiddle with the Bluetooth, the music all garbled and fuzzy. I switch to the radio, but it doesn't sound any better. With an annoyed sigh, I turn it off. Pull my messy bob back into a knot, just to have something to do with my hands, twitchy because we're here. Almost. I've replayed this meeting in my head several times, and I still don't feel prepared to meet my grandmother Agatha. Why didn't she ever reach out before? Will we like each other? Will we laugh about my dad? Cry about him? Will she tell us all the truths he couldn't?

The skeleton-like trees wave at me as we zip along the last couple of miles. The longer I stare at the woods, the more unsettled I feel, and it's not just nerves, not just the shock of the starlings, reminding me of so many things that hurt right now. It's also something unnameable, niggling at me.

Probably a trick of the light, I finally decide, the shadows fighting to survive on the cusp of day, the breeze transforming tree boughs into moving arms, the trunks wide enough to be torsos. The last of the stubborn dead leaves whirling to the ground.

Just the wind making noise, and not some haunting voice whispering my name.

How could I hear anything anyway? I tell myself. The windows are shut; it's cold out.

Active imagination, I remember in my dad's voice. *Does not pay attention in class,* I hear in my teachers' voices. *Head in the clouds, always.* My mom's affectionate whisper, threaded together with my knowing; the love for all she's done, all she keeps on doing. The way she tucks my hair behind my ears, the way she still calls me "baby" even though I'll be eighteen in a few months. We butt heads about my grades, my messy room, but I don't just love her. I like her. We are two blackbirds, connected by the wings. She's all I have left, the only one who can light up the dark and chase my nightmares away.

But if I told her all the ways I hurt, all my fears, it would drown her. And there's no way I'm letting that happen.

We zoom past the endless woods, and I can't look away from them, no longer nervous but foolishly afraid. Afraid of everything and of nothing.

Of wild animals that lurk inside the woods. Of hungry beasts, sprung out of the most twisted fairy tales. Of red eyes glowing in the night.

Wolves that wrap themselves in deceit and eat little girls.

But then I think of grandmothers, and inevitably, of mine.

How could my dad lie about his own mother being dead? He kept her from me. How could I not be hurt? *She* must be. Her letters said as much. She's waited for me my whole life.

A hand, a gentle one, fingers ink-stained blue, rests on mine. I squeeze it back and face front, away from the shadowy woods and what lies within. I push away the questions. I don't look for frightening things anymore.

Except somewhere, in the deepest recesses of my bones, I feel like they still look for me.

CHAPTER TWO

Rosemont looks like a film set, like a town from one of the old movies my dad loved. I almost expect to see Gene Kelly swinging around one of the streetlamps. We drive through the quaint streets packed with shops and restaurants, boutiques, a café, and my mom oohs and aahs at the charm of it all. I sit with my clammy hands squeezed in my lap and try to make out the names on the storefronts.

"There's a gallery," I say, pointing out a green building. "Is that the one?" Mom slows a minute, looking over her shoulder, and nods. "I think so."

That's just a perk of coming here; when Agatha wrote, she told my mom the gallery wanted to meet with her. I didn't read their letters, but I know the gist, how, two months after my dad died, Agatha reached out and dropped the bombshell that she existed.

I got one letter myself. A short one.

I cannot believe that after all this time you're finally coming to Rosemont, one line read. *I will be counting down the days. I've been waiting for you forever.*

"Oh, there's a festival!" At a stoplight, my mom smiles, leaning forward.

I peer through the windshield, following her gaze to some workmen stringing a banner between two tall light posts out ahead of us. *Crowning Day Festival,* it reads in fancy script, roses drawn on either side, then the dates—*January 1–3.*

She sighs, disappointed. We're leaving on the twenty-ninth. We'll just miss it.

On the edge of downtown she slows and announces, "This is it." She does a Y-turn and pulls up to a large building, eyeing the GPS, which she muted back in Minnesota and which I realize isn't working now anyway. She parks on the street, across from a restaurant.

I stare up at the apartment building, the brick worn with time, faded advertising lettered all along the side. It was a factory, once.

"It's neat." She sounds eager. The anxiety from before has passed, at least outwardly. She hopes—we both do—that we'll get closure here, that we'll get some insight into my dad's past before we go home and restart life. A new year and a fresh beginning. Back to school. Back to reality. Eight days to learn everything I can about a woman I should have known forever.

Eight days to find out *why, why, why.*

I pretend I'm staring in the face of some grand quest, which is why I'm hesitating, instead of feeling completely pathetic to be so nervous, worrying about awkward conversation and getting by without good Wi-Fi. Or maybe I'm just scared to find out things about my dad he would rather have kept hidden. Still, some valiant heroine I am.

We get out of the car, and my mom heads to my side on the curb, slinging her faded leather tote over one shoulder. "We'll come back for the big stuff later."

With a nod, I grab my coat and my bag, packed with essentials: a journal and matching pen in the colors of the bi pride flag; a couple of books; my phone charger; lip balm; gum; a smooth palm stone; a strip of lavender velvet too impractical to be considered a scarf, but that I wear anyway; an antique photo of a girl holding a bouquet. Of course, my dad's pages as well. Those I'd tuck into my heart if I could.

The winter wind teases our hair as we walk up the path to the building, and I take a long, deep breath, for courage. Or hope.

The entrance door opens with a creaking groan, and we enter a foyer with metal mailboxes, rows of buzzers above them. It all feels luxuriously retro, the brass nameplates shining in the light from a green enamel pendant lamp overhead.

As my mom studies the nameplates, the interior door opens, and a man wearing expensive-looking workout gear practically skips out of it, eyes bright in his pale face.

"Hi there." His sunny grin spreads as he nears us, gaze lingering on her. "You visiting? Can I help you find someone?"

"I can't make out some of these smudged names," she answers. "I'm looking for Agatha Starling?"

"Starling?" The man's expression is filled with delight as he says our name. His eyes move to me, and it's almost like there's a strange spark of recognition. His smile widens, stretching his lips thin. A ventriloquist's dummy. "You're her family. You're the Starlings."

Our name in his mouth, his leering expression, it makes my skin crawl. My mom clears her throat, and the man snaps out of it, glancing back at her.

"Sorry, she's number nineteen." He points, flushing.

"Thanks," she answers flatly, pulling me closer and pressing the buzzer.

He mumbles an awkward "Have a nice day" and jogs out the door, looking back at us as he hits the sidewalk. Looking at *me*. Once. Twice. Three fucking times.

"That was a little weird, that creep," she says, and I silently agree as she adds, "But it's a small town; everyone knows who everyone is. I'm sure they all know Dad's books."

The reference stings. We don't talk about him often; it still hurts too much. But it makes sense. I'm used to book nerds fawning over him, and everyone knows that small towns gossip. Agatha must've been talking about our visit, about the family of her famous author son. She's probably so excited. In fact, I know she is. *Counting down the days.*

There's no answer on the intercom, but a loud buzz fills the space, allowing us entry into a narrow hall that leads to an even narrower staircase, its wooden railing gleaming. An elevator with shiny metal doors stands opposite it.

"Wanna walk up?" She knows I don't love confined spaces.

"Yeah," I answer, even though my legs are tired. They're not just tired. They ache, like I ran a marathon or something. I shake off the discomfort and stubbornly stride up the steps.

When we reach the top floor—the fifth—we pause at number nineteen.

"Ready, love?" she asks, searching my face.

I let out a quick breath. "Ready."

She raps on the door, her modest diamond glinting in the light. My throat clenches at the sight of it. I don't know if I will ever stop hurting.

The door swings open, revealing a woman standing on the other side, blond hair pulled into a twist at her neck. She wears an oversized, crisp white blouse and trousers. Flat leather mules on her feet. Hands manicured and blue-veined, one giant black stone on her ring finger. A solemn look on her beautifully angled, minimally lined ivory face. Nothing about her is faded or soft. She doesn't look like the kind of grandma who bakes cookies.

"Oh my, Sally?" Reaching out, she takes my mom's hand before pulling her in for a brief embrace. "It's wonderful to meet you."

"And you. Thank you for having us," my mom says sincerely.

The woman looks upon me, eyes the same shade as my dad's. Does she see him in me, too? I'm suddenly ultra-aware of my baggy sweats and well-worn hoodie, the tendrils of dirty-blond that slipped from the knot to hang in my face, the smudge of eyeliner probably under my lashes. I try not to fidget, forcing my lips up at the corners as far as they'll go. Should I hug her? Will she hug me?

"Hello, Katherine," she says with a small smile.

"Hi," I answer, sounding nervous even to my own ears. "It's Kit, actually."

"Forgive me, I knew that. I'm Agatha." She reaches out. "It's lovely to finally meet you. Please, come in."

Her hand is sure as we shake, and I relax at the feel of her cool palm against my own as I smile back at her.

I follow them both into the apartment, which is large and open, loft-style, brick pillars holding the ceiling up. I take it all in, in snapshots: crystal candlesticks; bookshelves stuffed full; snowy white orchids in chipped pots; art in skinny, gold frames; sofa upholstered in a red-and-pink floral print, throw tossed over the back, a pair of creamy-white chairs opposite it; tassels on the silk curtains; faded Turkish rug; the smell of bergamot, which my mom diffuses at home. It's a pretty room, though there's no Christmas tree, nothing festive, which is fine by me. I'm not feeling very merry these days.

"I hope you don't mind sharing the guest room." Agatha turns to face us. "I never have company, so I chose a two-bedroom. It's easier for me to take care of, being alone."

She doesn't sound sad when she says it—more matter-of-fact—but I can't help feeling a stab of pity. All my relatives on this side of the family are dead, and not just extended family— her husband and both kids, including my dad. She must miss him, doesn't she? Doesn't the whole world? Sometimes when it rains, I imagine it as the earth crying for him.

"It's perfect, but are you sure it isn't a bother?" my mom asks. "The inn had rooms."

Agatha shakes her head a fraction. "I told you, that's for

tourists. You're family." Her words are directed to us both, but her eyes are only on me. Blue, blue, like my dad, blue. This here—her—is my last link to him, isn't it?

A war rumbles within my heart, anger and grief bloodying each other. They rage their battle on the grounds of confusion. I study Agatha silently, like I can figure things out just by looking at her carefully enough.

With a graceful about-face, she moves to one of the overstuffed chairs. "Come sit, and we can talk awhile and have a cup of tea, if you'd like." She motions to the coffee table, where a silver tray with teapot and cups, scones, and little sandwiches rests beside a huge vase of obscenely perfect bone-colored roses.

I sit on her chair's mate, sinking into its softness while my mom takes a spot on the couch.

Tipping her head toward the kitchen behind her, all white and shiny, Agatha says, "Or if you'd rather, something else? I don't cook much, but I can manage eggs and toast."

"Oh, no, this is great," my mom says, and accepts the tea Agatha offers.

I take some as well, warming my fingers against the cup.

"I'm afraid I didn't do much stocking up for your visit, yet," Agatha says, "but I'll have groceries delivered later." Fixing her eyes on me, she goes on, "I thought this afternoon we might all do some sightseeing, and you can get to know Rosemont . . . and me."

A thread stretches between us, shimmering with optimism. I find my voice, almost shyly. "Sure."

"Good." She settles happily in her chair, fingers wrapped around the handle of her delicate cup. The big, beetle-black ring glitters in the light. What would it have been like, having her as a grandma as a little girl? My mom's parents both escaped to the Florida heat decades ago, and I barely know them. I picture Agatha running her cool hands through my hair. Being a part of my life instead of being hidden from me.

And then there's my grandpa. My dad left everyone. Was he ashamed of them for some reason? Angry? Or just lost, finding his way into a new life that left no room for his old one? I imagine packing up my bags and leaving my mom forever.

Never.

"I'm very excited to get to know you, Kit," Agatha says, and time pauses as we share a long look. She seems to remember my mom after a second, and adds, shifting her gaze to her, "And you, of course. I've loved our letters. Although, I'm certain we could have gotten to share more if I had easier ways to communicate, like one of those cellular telephones."

I hold back a laugh at her old-fashioned terminology. She warned my mom about those things in her letters—that Rosemont struggles with terrible service due in part to all the trees in this rural area, and most people don't even have a computer in the house, let alone cell phones.

She adds, "Still, there's something quaint about letter-writing, isn't there? Sally, cake?"

"Oh, no thank you." My mom politely turns down the slice of pound cake Agatha offers.

"Thanks," I say as I take one, and the first bite practically melts in my mouth, a processed medley of lemon and sugar and butter—delicious, and definitely store-bought.

"You're welcome. You're a senior, yes?" Agatha asks me. When I nod—mouth full—she smiles and continues, "Then you're graduating in the spring. Though, your mother mentioned that you aren't sure of your plans after."

I swallow, my fork midair. "I want to be a writer," I say.

Like Dad. I leave it unspoken, but the words rest on the air, floating above us, and I know we're all thinking the same thing: he left here and never returned. Never spoke of Agatha or anyone else, other than to tell me and my mom they were all dead.

Yet her face is understanding when she murmurs, "He told me you might be a writer."

My mom and I glance at each other, holding our breath together before turning back to her.

"He wrote me, only once," Agatha says, "but he mentioned you. I've known about you for years. So you can imagine how much I value having you here before me. I only wish it weren't too late to see your father."

We all sit with that somberly. He *should* be here with us, on the couch next to my mom, hand on her knee, cake in his other hand. But he didn't want to be here. Not just in Rosemont.

Here. On this earth.

"More tea?" Agatha gently breaks the tension. "Sally?"

"I'm good for now, thanks," she answers, then gestures to the vase on the coffee table. "Those roses are beautiful, by the way. Are they the ones that are sort of famous?" Famous for Rosemont, anyway. Meaning a couple of online sites mentioned the natural phenomenon.

"Oh yes." Sipping her tea, Agatha gazes at the flowers

adoringly. "These are but a small preview of how fantastic the eternal roses are. I'm eager to show them to you both later this week, perhaps."

I appreciate her enthusiasm, but I don't really care about tourist attractions, not unless they involve my dad's life here. What I want to say is: *Show me what he loved. Show me where I can find him still.*

"And you have a festival coming up?" my mom asks. "We saw a sign on the way in."

"Yes," Agatha says. "It's such a special event for us. Rosemont is very excited for it."

"What's it for?" I ask, then guess, "The roses?"

"Yes, mainly to celebrate the bounty of our roses, the gifts they give us."

"I'm sorry we'll miss it," my mom answers wistfully. "I love festivals." And there were never truer words spoken. I can't count the number of festivals we've gone to over the years—cranberry and strawberry, sunflower and prairie rose, music fests, celebrations of heritages.

"I'm sorry, too." Agatha draws her eyes to look at me. My smile is regretful. I would have liked to go, too. She continues, "But today I'd like to bring you to my favorite place, my old home. It's a museum now, Starling House."

I raise a brow. "It's called 'Starling House'? What kind of museum is it?"

Her eyes flicker like a flame, brightly. "They call it a 'gem of historical importance,'" she quotes with pride. "We were one of the early families, and many of the original features of the house were maintained or restored, but I want to share it with you, Kit, as it's more than Rosemont history. It's *your* history."

"I'd like that," I say honestly. That means it was my dad's history, too.

With a smile, Agatha says, "Perfect. That's settled, then. Before you unpack and get situated, I'd love to see your portfolio, Sally."

"I left it in the car."

"I'll go," I offer. "I'll grab our stuff, too, Mom."

"Oh, honey, I'll help you," she says, setting her cup down.

"I got it." I shrug and stand. "It's only two bags. You stay and relax. Talk to . . ." I hesitate at the word and swallow it back down. *Grandma.* It isn't my word to use yet, is it? "Agatha."

I walk out the door and shut it quietly behind me. My phone dings just as I step into the stairwell, and I pull it out. Brenna. Guilt hits me when I see her name. Because I'm ruining our friendship, aren't I?

You almost there? Thinking about you.

My fingers hover over the screen. Things are different now, which is my fault. I tap out, *Here safe. More later,* keeping it brief. I hit send, but it fails. I wait with frustration, and try two more times, until it finally works. Then I add, forcing it letter by letter, *Miss you.*

I *do* miss her, desperately, our friend Leo, my old life. Our queer theatre trio has been strained because of me, because it's too hard pretending, and it's too hard being real. I delete the last two words, hiding my feelings away. I can't show her how I hurt, because I'll hurt her, as well. It's better to step back a little. A lot. This is also why I can't really talk to my mom about him. Not yet. Agatha and I will one of these days, when we're alone. When I don't have to zip myself up and stay stoic. So I don't hurt my mom with my own pain. She has enough of her own.

I take the stairs and head to the foyer. At the car, I pull out my suitcase easily, but my mom's—she's a notorious over-packer— is too heavy. My bladder is full, and my body aches from traveling, and the more I yank on the luggage, the heavier it seems to get. Damn it. How did she even get it in here? Now it's wedged between the front and back seats.

"Um, need help?" a boy's voice breaks through my internal cursing. I turn as he's jogging over from across the street— I'm guessing from the diner. Behind him the door is swinging closed, the scent of breakfast teasing the air. HAROLD's. The fluorescent sign blinks against the seafoam siding.

"I'm okay." I probably sound bitchy, but I'm sweating and irritated now.

"You sure?" He raises his brows, at my side, his golden-brown hair shifting in the wind. "I don't mind. Looks like it's pretty stuck, huh?"

I stand back and let him give it a try. He works at it for a few seconds and suddenly pulls at just the right angle, and the bag comes free.

Tilting my head to look up at him, I soften and say, "Thank you."

"You're welcome." His eyes are the color of melted chocolate.

The dark-rimmed glasses are cute, a little nerdy. "I'm Barrett. Bear for short," he says.

Bear? Yep. Adorable. "I'm Kit."

"Moving here?" His question is tinged with curiosity.

"Just a visit," I answer. By reflex, I glance at the apartment.

"I'll help you carry them in," he says, and before I can argue, he flashes a grin, a dimple on the right side of his face. "I insist, come on. That bag is heavy as shit."

I laugh. I can't help it. My defenses falling despite my best effort. "Yeah."

"I probably shouldn't ask where you're visiting from, or you might think I'm being nosy," he says as he takes my mom's luggage.

This boy. Too cute. I smirk, grabbing my bag. "Well, I probably shouldn't ask how old you are, or you might think *I'm* being nosy," I say playfully, and observe him again, trying to gauge it. With his sort of face, he could be seventeen or twenty-three.

"Eighteen," he answers. Then waits a beat on the step.

"North Dakota. And seventeen. A senior. In high school," I add, as if it weren't obvious.

As we move inside, I take the bag from him. Now it's just a matter of wheeling it all into the elevator. "Thanks again," I say as I press the buzzer.

"Anytime." Another damned cute smile. "Nice to meet you, Kit from North Dakota."

"You too. Bear," I say. The nickname feels silly, but something about him does remind me of a teddy bear I used to have, with golden-brown fur, big, dark eyes. Even though it's not true, I add, "See you around."

Bear gives me a wave and pushes out the door, then thrusts his hands into his coat pockets. He heads down the sidewalk. I get buzzed in and drag the luggage into the teeny elevator. The ride up is quick, but I don't breathe easily until I'm on the fifth floor, feet on steady ground again. I haul the luggage down to number nineteen, and when I enter the apartment, my mom and Agatha break their conversation to look at me, low voices drifting off. I have a feeling they were talking about *him.*

"Thanks for getting the bags," my mom says, face brightening. She blinks away the tears in her eyes, and I pretend not to notice.

"How about a tour?" Agatha says, rising. She's asking us both but only looking at me.

She shows us the kitchen—just as white and shiny from a closer angle—then on down the hall. Linen closet, her bedroom (we only peek inside), the guest bathroom tiled in white and green, and finally the guest room, wallpapered in blue flowers.

"It's very pretty," my mom tells Agatha as we hover in the doorway.

"Thank you," Agatha says. "I'll let you unpack now, and we can look at your portfolio, or you can relax, if you'd like. I have a few calls to make. Then we can get ready, rendezvous for a light lunch, and go out?"

"Sounds great," my mom says as she unzips her bag.

I'm not an unpacker, but I smile in agreement. I watch Agatha walk down the hall until I can no longer see her.

"I like her." A whisper, my mom's fingers paused with a pair of old pajama pants in them.

"I like her, too," I say. "She's different than I thought."

22

But then again, what did I think? I had no preconceived notions except that she was dead. A lie. I grab a fresh outfit and go to the guest bathroom to take a shower and wash the stink of the road trip off me. As the water runs down my skin, a memory washes over me at the same time.

"My parents died . . . ," my dad told me gruffly. "A long time ago. They never even got to meet Mom."

I was young when I heard that false truth, but the story never changed over the years, and we didn't talk of it. What was there to say? It made him too sad, I thought. His parents were dead. His sister, too. That part was true—she really did die before I was born. But the rest?

I hurry and wash myself, ready to begin our day together, hoping I can carve out some alone time with Agatha, so I can start getting answers. So I can finally understand why, for all these years, my dad lied to us. To me.

CHAPTER THREE

The three of us sit together at the kitchen island, a platter of gourmet-looking sandwich wraps before us, but my mom's hardly touched her lunch.

"What's wrong?" I ask in concern, noticing how pale and quiet she's grown.

"Just a headache." But she winces. "A bad one."

I frown. "You never get headaches. I hope you're not getting sick."

"I'm fine." She squeezes my hand. "But, Agatha, do you have any Tylenol? I don't think I brought anything."

"I do, just here." Agatha stands and rummages through a cabinet above the coffee machine. She pulls down a bottle and hands it to my mom, who smiles gratefully.

"I think I might take a rain check today," she says. "Kit, is that okay with you?"

"Are you sure?" I ask, darting my eyes to Agatha. I do want

time alone with her so we can talk. "I don't want you to miss out, Mom."

"I'm sure. I'll take these and lie down. I'll feel better later."

"It's probably the traveling catching up with you. I'll take you to Starling House another time, if you'd like. In fact"—Agatha pauses to smile at me—"I think it will be especially meaningful to share it alone with Kit today. The house is my favorite place in Rosemont."

A relieved sigh, and my mom stands, nodding. "I'll go rest. Have fun, you two."

"Feel better," I say as she brushes her hand along my shoulder on her way past.

She turns back once, a look that says a million things to me. *Don't be nervous. Use this time with Agatha. Have fun. Be safe. See you later. I love you, I love you, I love you.*

"Ready?" Agatha tucks the platter of sandwiches away into the fridge.

"Yeah," I answer, grabbing my bag, smiling.

I follow her out of the apartment and down to the tenants' private lot in the back, where her car waits—a pristine white Mercedes. The inside is just as pristine.

As she drives—hands carefully at ten and two—I stare out at the downtown buildings and comment, "It's really cute, Rosemont."

"I think so, too," she says proudly. "You know, I would've loved for you to see the festival. It's quite something. All the girls wear white dresses and flower crowns. It's going to look so beautiful, especially if we get more snow."

25

"Maybe I can come next year," I suggest. It's not a bad idea. I'd like more time with her.

"I'd love that, though it just occurred to me that there's a way to include you, even if you're leaving in a few days. We'll make a quick stop now, if you don't mind." She's already pulling over into an angled parking space.

"I don't mind," I answer as she parks. I unbuckle my seat belt and climb from the car.

Waiting for her on the sidewalk, I tighten my coat around myself and watch the people passing by, doing holiday shopping and working and living, shoulders hunched against the cold. An ancient paper-skinned woman with fluffy white hair like a snow cone shuffles by; then a thirtysomething mother with precocious twin boys; next a model-handsome guy in a navy suit, black hair slicked back from his face, his movements all hurried as if he's late for some important meeting. A man carrying a bundle of roses in his arms, the flowers nearly the same shade as his lavender-gray suit, his wool overcoat flapping in the wind. When he sees me, he gives a broad and friendly smile, white teeth bright against his deep-russet skin. I return the smile until Agatha gestures, drawing my attention back.

"Our stop," she says, motioning a few doors down.

Vivienne St. James, Seamstress & Designer, the curlicued font on the sign reads.

When we get inside, I let out a low breath. Gentle classical music plays, and the air is scented with the lightest spritz of rose and lavender, walls painted pale sage, antique wood shelves and racks everywhere. Behind the counter is a display of spools in every color thread you could think of, and then, only slightly less showstopping, a woman, probably in her late forties, with the blackest-ink hair, tinted almost indigo under the store lights.

"Good morning, Mrs. Starling!" she says, rolling up a bolt of fabric across her counter and setting it aside, next to a gold vase with a single peach-colored rose. "Mending today?"

"Not today, Vivienne." Agatha pulls me close to her side. "You see, my granddaughter, Kit, is visiting, and we need—"

"A dress for Crowning Day?" she says breathlessly. Her eyes are Elizabeth Taylor lavender blue, her tweed dress nearly the same color. Gold buttons down the front shining. She's pretty, in a pinched sort of way. Like one of those fancy dogs, sleek and narrow-faced.

"No, no." Shaking her head, Agatha corrects, "Kit won't be here for the festival."

The woman's face falls. "Oh! But—"

"But I would still like you to make her a dress," Agatha cuts in firmly, then turns to me. "I'll have it shipped to you, and you'll have a piece of Rosemont with you always. Consider it an early birthday gift."

"Oh," I say in surprise. "Okay. Thanks."

"Go on, go look through the white fabrics, see if anything calls to you," she says.

"Anything? Like, it doesn't matter what kind?" I ask. I have no clue what sort of dress it's going to turn into.

"Pick something beautiful." Agatha's eyes sparkle, and I read the underlying meaning: *money is no object.*

I cross to the other side of the shop, where bolts are stored on long rolls set into wooden cases, and I move past the black fabrics, then the candy-colored, then jewel-toned, and finally stop at the pale shades. As I rifle through them, the two women converse in quiet voices, whispering almost. I lift a couple of selections off the racks and stack them in my arms.

"I thought he . . ." Vivienne's voice drops off.

"*No.*" Agatha's severe reply. Then, quieter, "Please."

When I glance over, the seamstress's face is flushed, but she is nodding at Agatha, voice hushed. "I understand. I'm so sorry."

They notice me looking and both smile, Vivienne almost sympathetically. *He.* They were talking about my dad. My heart goes heavy.

Suddenly my arms feel heavy, too, holding up these bolts of fabric, a simple cream silk and a white lacy one with roses and leaves. I bring both up to the counter, uncertain. I say, "I don't know which, but I think the silk is more me."

"It's stunning." Agatha nods her approval.

"I can definitely work with this," Vivienne gushes. "Now, can you come over this way? I'll need to measure you."

I trail her to the back area. A set of mirrors stands curved in a semicircle around a low platform, with a row of three dressing rooms opposite it. Agatha perches on one of the blush-colored velvet chaises in the middle, handbag in lap. I don't know the designer of the purse, but I'd bet anything it comes with a matching dust bag. Brenna would know. She'd be nudging me now, wide-eyed. The signs of wealth are there, but it's also the way Agatha holds herself. She commands respect, which could be related to the name Starling but could also just be . . . her. Like a queen, there's something regal about her. I don't even know where her money comes from. What she used to do. What my granddad, her late husband, did. I don't know anything, really.

But I will. I'm already learning.

Vivienne instructs me to step up onto the wooden platform, but to take off my coat and shoes first. I do, and notice that one of my socks has a hole at the toe. Agatha is watching me, and I know she sees the hole immediately. Embarrassed, I turn back to Vivienne.

"I can hardly see your shape in that big sweater," she says disapprovingly as she pulls her measuring tape out. "But you're small," she adds, smiling, teeth almost bared as she wraps the tape around me in various ways, jotting numbers in a notepad. "Nothing too long, or it will overwhelm your frame."

"Kit, do *you* like long dresses?" Agatha asks, tone clear. Vivienne is not in charge here, I realize. Agatha is. Even to some lesser extent, *I* am.

So I smile at Agatha in the mirror and answer honestly, "Better too long than too short."

Her sigh is minute, but Vivienne tips her chin, studying me. "I'll get started immediately and get you the sketches, Mrs. Starling. Don't worry about a thing—it will be gorgeous."

"Thank you. Ready, Kit?" Agatha says briskly as she stands from the chaise.

I step off the platform, slip on my shoes and coat, thanking Vivienne as well. I have to quicken my pace to catch up with Agatha as she walks from the store to the car.

"Thanks again for the dress," I say as I get back into the passenger seat. I don't know where or when I'll ever wear it. I suppose it could work for prom. But still, it's a thoughtful gesture.

"I'm happy to give you it. The festival means something to me." Her lips twist a little. "I'm only disappointed I won't see the dress on you."

"I'll send you a picture," I say, before remembering. She has no cell phone, no computer, and no email. "I'll mail it," I amend.

"That would be nice." She smiles, pulling onto the street.

I look out the window as we drive through the picturesque downtown, and she points out things along the way—a florist, her favorite boutique, an old-fashioned cobbler shop that's been there since 1820. Only a few blocks down we turn onto a residential street, and the stores become houses. Some huge, some old, with rows of tall windows like teeth against the flat fronts. Painted crisp white with navy shutters, or butter yellow, or clad in tasteful taupe siding, decorated with white lights, and all with big front yards and giant trees that kiss the sky. Inside some of these houses there are families. Children, with their fathers. But I won't have mine. Not this year. Not next. Not ever. When will I know why? Why am I afraid to just ask? Then again, maybe she doesn't even really know.

I give Agatha a sidelong glance, but I don't say anything. Not yet.

We've driven for only a few more minutes when she pulls the car to a stop. I look up at a stately marigold-yellow colonial, a wooden sign out front that reads STARLING HOUSE. The shutters and the door are painted a deep green, and I can see what looks like a proper, enormous garden in the back, vines creeping over the edge of a gate. What's inside? Things my family members touched, long ago, my dad, maybe.

My heart leaps at the thought. I can't help it. Anything connected to him is something I need to see. Agatha takes the lead, up a walkway to the house. At the front door she stops and gestures to the other side of the street, toward a park. "The roses are that way."

"Okay." I turn back to the house, not caring about that. "You grew up here?"

She nods. "I did. The museum part is new. It was a family home for centuries."

"Centuries?" I ask, surprised. She did say we were one of the early families, but I guess it didn't connect. I had no idea Starlings were here so long. I try to remember the date on the sign into town, but it blurs in my memory.

"I donated it many years ago." Agatha adds, "To the historical society. It's an important part of your heritage that I want to share with you. You'll love it." Her voice goes thoughtful. "Your father did. He lived here, too."

A twist in my heart at the mention of him.

With that, she opens the door. I inhale deeply and go inside. It's a little crooked and also more colorful than I'd have expected, woodwork painted robin's-egg blue, sky blue, cheerful green, canary yellow. Voices from somewhere as Agatha and I wait inside the foyer, a large staircase opposite us.

"There must be a tour going on. But we don't need to wait," she says, leading me left, down a ways, and into a kitchen with an open stove for cooking, clean pots hanging on iron hooks over an enormous brick fireplace.

There's also a refrigerator, a microwave, an oven, a dishwasher, and a sink shoved into the room. It's like two different centuries met up and decided to get married but never quite fit together right.

"Some kitchen," I say, running my hand along the brick of the fireplace. Then I pull it away, mortar dusting my fingertips. Hastily I wipe it on my jeans. "I'm not sure what time I'm in."

"The house dates back to 1786, but we all added modern conveniences over the years," Agatha says. "I remember when my mother had our first dishwasher put in. Though we tried to keep the spirit of Starling House intact, we all put our mark on this home along the way."

Her face is lit up, almost reverent. Her adoration for this place is evident.

"Why did you give it away?" I ask as I trail her up a slender staircase at the other side of the kitchen.

Pausing, with her hand on the rail, she doesn't turn to me, but her voice gets tender. "With both my children gone, it didn't seem like a family home any longer. So I donated it, as much as I loved this place. I felt selfish keeping it when it's such an important symbol to Rosemont."

As we quietly continue the climb up the stairs, the pain is dull and familiar, a pit in my stomach as I ponder the losses. Not just my dad but his sister, Juliet, who I never met. Both gone, and then Agatha was alone, or at least alone with my grandfather, until *he* died, and who I still know nothing about. I need to ask about him, but I have so many questions that they're melting together, making my tongue heavy and useless.

On the second floor, we walk a long hall. I poke my head

into the bedrooms. They're all filled with ornate furniture, beds formally made up. It looks like nothing has changed in years.

"There are six bedrooms," Agatha explains. "That was a large number for that day and age, even though most people had a lot of children."

I lean into the doorway of a blue room, shut my eyes, breathe deep, like I could sense whether my dad slept here, like I could smell him somehow still in the air.

"Your instincts are good." Her hand rests lightly on my shoulder as she stands beside me. "This was his bedroom, and my younger sister's before him, and before that, one of my aunt's."

I let the breath come, in, out, in, out, easy and even. I'm not going to fall to pieces over a simple room, am I? It's just a room.

"I wish—" I find myself saying. But the sentence is endless. I have too many wishes.

Her low reply: "I wish, too."

The voices in the house grow louder, breaking the moment, and her hand falls away. Agatha takes me to a second staircase, a grander one that opens up again in the foyer of the house. At the bottom, there's a woman with a name tag speaking to an elderly couple. She barely looks our way, like she can't be bothered to stop her conversation. But then she snaps her attention back to Agatha, eyes widening in recognition, face lit up with glee.

"Hello! I didn't know you were coming today." The tour guide smooths her wrinkle-free skirt with excited hands. "And you brought someone?" When she sees me, really *sees* me, her mouth drops into a rounded *O* and she grabs my hand, jerking me away from Agatha.

"Katherine Starling, is it really you?" Her face is splotched bronze with fake tanner at the apples of her cheeks. "I'm Kristi Johannes, head guide of Starling House! Welcome!"

"Um," I manage, surprise and confusion making me mumble. "Thanks?"

"You must be so curious! So much to catch up on, but we're grateful you're here."

"Who's we?" I ask, looking from her to Agatha, then back, catching the way the couple behind the guide crane their necks to listen in.

"Well, everyone, of course." Kristi leans in, voice conspirator-whisper low. "The whole town's been buzzing about your arrival. We're honored, not that we expected different. After all that's happened, well, your line is built for honor. Apart from a few black sheep in the bunch."

Agatha coughs behind me, and all at once I despise this woman. Black sheep? I pull my hand from hers.

"Join our tour?" she asks, holding her breath as she peers over my shoulder at Agatha.

"No, thank you" is Agatha's cool reply.

The woman's hungry face drops. She's crestfallen, but she buttons herself right back up and gives us a cheerful smile. "Well, come back anytime, of course, and we can talk more," she says in a too-loud voice before leading the couple away, her navy heels clacking on the wooden floor.

I ease myself back to Agatha's side and follow her into another room. Before I can even ask, she turns to me, sighing.

"Unfortunately, there are a few members of the historical

society I don't care for, and it just happens that my least favorite was present today," she says. "You see, Kit, some people are so enamored with our family, they tend to lose any decorum the minute they get near me. It's a nuisance, really. Anyway." Agatha brightens, motioning to the papered walls beyond the stiff-looking furniture. "This is where we keep the family portraits."

Pulled forward, I cross a rust-colored rug, studying the oil paintings. Then, as history fades and modern photography takes its place, black-and-white photos, followed by color. Mesmerized, I see my own features in some of the subjects, recognizing the lift of the chin, the fair coloring—mostly blondes or redheads—the eyes. There are so many individual portraits of the women, including one of Agatha, with big curling-iron curls coiffed perfectly, a slash of pale lipstick.

She points out a miniature black-and-white picture in a frame—a girl in a wreath of glorious flowers. "This is me as well," she says, smiling. "At the Crowning Day Festival."

"Pretty," I murmur as I take in the grainy photo, the pride on her face, the smile. Then I move on, searching along the wall at a couple more portraits and wedding shots, family photos. When I look closely at one, I finally find him. *Dad!* my heart cries—there he is, as a preteen. There's no mistaking those eyes, that smile, even if I've hardly seen any older pictures of him when he was young. He didn't carry much of his past with him.

When I hover my finger above it, Agatha dips her head in confirmation.

I let my hand fall, confusion overwhelming me. The words echo. *Black sheep?*

"What is it, Kit?" she asks, searching my face.

"Why did my dad leave here?" I ask the question before I realize it.

She takes a low breath, nodding to herself, like she knew I'd ask, like she was waiting but still isn't quite ready. "We had a falling-out, many years ago. Daniel was a wonderful boy, yet we'd never agreed on even little things. His friends, his music, his hobbies, his girlfriends. We had differing opinions about what he should do with his life, once he was grown. In the end it wasn't one big blowup but a series of small ways that we couldn't see eye to eye. He wanted to write, he wanted to see the world, he wanted to live this sort of romantic, artistic life. I—" Her voice falters. "I put pressure on him, too much pressure. We were afraid he was giving up security and legacy for a dream. Your father didn't want to conform to the life we'd laid before him, and he made his choice, despite our protests."

"So . . . you cut him off?" I hold my breath, keeping my emotions in check.

"No, no." She shakes her head. "It wasn't like that. He was always, always welcome to come back. This family *is* his, no matter how he felt about it. You don't know how I pleaded, Kit. I tried to keep him. I only wanted to be a part of his life. But I think he was ashamed of himself, or even us, or he was simply angry, perhaps let down because he didn't get one hundred percent of the support and encouragement he thought he deserved. I wasn't a soft mother, in hindsight—though I was much harder on Juliet than him—but Daniel had a habit of making decisions only with his heart, with passion, letting reason fly out the window."

It hurts, how much that sounds like my dad. "Was the guide talking about him when she said 'black sheep'?" I ask.

Her lips purse distastefully. "I don't presume to make sense of half of what she says, but likely, yes. I don't care to think of him that way, though. I'm still proud of him. I would have loved to share our family legacy with him for longer. He simply did not want it anymore."

I look back to his photo sadly. After a moment, I admit, "I don't really understand what you mean by 'legacy' or why everyone is so enamored with our family. Before, you said this house is an important symbol, but a symbol of what?"

The guide ushers her guests up the stairs with a harsh resounding laugh, and then their muffled footsteps are above us. The downstairs falls quiet. Our eyes connect.

"Well, I suppose to understand it, you'd have to know where it all began. With her." Agatha focuses behind me.

I swivel, turning to a fireplace, and my eyes lock on a portrait hung above the mantel. My mouth goes dry. It's like staring at my own face. Hers is sharper, like Agatha's. Her hair is red and I'm blond, but otherwise . . . Her eyes, green, the exact shade as mine, narrowed, her smile a touch cruel. A cold calculation is visible in her expression. Still, it's like looking into a mirror. It's like looking at a version of what I could be, maybe, if I let myself harden.

I clear my throat. "Who is she?" My voice comes out strained.

"Her name was Frances Black Starling, though to me she's

always been Franny. She's the matriarch of our family. The root of us." The respect drips from Agatha's voice.

"Something about her . . ." My voice trails off into nothing, a wisp of a thought I'd feel foolish saying out loud. I stroke the edge of the heavy wooden mantel, where a corner was broken off, ages ago. It's worn down. My stomach tightens, turns over. I lift my eyes back to Frances's portrait and shudder.

"Yes?" Agatha asks.

"Nothing." I shake my head. I was going to say *scares me a little.*

"I think I've memorized her face. I have been staring at that portrait since before I could speak. You remind me of her."

Something about that makes me want to cringe, but why? "So, what's the deal with her?"

Agatha moves about the room, comfortable. Touching this or that, easing herself into a sturdy embroidered chair like she's sat there a million times. Of course she has.

"In the beginning—the early days of Rosemont—there was a harsh winter, and the people were starving," she says. "It was a horrific time, with many casualties. Frances was wealthy and generous. She brought in money and food and goods, and saved hundreds of people. She had this house built not long after, as her wealth further increased. Nobody has forgotten what she did for the town. That gratitude doesn't simply die in a generation."

"Or even a couple of centuries," I murmur. "It was so long ago."

An amused gleam in Agatha's eyes. "Our family has been blessed for just as long, and wealth and prestige certainly don't hurt in this day and age, either. People look up to us. There is so much of your legacy I'm looking forward to explaining more in depth. For now, though, perhaps we head out? Before that nasty tour guide comes to snatch you up again."

A laugh escapes me, and Agatha stands, smiles at me as she crosses the room. Before I follow her out, I sneak one last peek at Frances. Her eyes seem to shine right into me, and with a shiver I walk out. I shut the door of the portrait room, my stomach lurching, the wrap I had for lunch suddenly threatening to come back up.

When I join Agatha in the hallway, she eyes me with concern. "You look pale."

I manage to push aside the nausea and say, "I'm not feeling great all of a sudden. I'm sorry. I don't mean to cut today short. I just . . . don't feel right."

She pulls up her smile before it falls. "Of course, let's head home. We have all week."

Agatha turns to go the way we came in, ignoring a hallway and a glass-doored room behind it, and I have to ask, "What's back there?"

"There's a gift shop that way," she says, dismissing it, then adds, "It's not necessary to see if you're not feeling well."

Right. And I don't want to walk out with a coffee mug or tote bag embroidered with "Starling." That would be weird. This whole house is a little weird, isn't it? Or it just gives me a weird feeling. At least the portrait room did, the worn chunk of mantel, those green eyes blazing down at me.

But my dad loved this place. Agatha said so. And he looked happy in the picture, and didn't he tell me *some* things about this life that were true? He had a sister named Juliet who died, and he had a mom and dad, and even though they weren't dead at the time, like he said, they did exist. One still does. Agatha was dead my whole life, and now she's not. This is a gift.

I look into her eyes and I see him. I'm not going to lose her, even if this week goes by quickly. I'll come back, like I told her, maybe this summer. Then we'll get more time together; we will soak it up like cake in milk.

So, who cares about a house that makes my skin prickle, about a portrait of some red-haired doppelganger? Not me. I shove a piece of mint gum into my mouth to help combat the queasiness and turn to Agatha, open and willing. Smiling.

She says, like she's been holding it in, "I just wanted to tell you I'm sorry, Kit, for your loss. I can't take back our past and make amends. But I can renew my family again. With you."

I find myself wordless, suddenly feeling like I might cry, but I manage to nod, staring into her eyes. My grandmother's eyes, meeting mine. An ocean, a sky, a blue flame, flickering, bright and bright and bright.

CHAPTER FOUR

When we get back to the apartment, my mom is still napping, snoring soundly, so I quietly shut the guest room door and leave her be. It's strange to see her sleeping in the middle of the afternoon, but I'm glad she's getting rest.

While Agatha puts away the groceries she had delivered, I curl up in the living room with my book, first peeking at my phone, but nobody has texted me since Brenna, and my service is still beyond sketchy, the battery draining almost as I charge it. I set the phone on the coffee table next to that ridiculously beautiful vase of roses, and try to lose myself in my novel. This time it's easier, Agatha quietly opening and closing cabinets in the next room, snowflakes gently falling outside. I feel better now, since returning from Starling House.

As I drift into the dangerous world of fae and marvel at the use of language and atmosphere, I snuggle deeper into the couch.

When there's a knock at the door, Agatha asks from the kitchen, "Can you get it?"

"Sure," I call, and rise to go answer the door. On the other side stands an elfin-looking girl, with friendly eyes and a delicate heart-shaped face. In her hands, a pie smelling of warm berries and buttery pastry.

"I'm Charlotte." Her voice is breathy. "You're Katherine Starling?"

The way she says it is just like the other people we've talked to so far. I get why, now. I answer, "I'm Kit."

"Well, hi." She offers me the pie proudly. "My mom made this for you and yours and asked me to bring it up. We heard you were visiting Mrs. Starling, see." Looking into the apartment, she waves. "We're number eight," the girl, Charlotte, adds.

"That's really nice," I say, taking the pie from her. The pan is still warm.

"That smells delightful," Agatha cuts in. She sweeps to my side and scoops the pie from me as she addresses Charlotte. "Thank you. I'll be sure to thank your mother, too."

"You're so welcome," Charlotte says sweetly. She looks back at me, beaming. "Hope to see you again, Kit."

I smile, and she chirps a goodbye, turning so her chestnut waves bounce, and I close the door behind her.

"Pie?" Agatha says.

"Definitely." I go with her into the kitchen and sit on one of the stools surrounding the marble-topped island. My stomach feels fine now.

Agatha cuts a perfect slice and slides the plate to me. "Milk?" she asks. "Coffee? Tea?"

"Milk is good, thanks," I say, tucking in. The first bite melts in my mouth—this is definitely homemade—and I follow it with a swig of cold, cold organic milk and watch Agatha cut her own sliver and take a dainty bite. Then she frowns, swallowing.

"You know, I forgot. I meant to run an order to the florist tomorrow morning, but I have a charity meeting I unfortunately cannot miss, even with family in town. I would hate to have the order be late. Would you mind terribly dropping it for me when you wake up? Maybe you and your mother would like to take a walk there?"

"Sure, that's fine," I say. "I don't mind."

"Thank you. That would be so helpful." Agatha smiles at me. "Now, what would you like to do tonight?" she asks. "I don't cook much, though I've mastered a few select recipes. Or we can order in. We could play poker or watch a movie."

"You play poker?" I can't hide my surprise.

Agatha's lips tug up. "I do. My father had a penchant for it, and he taught us all how to play cards young. My mother didn't approve. But I enjoy it, and I *do* like to win."

"Do you like pizza?" I ask. "Pizza and cards sounds fun. My mom will like that, too."

"Pizza sounds fine to me." She covers the pie with a piece of tinfoil and tucks it away on the counter. As she moves around the kitchen, I find my eyes drawn to her right hand, the pinkie bent at an odd angle, the tip a purple bruise. She notices me looking and says, "Believe it or not, sometimes I can be clumsy."

"That's almost harder to imagine than you playing poker," I say, lightly teasing her.

She laughs as she puts the milk away. "Tonight will be lovely. A quiet night at home with my granddaughter. I can't think of anything I'd rather do."

"Hey," my mom's voice pulls our attention as she walks into the kitchen, sleepy-eyed, cheeks flushed, smiling sheepishly. "Sorry. I didn't know I'd pass out like that. I had such a bad headache. But it feels better now."

"Oh good," I say, relieved.

"Well, that's wonderful. Kit and I were just discussing ordering pizza but if you'd rather go out?" Agatha asks her, smiling.

She shakes her head. "Here is great. Maybe we can go out tomorrow instead."

"Of course." Agatha nods. "A neighbor girl brought over a pie. Would you like some?"

My mom's eyes light up, and I release the last of my concern. She grins. "I'd love some."

The rest of the afternoon goes by quickly, pie and good conversation. We eventually order in and eat our pizza as planned, play poker by candlelight with a giant jar of coins Agatha procures for us to use. We laugh and talk, but nothing is said about my dad, which I'm grateful for. The worry for my mom returns as the night wears on, though. The more I look at her, I can't help but notice that the skin below her eyes is shadowed blue, darker than normal. She says nothing, but I can tell when her headache returns, and I make an excuse to go to bed early, hoping she'll soon follow.

I close the guest room door, exhale. As I stand, back pressed against the wood, I take in the details I overlooked before: painted paneling below the wallpaper on the bottom half of the walls, a honey-toned armoire and matching dresser, neat curtains framing the large window, and a nightstand between two twin beds—my mom's claimed the one closest to the door. Unlike the living room, there's absolutely nothing personal, or even interesting, in here. I pull on a big T-shirt, and fling my clothes onto my open suitcase.

I turn out the lights, climb into the bed by the window, and pull the covers up over my legs. It's quiet and calm, but I can't turn my mind off. Not long after, my mom comes in and gets into her matching bed. Time passes and I toss and turn. I can hear her struggling to find her way to sleep as well, moaning. A bad dream? I get up and shake her gently until she stops the anguished mumbling; then I dig through my bag for my dad's pages. When I get back into bed, I slip them under my pillow and lay my fingers atop, the way a baby clutches at a blanket.

In the morning, when I wake, it takes a moment to orient myself. To remember. I'm in Rosemont. I roll over to see my mom is sleeping deeply, so I climb out of bed quietly and dig through my suitcase for clothes. I'll go to the florist to run Agatha's errand on my own so my mom can sleep longer, and by the time I'm back, I'm sure she'll be awake.

Once I'm ready, I stop off in the kitchen to find that Agatha left the florist order for me on the counter, a sealed envelope labeled, simply, *order*, along with the spare key. Next to it, a note for me saying thank you, the bottom signed with just the letter *A*, just like the letter she wrote me. I jot down a quick note for my mom in case she wakes early, letting her know I'll be back shortly.

I grab the envelope and key, and head out, locking the apartment behind me, and taking the stairs. As I push the foyer door open, the fresh, crisp air blows against my face, and I go down the street, enjoying the morning walk to the little storefront Agatha pointed out yesterday. The sun shines brighter today, no sign of snow to come. When I reach the florist, the bell rings as I push open the shop door, and my breath catches at the sight before me. Heaps and heaps of roses in buckets stacked on tiered shelves, reaching almost to the copper tin-tiled ceiling. Red ones, pink, yellow, coral, white veined with thin purple skeins, the palest ivory, the darkest plum, stunning against the emerald-green walls. Other flowers dot the perimeter of the alternating-bronze-and-ivory-tiled room—some in refrigerators, some out in tin buckets—tulips and peonies, greenery, lilies, but the roses steal the show. The air is wet and fragrant with them.

I can't move until a voice breaks me out of my thoughts. Someone in the back is singing "Baby Dream Your Dream." Then, "Oh, hey there."

A man is peeking his head out from what must be a back room, smiling at me. I recognize him from yesterday. He was in the lavender suit, a bundle of flowers in his arms. Today he has on a Henley fitted to his muscular torso, sleek trousers paired with it, and a pair of glossy black Chelsea boots I covet. His diamond nose stud glints. "Can I help you find something?"

I step forward, smiling. "Hi, yeah, my grandmother gave me this order to give you?"

I hand over the envelope that Agatha left for me, and he sets the bunch of dried flowers in his arms on the counter, then rummages in a drawer for a letter opener and slits the seal.

"I see." He pauses to read it, glancing at me, then tucks the paper away into a drawer with a nod. "Let her know I'll have it ready by then."

"Thanks. I will." Then I blurt out, "I liked your song. I like *Sweet Charity*."

"Do you?" The man looks pleased. "Any others?"

"I mean, *Chicago, Hamilton*. There are a lot."

"What about *Cats*?" he says.

I cringe involuntarily. "Can't do it. Way too creepy."

We both laugh, and he tilts his head. "I'm Miles Jones, by the way. This is my shop."

"Your shop is really beautiful," I tell him happily. "I'm Kit."

"Kit Starling, I take it," he says. It's not a question, which makes sense. He just read Agatha's note. "And you are visiting your grandma?" Miles asks as he gets to work on the flowers he put down. "How are you liking Rosemont?"

"It's nice," I reply. Images of adorable stores and smiling people run through my mind, the quaint old-fashioned vibe of it all. I push aside the uneasy feeling I had at the museum and add, with a smile, "Charming."

Watching him is soothing, the way he weaves the dried

flowers into wreaths—or crowns, I guess. Didn't Agatha say the girls in town wear flower crowns for the rose festival?

"Are those for the festival?" I ask.

His hands pause a moment before he answers, "They are."

"Oh," I say. Out of slight curiosity, I ask, "Do they mean anything?"

Again that hesitation, though his hands continue on, sure and confident as he points each flower out. "The yarrow is for everlasting love. Peonies for prosperity, cornflowers for good fortune. The hyssop and poppy for sacrifice and remembrance. There are others, too. Flowers have a language all their own. Some given by humans, and others, well, just look at a pansy and tell me it doesn't make you want to smile."

I smile at his clear fondness for them. I look around the room at the roses exploding in color. "What about roses? They mean love, don't they?"

"Sit, if you'd like," he says, gesturing to a turquoise metal stool at the counter as he busies himself with the delicate wreath-in-progress. "We can talk while I do this. You can help, if you want." He looks up at me, weighing my response.

"Sure," I say, happy for the invitation—I like it in here. I take a seat, and he slides over a pair of small clippers. Then he puts in front of me a selection of dried flowers gone brown and fragile. "Just snip off the bottom quarter of leaves or so, but leave the stem intact so it can be woven in." As I start on that, he explains, "A lot of flowers have multiple meanings, including the ones I mentioned, and roses can mean different things depending on their color."

"That makes sense," I say. "Do all the crowns get roses? You're famous for those, right? I mean, Rosemont is." I snip off a trio of leaves, then glance again at the rows and rows of roses. They *are* remarkable.

Miles keeps his eyes down. "Well, no—to your first question. Yes to your second. One girl gets only white flowers in her crown, live ones, roses included. They stand for purity, innocence, honor. That sort of thing."

"Why are the other ones dried?" I gently sort the finished flowers in front of me.

"They symbolize death. The festival celebrates balance. Life and death."

"Huh," I say, curious about this alternate explanation. "I thought it was to celebrate the roses." Isn't that what Agatha told us? "Or mainly the roses?"

"Those as well," he says, then adds, "I've actually not been to the festival yet. I've lived here five years, and this will be the first for me."

"Oh," I say, surprised. "I assumed it was every year." Which seemed logical for a festival like this.

Miles puts his focus back on the crowns. "No, but maybe that makes it extra special—"

The ringing of the old-fashioned phone at his side cuts him off, and he smiles apologetically as he lifts the butter-yellow receiver to his ear. His other hand rests on the dried flowers, almost protectively. From what I can gather, it sounds like the conversation won't be a quick one, and I'm finished with my task anyway, so I motion to him that I'm going to leave, and he whispers his thanks as I stand. I give him a little silent wave and leave him to his business. I don't need to take up any more of his time.

Out on the sidewalk, I turn left, in the direction of the apartment. I look at my phone, which is roaming. No new messages. Not that I expected any, really.

Cheery shoppers laugh as I move past them on the sidewalk, bells ring, expensive cars line the curbs, at least a couple I would guess are from the fifties or sixties. A man exits a building across the street, and when he looks at me, he trips a step. I turn back to find him watching me, staring, really. Is it because I look like the girl in the portrait? Frances? I frown, and he snaps out of his reverie, keeps walking.

The smell of good, strong coffee floats from the place he just left, and as I get closer, I realize it's a café, which makes me cross the street, almost automatically. I sigh, noting that the handwritten sign on the door says, *No Wi-Fi, sorry!* But I go inside anyway, pulled by the scent and my sweet tooth. Agatha had fruit and yogurt delivered for me, but I would kill for a cinnamon roll or something chocolatey and creamy.

Inside there's Christmas music playing over fuzzy speakers, and I can't help but be delighted by the swirly vintage tile floor. I step up to the counter, fuchsia-pink roses in a vase to the side. And behind it, a girl with blue corkscrew curls, the color popping against her sepia skin, her eyes wide as she takes my order. A chocolate muffin big enough to split with my mom when I get back, and a rose-syrup latte—the signature flavor here. When I hand over a ten-dollar bill, the girl, whose name tag says *Angelika*, bites her lip.

"Oh, I couldn't," she says, hands fluttering. Red roses decorate her perfect, long, coffin-shaped nails, and her gaze locks on mine. I try to find flaws on her face, but there are literally none. She smiles, and for a second, I think she's flirting with me, heat rising to my cheeks, but too quickly she dashes that unlikely hope, adding, "It's on the house. You're a *Starling*."

She passes the money back to me, and I fumble it before shoving it into my wallet. "Thanks," I say, hesitating. I still don't totally understand. But if it weren't for Starlings, some of these people wouldn't exist, right? Still, it's strange reaping the benefits of this family honor when I only got to Rosemont yesterday.

I step off to the side to wait, awkwardly scrolling through my roaming phone, but it only takes a few minutes for my order to be ready, and I grab a bag with my muffin off the counter and take the cup—one word written on it: "Starling." I take a tentative sip on my way to the door. It's surprisingly decent, the rose syrup.

Before I leave, I dart one last glance at the pretty girl behind the counter. She's watching me. Our gazes connect, and she mouths *Thank you*. I push through the door, my smile dropping. Thank you? For what? I puzzle over it as I walk down the sidewalk. I must have read her lips wrong.

"Hey," someone says, and I stop just before I bump into them. "Kit from North Dakota."

I recognize the voice and look up in surprise—*pleasant* surprise—just inches from running into his chest. "Oh, hi, Bear," I say, feeling the corners of my lips turn up.

"How are you?" he asks, flashing me a bright smile.

"I'm good," I say, and jerk my head toward the café, adding, "Just got a coffee."

"Food?" He glances at my bag. "Tell me you got a bacon sandwich. They're the best in town, but you gotta get extra bacon. It's a rule."

"I'm a vegetarian," I offer drily, trying to keep a straight face, but something about him just makes me want to grin, damn it.

"Well, good, more for me, then. Too bad I already had breakfast at the diner."

He looks so comically disappointed, I laugh, then notice the people turning to do double takes as they pass us. Whispers at my back.

"Do you know who that was?" someone says.

Slightly embarrassed, I take in a breath of cold air. Just because I get why people are noticing me doesn't make it any less uncomfortable. I don't love being the center of attention. Distracted, I nearly drop my bag, when Bear says something.

"Hmm?" I turn to glance at him. He's standing there with that buttoned-up plaid shirt underneath his jacket, a hint of nerdy in his glasses, and it hits me that he's remarkably cute.

"I asked if you'd seen the eternal roses yet," he repeats.

"No." I adjust my answer. "Well, I saw some at the florist. But not the actual ones." I look up, curious. "Why?"

"Want to go now?" Bear asks. Then he drops his eyes, suddenly shy. "To be honest, I'm working on a story. I've been stuck on it for a while, and I'd like to see the roses, see if I can figure out another angle, you know? And I'd like to take you."

"You're a writer?" I ask, gazing at him with new interest.

Good-looking *and* he writes? How could I *not* be intrigued? "I write, too," I say brightly.

"For real?" His eyes seem to light up. "What do you write?"

"Fiction. Fantasy, mostly," I say. I consider him for a moment. And I know Agatha wanted to take me to the roses, but . . . "I guess we could go," I say. "Just let me run this food up, 'kay?"

"Sure," Bear says.

He walks with me the block to the apartment building, and I leave him waiting on the front step for me. When I get up to the apartment, my mom is sitting at the island, head bent over her sketchbook as she draws. I'm relieved to see she's awake. She has a coffee in front of her, probably her third cup by now, even though I wasn't gone that long. *Caffeine addict,* I think lovingly, and as her pen moves, her face is intent, focused, and calmly happy. I could watch her draw forever.

"Hey, Mom," I say. "Agatha's still out?"

She looks up and nods. "She had a second charity thing she couldn't reschedule, but mentioned we'd go out tonight for dinner. I said that was good." She spies the bag then, and asks, "What'd you get?"

"Muffin," I say, dropping it onto the counter. "You can have it if you want. You feeling better?" I hold my breath until she nods, and then I let it out, glad. "Good," I say, then go on hesitantly, "So, I got invited to see the roses. You don't think she'll mind much, do you? I know she wanted to bring us sometime."

Shaking her head, she says, "I don't think she'll mind. It's not like we haven't seen them," she says, pointing her pen in the direction of the giant vase of roses. "Who invited you?"

"This guy." I fold too easily, breaking into a small smile. "Just a friend," I add before she gets too excited about it. "Sort of."

I picture his playful grin and know I'm blushing. She doesn't give me any shit, just one raised brow like she's thinking about it.

"Okay." She smiles. "Have fun, be safe, all that."

"Please, Mom. Rosemont is probably the safest place I'll ever go." I laugh, then add, "It might be boring, but I thought it would be nice to go with him."

"Ohhh, that is just so *nice* of you," she teases as I get to the door.

I turn around and stick out my tongue as she smirks.

"Love you!" she says.

"Love you more," I call back as I close the door to the sound of her laughter. I jog downstairs, making sure not to spill coffee on myself.

When I meet Bear back outside, he climbs to his feet. "Good to go?"

"Yeah." I return his smile as we veer to the right, to the sidewalk.

"The roses aren't far," he says, "just a few blocks. I like walking, if that's cool with you, and sadly, I don't have a car right now."

"Walking is good," I agree, even though I could've driven our car. Today is warmer than yesterday, the sky blue, clouds white cotton. I wouldn't even mind shrugging off my coat. "I kinda know where they are; I saw the museum yesterday, with my, um, grandma. It used to be her house, I guess."

His eyes widen just a fraction. "Oh. Starling House." His gaze lingers on me for a long moment, like he's putting two and two together. Like he's realizing exactly who I am, but to his credit, he just offers me a gentle smile. "Yeah, I've been there."

"Yeah?"

He laughs. "So many field trips, you have no idea, Kit. Dozens. *Hundreds.*"

"That's so strange," I say, half cringing. "Like, knowing people have been in my family's old house, touching their stuff and staring at their pictures. All that."

He considers that a minute, then thoughtfully says, "I never thought about it like that, but yeah, you're right. My family's old homes would be boring as hell, though. At least you have some cool stuff in that house. All those antiques and everything. It's like it was frozen in time."

"Let me guess, you write historical fiction?" I tease, finding an easy comradery with him.

"Sometimes, yeah," he says. "I also love mysteries—like secret tunnels and safes hidden behind fancy portraits. But actually, I'm working on fantasy now." As we move along, a man in a uniform wheels a dolly out of a shop, brown boxes stacked up to his chin. He loads them into the back of his truck, adding to dozens more inside just like them. A floral scent snakes from the shop, overpowering my senses.

"The perfumery," Bear explains. "They export their rose oils, mainly."

"That's a lot of boxes." I look again. "They do well, looks like."

He flushes. "Everyone does well here."

I file that away. "Can we go in?"

"Absolutely," he says, and we walk into the shop together.

From the floor tiles to the walls to the heavy velvet draperies framing the display window, all is pink and red, like Cupid puked everywhere. The glass shelves are trimmed in gold, loaded with rose beauty products: bath bombs, sea salt scrubs, soaps, lip balms.

A woman behind the counter gives me a generous smile. "Welcome to my shop. Let me know if you need anything."

I thank her, noting that her face looks like an older, slightly rounder version of the girl with the pie's—Charlotte's. I'd bet anything she's her mom.

"They have a little gift section, with minis," Bear points out at my side.

"No, that's okay. I'm good." I smile, easing us out the door. The smell is too overwhelming to appeal to me. I'm starting to get a headache. I mentally note to tell my mom to steer clear of the perfumery.

We continue walking through downtown, passing more shops that look like they fell from Stars Hollow, plus more people. Some of them stare when they see me, which I try to brush off, embarrassed. But the rest are just living their lives. A couple of carrot-headed preteen boys run into the single-screen movie theatre. A woman pushing an old-fashioned stroller, a slash of fire-engine-red lipstick against her white face, as she clips down the sidewalk, looking both gorgeous and dangerously maternal. We have to scoot out of the way to avoid her running us down.

"Jesus," Bear says. "People are brutal." I laugh, and he motions to the right. "We'll turn here. If you kept going, you'd find a few businesses, but there's not much that way."

"What's that building?" I point to the ornate architecture

across the intersection, fancy scrollwork on the plaster, lion statues protecting the tall wooden doors. "A church or something?"

"It's actually an old schoolhouse. It's been converted now to a funeral home," he says, then adds, "Rosemont doesn't have any places of worship."

That's sort of strange, but it's a small town. I'm not religious at all, but I suppose if anyone here is, they go to a bigger town nearby.

"What do you do here?" I ask him. "Like, for fun?"

Bear shrugs. "Hang with friends. Go hiking."

"In the woods?" I sort of flutter my hand behind me, in the direction my mom and I drove through to get here.

"There's woods surrounding the whole town, basically. A river, too, to the northeast." He stares off beyond the houses, and up ahead of us, I can see trees in the distance. Bear frowns. "But it's not good for swimming or anything. In fact, it's kinda dangerous. Plus, I write, which is mostly fun but can also be frustrating."

I take a sip of my latte and grin. "I get it."

We talk the woes of storytelling, but also the good. Bear is animated as he tells me his novel idea, about a kid botanist who creates a new type of flower by accident and finds out the flowers have poisonous properties—and honestly, the story sounds amazing.

"What about yours?" he asks.

"Um . . ." The story in my heart beats. The snarky Mackenzie Braws. Devilish Ryder Bailey. The treasure they stole from the awful Captain Fanshaw. But that isn't my story, no matter how much my dad would sneak early pages into my school-books for me to read secretly, no matter that he'd often ask my opinion, no matter that I helped name five of the characters, no matter that I was his first reader, his most loyal one. It's not mine.

"Your face." Behind his glasses, his eyes are wide with concern. "You all right?"

I should shrug it off, but for some reason, I don't, stalling on the sidewalk. "I was thinking about my dad. He, uh, died a few months ago. He was a writer."

Softly Bear says, "I'm really sorry. I did hear. I'm . . . Do you want to talk about it?"

"Not really. Not now. But thanks."

He takes my hand. I let him, surprising myself, and by the look on his face, I've surprised him as well. We move on, walking into a residential area, hand in hand, my face heated. It takes me a moment to ground myself as we continue on, speaking of only benign things. After a couple of blocks, I recognize some of the houses from yesterday.

I finally break the silence. "I'm not sure what I want to write. I started this sort of demon siren thing before. But now I don't know. I keep thinking about my dad's last story, the second in an intended trilogy. He died before he finished it, and I almost wish I could keep writing it."

"I loved book one. I don't blame you," he says, squeezing my hand. And my heart, in a way. He's read my dad's work!

We went into the sapphire water with our pockets stuffed full of jewels.

"So, you're eighteen?" I ask Bear, changing the subject. "Are you in college?"

"Actually, I'm taking the year off, doing odd jobs and writing. I know it sounds pathetic. My parents aren't thrilled."

"I don't think it's pathetic. You don't have to have things figured out yet." Which I understand more than anyone else. "I'm going to take a year off also. I haven't applied for colleges. I don't know if I even *want* to go to college," I confess.

"Same. I'd love to travel." His jaw tightens. "But I can't."

"Why not?" Curiosity makes me pry.

"It's my family. My dad. Writing isn't good enough; traveling isn't, either. Nothing I want is." He leaves it at that, but I catch how his shoulders slump. How the light in his eyes dims.

"He expects a lot from you?" I guess. It makes me think of Agatha, how she didn't like what my dad wanted to do. I can't imagine that pressure. It makes me sad for Bear.

"Everyone does." His tone gets lighter and he shrugs like he's unbothered, but I can read him clearly, like I've known him for years instead of mere hours. "What do you do outside of school?" he asks, changing the subject. "Sports? Work?"

"Plays, sometimes, stage crew," I answer. "I, uh, was working at a bookshop for a while." Before I missed three shifts in a row because I couldn't get out of bed. Before I scared my mom half to death herself. "I'm going to apply for something new when I get back."

Miles's floral shop comes to mind—maybe I could get a job at a place like that at home.

In the front yard of one white house, three little girls—

sisters, by the looks of their nutmeg hair and round eyes—hold mittened hands as they dance in a circle, singing. The tiniest, wearing a kitty hat, smiles at me. Their small voices are melodic and sweet, and I catch just a bit of their song.

". . . all their daughters fair and dark and in between . . ."

A woman comes out of the house, scolding, "Shh! He'll hear you." And the kids giggle, breaking their circle apart to play a quieter game—maybe keeping their third-shift sleeping dad in mind.

Smiling at the adorable children, Bear lightly squeezes my hand, nodding ahead. "Here's the park."

Farther up the block, I can glimpse Starling House to the left, but it's the grand-looking park to the right, which Agatha pointed out and I overlooked yesterday, that draws my focus, with a tennis court, a wooden-castle playground that is probably as big as my house, and neat picnic tables in a row in front of a brick community center. The kind of community center where they clean the bathrooms regularly and you won't find graffiti or shit smeared on the walls.

Side by side, we cross the lightly snowy grass, walk under an arch of a gate entrance and onto a manicured cobblestone path, then past a crisp white gazebo, so bright that it looks as if painters laid a fresh coat only yesterday. This is the kind of park where people get married, where over-the-top proposals happen. I'm surprised I haven't seen it in a hundred social media posts before. Then again, I'd never even heard of this town until a couple of weeks ago. "A well-kept secret," my mom called Rosemont. With the lack of technology and what I'm assuming is an old-fashioned mindset, it all makes sense now.

"This is like a tourist spot? Rosemont?" I ask, gesturing, "All this?"

"It's no Bali or anything like that, but we have enough tourists come through to see the roses, or who drive in accidentally."

"Yeah. Well, it *is* charming," I say. "And a little irritating," I add, with a laugh. I sneak a glance at my phone to see that the battery is drained even though it was fully charged this morning. I slide it back into my bag, dead.

"Definitely can be," Bear says.

"Agatha, my grandma, doesn't even have a cell phone," I offer, then explain because I didn't actually say who I'm staying with, "That's who my mom and I are visiting."

"My parents don't, either," he says. "And I know who she is. Everybody knows Agatha Starling. Small town, remember?" At that moment he stops, and I smell them before I see them, that heady cloud of rose. Not like rose-syrup lattes. Not like the stamped bar of small-batch soap in Agatha's guest bathroom, not even like Miles's shop or the overbearing perfumery. This is better. Deeper, stronger. Truer.

"Here they are." Bear gestures with a smile.

When I see the rosebushes, I can't help it, I'm awed. I stare at them, how they suck up all the attention, tumbling over the arbors, around the trunks of trees, spilling onto the ground, a carpet of blossoms.

"Wow," I say after a long moment. "They really are beautiful."

"Beautiful" doesn't do the flowers justice, but I'm lost for a better adjective. I walk closer, taking in the many shades: a deep burgundy, the color of rich, ancient velvet; classic red; friendship yellow; white; Georgia peach; blush pink. More. So many more. There's something sensual about them all, almost overly so. They put their cut counterparts to shame.

I swear under my breath. "I mean, no wonder you all celebrate. They are for sure festival-worthy."

He laughs. "You're talking about Crowning Day?"

"Yeah, seems like a big thing." I tip my face to look up at him.

"Rosemont celebrates the shit out of anything." He looks at the flowers for emphasis, light sarcasm tinging his words, but there's nothing malicious in his face. His eyes twinkle, like it's all one big joke to him. I get the feeling Bear laughs a lot, in a good way. "Lots of fanfare, which is a little strange, but I think all small towns are strange in their own way, plus we're so cut off here, you know? Are you from a big city?"

"No," I answer, staring back at the flowers. "We're like an hour from Bismarck. I always thought my town was small, but now that I see Rosemont, I'm not sure. So, how do these stay so nice?"

I run my fingertips along the velvety petals of one of the roses. Everything else is dead, plants and grasses flat brown, the color of old pennies. A current of reservation ripples through me as I stare at this brilliant exhibition of life. "I've never seen roses bloom in December."

"There's a hot spring."

"Really?" I try not to sound so unconvinced. I read the sign he points out, a wooden post with a golden plaque nailed to it, shining as if it were buffed only this morning.

The famed eternal roses of Rosemont have existed since the late eighteenth century. These particular strains of roses are especially hardy, but they owe their perseverance to the existence of a hot spring running directly below. This spring has created a geothermal pocket of warmth in which they thrive, no matter the weather conditions.

"Weird. But they still get snowed on, right?" There's less snow today, thanks to the sun melting some of it, but every other plant I saw on the way here had a dusting. What would it be like during a blizzard?

"Melts right away," Bear explains. Then he smirks. "You're right, it *is* weird, but I suppose we're used to it. Tourists like to *oooh* over them, though, taking pictures and stuff."

"Yeah," I murmur, unable to look away from the flowers, "looks like a real selfie spot."

Bear lets me gaze for a few minutes longer. Then he tugs my arm and I turn, walk at his side back down the cobblestones, before I remember the reason we came. "Did you get an idea for your story? Want to go look again?"

"It's fine," he says. "I'm so used to them they don't seem special anymore, but you sort of opened my eyes to them again."

As he walks on, I glance behind me, one more time at the brilliance of the flowers. They're radiant, beautiful. Something about them makes me hurt.

Bear doesn't see the woman stride over to the roses. Get down on her knees. Her mouth moves quickly, her eyes closed. There are no places to worship in Rosemont, apparently, but something about her here, at the roses, looks like worship. Like she's . . . praying.

Shivering, I almost bring it to Bear's attention, but I turn instead, picking up my pace to catch up with him. "Yeah, they're really special," I say.

The wind whispers, sending chills down my spine. It almost seems to call my name. Silkily, a caress against the back of my neck.

Starling.

CHAPTER FIVE

Bear and I have been wandering for a while around the block, when I think to ask where he lives.

"Um, there." He indicates a house a few down the road from the park and Starling House—a blue colonial, pristine landscaping, lights strung up neatly, a polished BMW in the drive. "Just me, my parents, my cat, Twinkie. But I'll walk you back, if you're ready to go. Not that I want to rush you," he quickly adds.

"Oh my God, Bear." I laugh, pushing aside the uneasy feelings from the roses. "That's super sweet, but you do *not* have to walk me all the way back." The second I say it, I wish I hadn't. He makes me feel lighter. I'd love to spend more time with him. "I should probably go, though," I say. "I think Agatha will be home, and I don't know what we have going on today, really."

"Are you sure? I don't mind."

"I'm sure," I say warmly. Walking back doesn't sound fun, no matter what. My legs ache, in a strange bone-deep way that they haven't since I had growing pains in middle school. I frown, shake off the discomfort. We didn't walk *that* far.

"All right. Listen," he says. "I know you're leaving soon, after Christmas, right?"

"Yeah."

"Well, if you get time when you're not with your family, I'd love to see you again." He looks down at his shoes. Bashful boy. Teddy Bear.

"I'd like that," I tell him. It's nice having someone I'm not expected to talk about old things with, but I can if I want to. He has nothing to compare me to. I grab for my phone, but remember it's dead.

Before I can just give him my number, he reaches into his pocket and pulls out a pen. "Writers are always prepared, right? Gimme your wrist?"

I look up at him, charmed, and hold out my left arm.

He pushes my coat and sweater sleeves up and starts writing his number on my wrist, and I like that he didn't just take mine to put in his phone. He's leaving the choice up to me.

"Thanks for bringing me," I say, smiling.

"Anytime," he says, and grins. "See ya, Kit from North Dakota." He walks backward up the street toward his house, his gaze fixed on mine. My heart does a little backflip at that smile, one last warm crinkle of his eyes, that damned dimple in his cheek. He turns and keeps walking, and I watch him go up his driveway and through the front door, the taste of rose syrup on my tongue.

I trudge back to the apartment, slowly and painfully, wondering what the hell is wrong with my legs. Wondering if I'm having a freak growth spurt at seventeen—I mean, I'm petite, so maybe that wouldn't be so bad, except for the pain. Maybe there's something going on with my bones that I need to get checked out. Should I call a doctor? See if Agatha has a thermometer? But when I swing open the door to the apartment building and step into the foyer, I forget all about any discomfort. There are three giggling girls in front of me, clustered by the mailboxes. They're all ridiculously pretty, like teen-movie stars. I recognize Charlotte, the girl who brought the pie, but the others I've never seen.

"Hi!" Charlotte's glossy pink lips turn up as she introduces me to the two girls standing beside her. "Kit, this is Molly Vue and Daphne Martinez."

"Hi," one of the girls says, and smiles. Her hair is pulled off her face into a sleek bun, silver leaves dangling from her ears. "I'm Molly."

The other offers me a restrained nod. Everything about her seems purposeful, the brown roots and honey highlights of her hair set perfectly against her sun-kissed skin, her guarded expression, her eyes fixed on mine. She looks like she wants to say something to me but is holding back.

"Hi," I say, expecting a quick hello and goodbye, but they make no move to leave.

Instead Charlotte settles in, leaning against the wall. "So, Kit," she says, "your grandma mentioned you won't be staying for the festival? I ran into her early this morning, coming down."

"Yeah, we'll be leaving next Friday." I nod, disappointed again about missing what everyone seems so excited about. "But she's going to send me one of the dresses, like you guys wear."

The three girls meet eyes. "That's nice of her," Charlotte says politely, then smiles. "Are you having fun so far?"

"I saw the museum, and the roses," I answer vaguely. I'm kind of having fun? But it's more complicated than that. Bear is fun, pizza and a poker-playing grandma are fun, but underneath it all is the ache, the wondering. This trip isn't for fun. It's for closure.

"They're so beautiful, aren't they?" Molly asks dreamily, and before I can answer, she adds, "I love painting them."

"Molly's an artist," Daphne says with a wry grin. "Don't get her started." Molly blushes, and Daphne makes a kissy-face to her friend and adds, "Just teasing, Mols."

"What kind of art do you do?" I ask in encouragement. "My mom's an artist, though I can barely doodle a stick figure. She's been into ink drawings lately."

Molly smiles at me, clearly happy to be asked. "The roses are just for fun," she says. "I'm a designer, really. I get my inspiration and color from traditional Hmong embroidery. Here." She digs into her tote and whips out a sketchbook, flips to a drawing of a sleek model wearing a dress with a hot-pink border, the pattern in blue and chartreuse. It's beautiful. "These are for prom. I'm designing us each one," she explains.

"That's amazing," I tell her, impressed. My mom would be impressed, too.

The interior door opens. We step out of the way, and an old

woman and her poodle move past us as Molly tucks her book back into her bag, grinning. "Thanks."

"So, what about you, Kit?" Daphne asks. "Are you an artist or . . . ?"

Silence settles around us because I know what she's getting at. Mom's an artist and they know who my dad is, who he was. What he did. Which means they all know he's dead now. Of course they know. It's a small town. The quiet turns to tension as I mumble, "Um, I write."

Charlotte shoots dagger eyes at Daphne. Hurriedly she says, "We were sorry to hear about your loss. My dad was a friend of your dad in school. He sounds like he was a wonderful man. I know Daphne's got all his books."

My chest is tight, and I can feel my throat closing up. "Yeah," I force out. "Thanks."

"Sorry," the others say in unison. Molly looks like she might die of mortification. Daphne stares down at the floor. Is she sorry she asked, or sorry he's dead? I can't tell.

Despite how nice the girls are—at least Molly and Charlotte—I'm an outsider. I want to come back to Rosemont to visit, but really, will I ever see them again? We're not going to be friends, right? This is just a moment in a hallway.

"Glad to run into you," Charlotte says, impulsively leaning in to hug me. It startles me, her hair tickling my cheek. "Sorry again," she adds softly. "I can't imagine how you're feeling."

"It's okay," I murmur, giving her a weak smile.

I follow the girls through the interior door. They head into the elevator, while I take the stairs, even though my legs are still so tired. I use the spare key to unlock the door, and I greet my mom in the living room. She's moved from the kitchen island to the couch, work spread all around her. She's busy making new pieces to show the gallery next week.

"Hey," she says. "How were they?"

It takes me a minute to place what she's talking about. Then the roses flash through my mind. The woman praying to them? "Pretty," I say as I kick off my shoes.

And kind of weird.

"And the guy?"

"Cute. Nice." My shoulders loosen, and I try to clamp down my smile at the thought of Bear. "Where's Agatha?"

"She called a little while ago from her meeting," my mom answers. "She should be back soon. Also, we have dinner tonight. Confirmed and reserved."

"Oh, right. Okay."

"Speaking of, I think I'll lie down for a while," my mom says. "My headache is back." She grimaces, reaching up to touch her temple. She's wearing my dad's oatmeal-colored sweater. I know its nubs and threads by heart. She wears it when she's sad and sick.

There are shadows under her eyes. Is it my imagination, or have they gotten twice as dark since we arrived here? It hasn't even been two full days.

"Go nap," I say. "I'll read for a while."

"Okay, love." She kisses the top of my head, and I watch her walk down the hall.

She's okay, I tell myself. But she never gets headaches this bad. And I haven't felt aching like this in my body since I was little. It's strange, isn't it?

I tell myself it's nothing and carefully move her drawings to the side, settling in on the couch to read. I open my book and force myself back into the fantasy world.

I read until a clock chimes, pulling me from the story, back into the apartment. Irritated, I search out the source and find the culprit on a bookshelf behind me. It's an antique gold clock, wedged in amongst books and other trinkets. I set my novel down and get up to look at the objects dotting the shelves: a dish with folk art designs; a tiny papier-mâché teacup that looks so fragile, I don't dare lay a fingertip upon it; a brooch framed with pearls, but instead of a cameo inside, it's a painted eye with a diamond teardrop; a monarch butterfly pinned to linen backing; a blood-red calico ceramic rabbit that looks ready to pounce.

I look over all the shelves, and it's not until I've examined everything that I realize what's missing. Agatha doesn't own my dad's books. Not one.

Black sheep, black sheep, repeats in my mind. She said she wasn't mad at him for leaving. But why wouldn't she have his books?

"Kit?" my mom calls, and I step backward, eyes still fixed on the shelves, starting to tear up for some reason. Why? Why not?

I brush away my tears and follow my mom's voice down the hall into the guest room.

Sleepily she smiles from the bed. "Sorry, baby. I think I missed my alarm. My phone died. And I was so tired." She stretches like a cat, pushing herself up. "My head is better now."

I settle on the bed beside her. "Good." But I'm worried about her, even so. And something feels *wrong*, but I'm not sure what.

"What's the matter? I can see it in your face," she says, as though she can read my mind. "You show it just like Dad."

Unbidden, a sob rises to my throat. I force it back down, give her a smile. "Nothing."

I don't even know why I'm so upset. What about the books not being here triggered me so much? Why does it make me want to climb into her lap and cry?

She reaches out and cups my face, turning it so that I'm looking at her. A couple of fingers stained blue run along my jaw, gently grasp my chin. "Hey. I love you. It's you and me, no matter what."

I clutch her hands. Stare into her shadowy eyes. Lose myself in the love within them, let it carry me away to somewhere safe, somewhere I can't hurt anymore. "You and me," I repeat.

"Oh, hi," Agatha says from the door, and I jump. "Sorry to startle you. I just wanted to let you know I'm home. How was your morning, you two?"

"Good." My mom smiles. "I got some work done, and Kit went out with a new friend."

"I'm delighted to hear it," Agatha says. "Dinner tonight still fine with you?"

"Sounds good to me," she answers, and I tip my chin in silent agreement.

Maybe Agatha keeps his books in her room. Maybe it just hurt her too much to see them on her shelves. *Maybe, maybe, maybe.*

I admit that I don't know enough about their history. We only have six days left, and I don't feel the closure I think I need to feel. Not yet. Because I can't help but hope that if I know everything about him, his past, his secrets, maybe then I'll understand why he left us.

Agatha turns and walks away down the hall, taking all the answers with her.

As soon as we set foot in the restaurant, the hostess exclaims, "Ah, Mrs. Starling. Your usual table is ready!"

Her eyes shift from Agatha to me, widen, and she smiles bigger, if that's possible, before she grabs menus and leads us to our table.

The three women walk ahead of me through the dimly lit restaurant, brick-walled and glossy-tiled, and nice enough to make me glad I wore a cute outfit and did my hair. If I'd guessed what a rural Wisconsin town looked like, I'd have guessed red flannel and hunter's orange and maybe a few dive bars. Not this. Not any of this.

The place is full, even by holiday-season standards, glasses clinking and well-dressed people laughing and talking, steaks bleeding across their plates, a single rosebud in a vase at the center of each table, all the deepest red. I pull out my chair and take a seat; I don't look around anymore. I can tell people are staring at us. At Agatha.

At me. All because my great-great-great-whatever somehow saved this town, over two hundred years ago. But there's a metaphorical itch under my skin that I can't get at. Something prickly.

I glue my eyes to the menu, and my eyebrows rise when I see the hefty prices. But Agatha's treat, she already said. A waiter comes by to tell us the specials, and they include things like "essence of" and "root puree" and "imported." Nothing like what I'm used to back at home.

Agatha and my mom both order a glass of red wine. I get a Sprite, *wishing* it was liquor, and sneak another glance around the busy walnut bar, at the couples cozying up. I catch a few furtive looks at me. I turn away, to the large front window, my own light reflection against the black night. When did I start looking so small?

When the waiter comes back, he asks Agatha cheerfully, "Your usual, Mrs. Starling?"

"Thank you, yes, Paulo," she answers.

"My pleasure." He faces me, grinning, studying me. "For you, miss? We have just two of those rare steak medallions left tonight."

I shake my head politely and order the salad with berries, goat cheese, and sourdough croutons. After my mom places her order, he plucks up the menus and smiles again before leaving us. One backward glance at me. My throat is thick, dry, and scratchy. I reach for my drink and take a long swig that breaks into a choking cough, and I almost drop the glass.

My mom reaches over, eyes huge with alarm, ready to Heimlich-maneuver the hell out of me. "Went down the wrong pipe?" she asks, handing me a linen napkin. I wipe my mouth.

"I'm fine," I gasp. Then, between coughs, I ask Agatha, "Where are the bathrooms?"

She gestures to the back, next to the bar, and I stand, move through the restaurant, past tables, which go quiet when the diners see me, past the kitchen, where someone yells directions, pots bang and clang together, and steam rises, carrying the smell of meat.

I push into the bathroom, and I'm enveloped in quiet, save for a light, tinkling sort of music. I lean forward into the fancy sink and splash water onto my face, uncaring about my makeup. Why do I feel so odd right now? The door opens and heels click across the floor.

A thirtysomething woman walks in, giving me a strange look in the mirror, head craned as she passes behind me, stumbling forward. I vaguely notice a rose tattoo on her arm.

Just as she's about to step into the stall, she turns and asks, voice slurred, "Are you nervous?"

"Me?" I point to my own chest, no idea what she's talking about. But I'm the only other person in here.

The woman laughs, slowly. She's drunk. I roll my eyes, but honestly, good for her.

"Sorry," she says, the word liquid as she bumps against the door and spins into the stall with a boozy flourish, even doing a jazzy little kick with her foot at the end.

Huh. I dry my hands and face and pause when I hear her singsong voice from the stall.

"*Staaaaar-ling, Staaaaar-ling,*" she croons under her breath.

Goose bumps dot my skin as I listen to her sing my name, and as I hurry out of the bathroom, she's still singing. I make my way back to the table, uncaring about the prying eyes on me this time.

I'm staring at my glass, thinking over the strange encounter, when the woman slowly passes to return to her table, glazed stare fixed on me. She rejoins her group, and without shifting her attention from me, she starts talking to them, a lazy smirk hanging off her mouth. She's talking about me, I can tell. Now they all are.

Her song echoes in my mind as I try to understand. Not just this but everything. Time feels unset. The room unfocuses and I remind myself, *Pick up your damn pop and drink. Smile now; Mom is looking. Laugh at Agatha's witty remark. Thank the waiter for your food. Grab your fork and start eating.*

I can't taste the salad. Something isn't right, but I can't put my finger on what it is. I glance one more time at the woman across the room. Her mouth is moving, slowly, her eyes stuck on me. Though I can't hear her words, I know what she's singing.

"Staaaaar-ling."

CHAPTER SIX

The pain has returned with a vengeance. I thought it was two long days in the car, then walking across town, that had maybe aggravated my legs. I toss and turn, stretching out my toes. Sharp daggers shoot up my shins, up my thighs, down my ankles.

Since my dad died, I can be a rock, unmoving and hard. Other times I let loose a violent rush of words so sharp that I think I'd cut a bad-mouthed sailor with them. In my weakest moments, like now, I cry, pitiful. Like a wounded bunny, a sad little kitten. Like a child.

I roll over and shut my eyes tight. I'm trying to breathe through the pain when my mom whimpers in her sleep. Louder now. Once more. A scream shatters the darkened silence like ice cracking across a frozen lake, and I leap from the bed.

"Mom!" I shake her awake, and she clutches me to her, sobbing against me like she's the child and I'm the parent. "Mom, wake up. It was just a dream."

In answer, her shuddering breath comes first, fingers digging into my shoulders. Then she swallows, says, "A nightmare" in a hoarse voice. The moonlight shining onto her face.

"Are you okay?" I ask. "What was it about?"

Her mouth is a stubborn line. "Nothing." But then her voice softens and she reassures me, "It was just a nightmare. Sorry to wake you."

"You didn't. I was awake. I think I need some Tylenol. My legs really hurt," I say.

"Growing pains?"

"I haven't had growing pains since I was, like, eleven," I say, more to myself than to her. That's what the aching feels like, sort of, but it isn't quite like I remember.

She sits up, her eyes lit by the moon. "I could use some, too. My head . . ." She trails off, squeezing her eyes closed.

"I've got it," I say, standing before she can. I slip out of the bedroom. But the floorboards in the hall creak, and when I tiptoe past Agatha's room, careful not to wake her, the door opens anyway.

She flicks on the hall light. Her silk robe flaps open, a matching nightgown beneath. Concern draws her brows together. "Everything all right?"

"Yeah, sorry. We didn't mean to wake you." I smile, shifting the weight in my legs. "My mom had a bad dream, and I've got growing pains." So funny. Growing pains, at my age? I may be short, but I'm seventeen. I wonder again, *How much more can I grow?*

"Not to worry," Agatha says, shaking her head, gently

tugging her robe around herself. "I'm a light sleeper. If she needs something to help her rest, just let me know."

"Thanks," I whisper.

"Sleep well, then." She disappears back into her room, easing the door shut with a smile.

I pad to the kitchen, get the medicine. When I reach the guest bath, I pause and stop in. It smells like a hotel. While I pee, I count eight of the tiny rose-shaped soaps in a pewter dish beside the sink. The tile grout is as white as bone, and fluffy bath towels and embroidered hand towels, each with a cursive *S*, hang on the rack.

I scan the hallway for the light switch, which is next to Agatha's door, and pause, hand on the switch. There are voices coming from inside her room. One deep voice. I freeze, listening.

There's another low murmur, and then it goes quiet. *Silly Kit. What do I think, that she's got a man in there?* Or like Brenna's grandma calls the old guy she's dating, her "man friend"? (Gross.) Now I'm hearing things. I just need sleep.

In the guest bedroom, my mom is waiting for me out of bed, standing near the window, arms folded around herself as she stares out at the moon shining in. I divide up the pills, and we each take a swig of water to wash them down.

"Thanks," she murmurs as I return to my bed. She reaches over and pulls my covers up. "Go to sleep, love. Sweet dreams."

Her tender words are my lullaby, her hand resting on my wrist. My dad's pages under my fingertips. At some point, her hand lifts from my skin, and the weight of the mattress shifts as she moves and climbs back into her own bed.

I struggle, restless, slipping in and out of a hazy sleep, so that even when I'm awake, it's a dream. The night drags on and on and on, endless, the pain barely easing. The shadows creep toward me, a man's deep whisper in my ear, his cruel laugh echoing its way into my subconscious, hurting me.

Hurting me happily.

I jolt upright, eyes open, heart pounding, bones still throbbing.

Just a nightmare. The room is quiet and dark, still. It's late. Beside me, my mom is asleep, breathing deeply. I take a sip of water to soothe my dry throat, to anchor myself in my body.

I'm fine. I reach my hand under my pillow and find my dad's pages. A good-luck charm. A protective spell.

I finally succumb to the seductive pull of sleep.

Still, it hurts. Even in my dreams.

When I wake, the room is misty with periwinkle light, the bed beside mine empty.

I get up, throw on a sweatshirt to ward off the chill in the air, tiptoe down the hall, past Agatha's closed bedroom door. I can't sleep now, either. I bet my mom woke early, made herself a cup of tea. I picture her blue-tipped fingers, wrapped around a steaming white cup. I'll join her and we'll sit in Agatha's big comfy chairs and talk.

Wandering into the main area of the apartment, I find the living room empty, though, and so is the kitchen, dim and quiet. Even the early light doesn't seem to brighten it today.

My mom's not out here, or in the bathroom.

She went for a walk, maybe, or to get a coffee. Or maybe ran to get me a gift despite our agreement to have a non-Christmas this year. We knew that coming here—it was part of the appeal, honestly.

Shivering with cold, I wrap the throw blanket around my shoulders and get comfortable on the couch, picking up where I left off in my book. I try not to think about Agatha not having my dad's books, or weird roses, or strangers who know my name. Strangers who sing my name.

But I can't. Tossing the novel down, I give up. I'm restless. If we were at home, we'd have cinnamon rolls rising, we'd have music playing. Here it's so quiet.

I wander and find cereal to eat, but it has no taste and leaves me even colder. When I'm done, I rinse the bowl and load it into the dishwasher. I'm closing the dishwasher door just as Agatha comes into the kitchen, ice-blond hair tousled glamorously.

"Oh, Kit, it's you." She even yawns delicately. "I thought I heard your mother."

"She's not here," I say. I know I sound irritated. "She must have gone out."

"All right. Tea?" Agatha asks.

"No, thanks." I turn to leave the kitchen.

"Kit?"

"Yeah?" I pause and look back at her.

Agatha smiles and says, "I know we're not really celebrating, but I just wanted to say I'm glad you're here."

"I'm glad, too," I answer. But to my ears it comes out

sounding hollow. "I think I'll go get ready." She nods as I move away, to the guest room. Not that we have plans today, other than hanging out here.

I pause as I reach the bedroom, my mind turning back to my mother. Did she go out for a drive? She wasn't sleeping well, and now I realize her purse is gone.

Frowning, I reach for my phone, which blinks a blue light. Of course she would've texted me if she went out. Of course, I should have known. My mind is thick with fatigue. I swipe open to see my texts and let out a breath I hadn't realized I was holding. There's one from Mom.

I sink onto the bed and open it. Except as I read her words and read them again and again, my breathing has stopped entirely. The air in the room has been sucked out.

I need some space. I'll be in touch. Stay with Agatha.
I'm sorry.

"She wouldn't just leave!" I insist to the sheriff, starting to lose my shit. It's been hours since I woke up and saw her text, and it feels like as many that I've been sitting in Agatha's living room, answering the same questions over and over.

"But her message said so." Sheriff Thompson's brows pull low on his weathered face. His thick mustache doesn't move when he talks. He stares down at my phone. "Looks like she sent it around one-thirty this morning. Then I see you called her *several* times since—"

"And it's now almost ten a.m.!" I push off the sofa angrily, fold my arms. "We've lost the whole morning, and I still don't know where she is. What if someone took her?"

"There are no signs of forced entry." The sheriff glances at Agatha, then back at me. "Uh, has your mother been depressed? Drinking maybe? Your family's been through a lot. You know, depression is a very—"

"Please don't lecture me about depression," I whisper, the anger seeping from my body. I look down. Spreading my hands. Picturing them as feathers, a pair of wings. Thinking of how people jump. I think about pills, and car fumes. Think about gunshots, ringing in the night. Think of my dad. "I know what it does to people." I know what it could've done if it had dug its claws into me. "My mom has anxiety, and she's open about that. But she's not depressed."

"It's easy to hide," he says.

I want to cry out. *I know, I know, I know, I know.*

"Be that as it may," Agatha says, intervening, "I called you to give us peace of mind and to look into this. The facts remain. Nobody knows where my daughter-in-law is. We need answers."

"It hasn't been twenty-four hours. *That's* protocol. Besides, her message—"

"She didn't write that!" My voice cracks. "She couldn't have. She wouldn't."

Agatha and the sheriff meet eyes again, silently.

Agatha twists her ring until only the ornate band shows, as her eyes flick to me, then back to him. "Well, what if she was drinking, like you said? Nearby authorities would tell you of accidents."

Drinking? Unlikely. But an accident? My breath catches.

I don't want that to make sense, to plant a seed of doubt in my mind. Reason pushes the roots of that away. I know she wouldn't leave me, and she would never drink and drive. What else could it be?

She went out for a drive and parked somewhere hidden, went for a long walk, fell, and sprained her ankle. She could be hurt. Lying in the snow. It's falling now, hard. Caking on the windows.

"In my heart I know something's wrong," I say, pleading with them both. "She's in trouble."

Again that silent exchange. Agatha wins whatever battle they seem to be having, and the sheriff nods at her, so small a movement that I almost miss it. Then he stands, giving me an overly toothy smile, his mustache shellacked into place. "Well, we sure will look into it, absolutely. Kit, if you get another message from your mom, let us know."

Another message. He still thinks she sent that text.

I stare after him as he leaves, misery a cloud above me, raining down. Maybe it hasn't been twenty-four hours yet, but I'm still sick with worry.

Agatha moves toward the kitchen. "I'll make some calls, see if anyone has heard anything, or seen her."

I watch her pull a phone book from a drawer—an *actual* phone book. Numbly I pick my phone up from the coffee table, where the sheriff left it, and I open the message, reread it. I call her again, and again, trying not to cry each time the call drops, each time she just doesn't answer.

Mom, where are you?

It's less than a half hour later when I put on clothes and decide to get down to business. Agatha is already getting ready to go to a meeting. If she and the police won't take this seriously, then I will. I'll go door-to-door to get answers if I have to. I'll start downtown. First stop, the diner across the street.

As soon as I walk inside, I'm quickly enfolded in the comfort of it—its pale salmon walls; the oldies music playing; the scent of coffee, fried eggs, and bacon filling the warm air.

People sit in the olive-green booths, a few of them watching me as I make my way to the counter. I flag down a waitress, a rounded beauty with Marilyn Monroe hair, red lipstick, and nails painted bubble-gum pink, to match her uniform. Her name tag says "Belinda."

"Hey," I say. "Have you seen this woman?" I scroll through my phone to find a picture of me and my mom together. My throat thickens as I tilt the phone toward the waitress. She stares at the photo, then at my actual face for a few uncomfortably long moments, and again I put it down to my unnerving resemblance to my great-great-great-whatever. The waitress has to know I'm a Starling.

"No, I haven't." She frowns, red-slicked mouth pulling down in sympathy. Her platinum curls are coiffed perfectly around her pretty, round face. "I'll keep my eyes peeled, okay?"

"Thanks." I try not to sag in defeat, just one stop in.

"Want something to eat?" she asks.

"No. I don't know." My voice breaks helplessly. I can't

remember the last time I ate something substantial, actually tasted my food. Pizza night, maybe.

Belinda jerks her chin to a booth and orders me to sit.

I pick at the scone she brings me, and drink only half the hot chocolate before I stand and go to the counter. Dig into my bag for money. "Thank you," I tell her with a weak smile. "That was good. I'm just not that hungry."

"No, no." She waves my money away. "It's on me."

"Why," I ask, "'cause I'm a Starling?" I can't keep the hostile tone out of my voice.

She raises a brow at me and answers, "No. Because of your mom. Thought you might need some kindness, is all."

Shame washes over me. "Thank you," I say. I smile again, humbled, and leave more grounded than when I came in.

Out on the street, I try texting Bear, but the message doesn't send. Could I have entered his number wrong, or is it just the bad connection? Frustrated, I continue on, into boutiques full of velvet blazers and beaded Gatsby-looking bags and hammered silver earrings made by Mexican craftswomen. Then the perfumery, and more and more places.

It hurts, the desperation chipping at me, at my surety that my mom wouldn't leave me. I beg people for information. *Have you seen this woman? Her car? My mom. Sally Starling. Yes, we're related to Agatha. That's my grandma. Yes, my dad was Daniel Starling. Yeah, I've tried calling. Thanks. Let me know.*

Some of the people are nice, some nosy, a little too interested when they turn and see who is asking, or when they hear my name. People respect our family, only this doesn't feel like respect. It feels like there are secrets I'm not a part of. Like it's not the museum or the wealth or the history or even my resemblance to Frances. It feels like something else.

One old man on the sidewalk smiles kindly at me when I clumsily explain my mom's absence, then presses something into my palm and hurries away before I realize. I look down and blink at what I'm holding. It's a hundred-dollar bill. What the hell? I stand, struck frozen, until I think to shove it into my pocket and keep walking, wishing with all my might I had a car to search the streets of Rosemont, to go door-to-door faster.

The gallery is empty, except for one gangly guy pondering a painting of a rose. The owner knows nothing about my mom being gone but seems genuinely concerned, frowning. "I'd be disappointed to miss our meeting," he says. "I hope she's back soon."

"Yeah," I answer thickly. Same.

Tomorrow is Christmas Eve. She'll be back by today, won't she? By tonight? She'll apologize for worrying me, I'll yell at her as I hug her, we'll laugh, we'll make up. It will be fine. Won't it?

Downtown is bustling, busier with each step I take, it seems. I push past the people chattering, laughing. I try to ignore how so many of them watch me as I scan the cars parked along the street, those that drive down it, trying to find our familiar vehicle. Next I go to the library, to print my mom's photo like they do in movies. I don't *care* if it hasn't been twenty-four hours. I don't feel like I'm overreacting.

With my arms stacked with papers with her picture, my number at the bottom so people can get in touch with me, Agatha's home phone below that, I pause at the foot of the stairs to go to the children's section. Just to see my dad's books, to touch them, will give me courage to go out and start stapling my mom's face to telephone poles.

There's nothing between *Stark, Allen* and *Starpen, Nia.* I glance a few authors over, assuming my dad's books were mis-shelved, but no. Maybe the library has a special section for his books. This *is* his hometown. I go to the local history section, just in case his books are wedged in there, but the shelf has only a handful of volumes, about roses, agriculture. I let out a frustrated sigh. The building is small, but I don't want to traipse through the whole thing searching for his books.

At the reference desk, I ask. The toad-faced woman behind it avoids looking me in the eye when she tells me they don't have any of them.

"They're all checked out?" I'm not surprised, but let down.

"No." She clears her throat, phlegm rattling in the back. "At this time, we do not have any of Daniel Starling's books in our collection. Did you want me to order them?" Her voice is doubtful, her bulging eyes shifty.

Shaking my head, I turn away. How could they not have his books? He was a Starling. Doesn't that mean anything? Or is the town punishing him for leaving Rosemont? It makes no sense.

Black sheep.

Mind muddled, uneasy, I remember the task at hand. Posters. On the way out of the library, I swipe a stapler off the desk, not caring how wrong that is. Along the streets of Rosemont, I get to work, stapling the fliers to light posts. A woman passes me, eyes cast down.

"Excuse me," I say, shoving a paper in her direction, "Have you seen her? She may have been driving a blue SUV?"

The woman shakes her head, walks faster, away from me. She's not the only one. Nobody knows anything; nobody will help me. There are too many hesitant pauses. Too many sidelong glances, or conversely, too many bright, toothpaste-commercial smiles, reassuring me that everything is fine. That she'll be fine. That it's lovely to meet me after all this time. That they're so glad I've come. That it's all *fine, fine, fine.*

But none of this is fine.

By the time I get to the flower shop, halfway back to the apartment, I have more questions than answers. More fear than hope. I shove open the door, and am immediately engulfed in the heavy, wet floral scent of the shop.

Miles looks up and grins. "Hi, Kit. How are you?"

I trudge inside and collapse onto the stool at the counter. Trying to hold back my tears, I explain about my mom, re-counting everything yet again. At least he's sympathetic. At least there's some softness here, in his tone, in his eyes.

Except even Rosemont gossip hasn't reached him yet.

"I'm so sorry, Kit. I'm afraid I haven't heard a thing," he says, then adds, frowning, "You all right?"

"No," I say, and to my horror, I burst into tears. "Shit. I'm sorry," I mutter.

He lays down the sheers he's been using, digs into his pocket, and passes me a clean silk polka-dot handkerchief—who carries handkerchiefs? But I appreciate his kindness.

"Sometimes you have to cry," he says.

"Thanks." I wipe my eyes, then hand back the handkerchief.

He sets it aside and begins tending to a bucket of roses, singing under his breath. I recognize the song from *Hamilton* immediately. But something about him is unhappy. His cheery blue shirt can't hide that.

"Are *you* all right?" I ask finally. "You seem sad, too."

"Of course." His voice is light, though there's a stubborn sort of melancholy shading his dark eyes, threads of bronze running through the brown. "I'm just homesick, I guess."

"How long have you lived in Rosemont? Didn't you say five years?"

"Yes. It was sort of an accident, coming here. I was doing genealogy research after I discovered—late—that I was adopted, and found I had family from Rosemont. I met someone in a roundabout way through that, and he convinced me to visit. We fell in love, but it didn't last."

"I'm sorry," I say, as though I know *anything* about falling in love. Crushes? Those I know. Bear's chocolate eyes twinkle in my mind's eye, and my face heats.

"It happens," Miles says. "Anyway, I couldn't bring myself to leave." A confused look crosses his face, and he chuckles finally, shaking his head to himself. "So, I decided to stay. The shop was empty, and I had studied floral design and been an assistant a few years prior. It seemed like fate. You know, actually . . ." He smiles. "We're a little bit related."

"Are we?" I ask curiously.

"Frances, your relation," Miles says as he fusses over some cream roses. "She had a half sister who's an ancestor of mine, Minette."

"So technically we're cousins a billion times removed?" I ask, managing to smile, despite the mention of Frances, despite everything. "I don't know how that works."

"Me neither, kid. But it's nice to know anyhow. I don't have many people here. . . ." He trails off, voice wistful. "I left Chicago and didn't look back, but sometimes I really miss it. And I get lonely here."

"Really? That surprises me. You're so—"

"Black and gay?" He winks, arranging the creamy roses effortlessly in a vase.

My lips quirk up. "I was going to say 'Nice and fun. Like you'd make friends easily.' But in a place like this, I can see how Black and gay might, um, be a hard sell for some people. Rosemont is a little Stepford-y, huh?"

"Mmm, yeah, and they weren't keen on me buying this place. It always belonged to Starlings—was built by one, in fact, and even though we share blood, I'm not a Starling." He looks down, and now it doesn't seem like sadness clinging to him. It seems like reluctance. It doesn't feel like a counter between us. It feels like information between us, the kind he won't—or can't—share.

I wait a beat, but Miles busies himself tending his flowers, his mouth shut. The moment has passed. I stand up to leave, somehow hurt, like I lost a friend I never got to have.

"Well, I'm sorry you're lonely," I say. "I hope you feel better soon."

"Hey," Miles says, "if I see your mom, I'll be in touch, okay?" His words ring with sincerity, and he wavers a moment before passing me the vase of roses he just arranged. "Here. Maybe these'll brighten your day, or give you luck. I'm not from here, either, but I know that Rosemont has a way of working in peoples' favors, usually. Especially your family."

He bites his lip and turns his face away from me. Again, he's holding something back.

"That's so nice." I thank him. Then, unsure what else to say, I step closer to the door, and a bronze floor tile, to the left of the counter, catches my eye. It's almost hidden in the shadows, but I read it clearly, seven letters spelling one little word: "forever."

Huh. I push the door open, leaving behind the scent of flowers, the sadness, and the secrets, too. I hold the flowers against my chest and step into the chilly wind, thinking suddenly of Bear. He'll help me. But when I pull out my phone, I see that the damn text I tried to send before still hasn't gone through.

My lower back is starting to hurt, and there's a new ache in my belly. I'm tired of walking, and my period is coming or has maybe finally arrived, by the feel of it, and I'm cold and afraid. I walk faster, back to Agatha's apartment, pushing hope forth with each step, forcing it. By the time I get back, my mom will be there, waiting. Won't she?

I hold in tears, bury my nose in the flowers and breathe. They're luscious, so full of life. Why, then, do I recall what Miles said the first time we met, oh so succinctly, about the dried flower wreaths, how they symbolized death?

CHAPTER SEVEN

I step into the apartment foyer, almost bumping into Charlotte.

She's on her way out and doesn't seem to notice the way I must look. I lower the vase and immediately zero in on her blotchy face.

"What's wrong?" I ask, anxiety rocketing in my chest.

"Someone *died*." The word breaks like a cry. "A girl."

Something sharp and poisonous stabs at me, and I go cold. "Who?" I ask.

"It was Daphne's sister, Corinne," she says, sniffling back more tears.

I still. The girls I met in the hallway yesterday with Charlotte, one was Molly. The other was Daphne. Her sister died? My stomach sinks.

"She was found last night," Charlotte says.

"Oh, my God." It hits me hard. Sympathy, deep and true, runs through me. "How old was she?"

"Sixteen."

Agony follows as Charlotte explains. Not only agony for the girl, for her family, but because I'm more terrified than ever. Someone in Rosemont is *dead*. She was found in the river. . . . Does that mean she drowned? Or something less innocent?

Could my mom be dead? No, no. I force aside the panic. I try to breathe.

As I stand there, speechless, Charlotte rubs her eyes and says, "Sorry. I'm a mess. I was just headed to see Daphne. She needs me."

"Please tell her I'm sorry."

"Your grandmother will probably be at the funeral. It's on Wednesday. You could go, too, if you want. But I suppose it would be awkward for you—"

"I'll go," I say with certainty, though nothing else is certain right now. *Mom, Mom.* My heart beats like a bird's wings. "I only met Daphne once, but I'll go."

At my dad's funeral it meant so much, seeing how many people would miss him. How many people loved him. How people came out to support me and my mom. I remember a sea of faces. Some of them crying hard, pressing their hot hands into mine during the receiving line. Some hugging me tight, strangers' cheeks against mine, their perfume scenting my hair for days.

I remember. I'll go.

"Take care," I murmur as she turns to leave. I head upstairs, and once back in the apartment, I stick the vase of flowers on the dining table. Agatha's gone, no surprise. I go to the bathroom and clean the blood staining my thighs.

As I'm washing my hands, I watch the water running over my skin, letting it hypnotize me, almost, the way it pours over my fingers. I think of water, the river. The woods.

Missing people end up in the woods all the time, don't they?

People *die* in the woods. Like Daphne's younger sister. They found her in the river. She might've walked in herself, pockets full of stones. She might have simply fallen, losing her balance, hitting her head, drowning. She shouldn't have gone near it. *Or.*

Or someone could have put her there. Someone could have killed her and discarded her like trash.

Active imagination, I scold. Mom is *not* in the woods, I tell myself logically. But I don't know that, do I? Not for sure. I only hope she's not. I don't really know.

I won't know unless I look. Bear's not answering yet. I'll have to go alone.

The woods are kind of dangerous. He said that one day, or something similar. And a girl just drowned in the river there. But fear makes me brave.

I'm going.

I leave a note for Agatha, and then I run from the apartment, panic making me go fast. I move like the wind. Flying down the street. I run past houses. I run, not caring that people I pass stare. Someone whispers "Starling" behind me, and it somehow still can't drown out the questions in my mind. Where is she? Where did she go?

Lost, lonely, sick? Kidnapped? Trafficked? I can feel myself unraveling from the thoughts spinning, the hopeless feeling heavying my already heavy heart. I have to keep my mind clear. I have to keep moving, heading in what I think is a northeast direction. I don't look like a runner, in my battered green Docs and ripped jeans, tears streaming down my face, ruining my eyeliner. I don't feel like one, either. My chest hurts and I'm out of breath, but I keep going until there are more trees than houses, till I'm no longer running on salt-crusted sidewalk but through snow. I run until I find myself at the edge of a woods, not the ones we came through into town, but a wider, wilder forest, the one Bear pointed out from the sidewalk the day we went to see the roses. I'm only minutes from the apartment, maybe ten, fifteen, but it's a different world already.

The trees throw shadows toward me, brimming with nature's secrets, and I hesitate. I've read enough books to be wary of entering the woods by myself. And, Jesus, a girl just died. Drowned—probably—but still. There's something here, something in the air, a danger that teases my senses. But it only emboldens me. Truth or dare? I pick dare, defying my own fear.

I would defy anything to get my mom back safely.

Chained off, the woods carry with them a warning: PRIVATE PROPERTY. DO NOT TRESPASS.

I glower at the sign, just another barrier. Do not trespass? Says who?

I duck under the chain and into a sort of peace. Without people staring, or whispering, without judgment. Maybe I'll just disappear in here entirely. If my mom doesn't come back, well, who would there be left to care if I was gone? Who would be left to care for me? Can I count on Agatha?

Where is she now, when I need her most? At some meeting

for Rosemont. And I'm here, alone in the woods. But that's my fault, I suppose. Still, I move on.

My face is cold, my toes chilly, but my body? Hot, clammy. I push up the sleeves of my sweatshirt, realizing I didn't even bring a coat. I let loose a jagged hiccup. My heart is still racing, darting forward in fear.

Slowing, I remind myself to pay attention. Maybe I'll see a sign like they do in mystery books: strands of her hair snagged on a bush, a footprint. I call for her, my voice going hoarse the more time passes with no sign of her. Of anything.

I walk on, making tracks in the snow, looking for something unattainable, taking in the crisp air, the wild tang to it on my tongue. Eventually I come to a river, and I stop to watch the water rushing over smooth rocks, foaming along the banks. I stand among trees, and even with my cursory knowledge of nature, I can pick out blue spruce, maples that will bleed sap come spring. There are others, too, bigger trees, one with a trunk so dark it's nearly black, and to my right, a birch with papery bark peeling away from itself, like a snake shedding its own skin. I run my hand along one smooth spot and stare at the river. Something prickles at my neck; goose bumps dot my arms. They just pulled that girl out of there. It must have been so cold.

The image chills me to the bone, and I shiver before turning away. I make a wide circle back in the general direction of where I entered the woods, keeping to a semi-path marked with spiky old vines I have to push out of the way. Prickly branches tear at my sweatshirt, poking me through it. One cuts me across my hand, breaking the skin, and it stings. I ignore it; the scratch is minuscule. I call for my mom harder, rasping out her name, sending it off into the wind even as I tell myself there's no point. She's not here.

I squeeze between trees, pushing along the now crude path, unsure where I'm going. How far can I go before I get lost? Do I want to get lost? I step over a fallen tree, and my foot catches, hooking on a twiggy branch poking from the trunk, just as a surge of dizziness hits me. I fly forward and fall, landing hard on the snow-covered ground, gasping as my body makes contact.

It takes a second to realize I'm bleeding. It doesn't hurt badly at first, a cut on my inner forearm, above my wrist. There's a rock jutting up from the ground at just the right angle to have cut me, deeply. In an instant, pain rips through my haze, stunning me with its fierceness. I stare as my own blood drips down into the base of a towering tree—an oak, I think, red against white. Now it doesn't drip. Now it pours from me.

Have I hit a vein? I hurt myself pretty badly. I think, half-numb, *Maybe I'm going to faint. Maybe bleed out. Maybe die.*

A terrible, secret, mostly-but-not-entirely-lying part of me reasons, *Would that be so bad?*

And the earth shivers beneath my body.

I gasp, panic taking over, and I jump up, grabbing the trunk of a tree, steadying myself as though I could steady the world below me. There aren't earthquakes here, not in Wisconsin. Logically I understand that, but it doesn't stop the trembling, of the ground or my body.

Run! But I don't run. Something comes over me, a wave of

something. A whisper, a memory, a knowing. The trees shudder, the ground in front of the oak tree yawns open.

Then a stillness. Everything is holding its breath.

I can't even hear the river. And then the pause breaks, and the roots of the giant, old oak are unfurling, untwisting, revealing something inside, like a bird in a nest.

Curled in the roots.

A girl.

CHAPTER EIGHT

The girl in the ground turns her head, meeting my eyes with one electric zing. Beneath a layer of grime, her bare milk-white arms are bound by the roots at the bony wrists. Her chapped mouth opens, gasping, a silent cry. She stares at my face, her huge liquid-metal eyes drilling holes into me. Curiosity runs its spindly fingers along my spine, beckoning me forward.

I can't explain it. I don't fully understand it. I'm scared because there's something *wrong* about her, about all this, but I do it anyway, creeping closer. She needs help. I disregard the wrongness of this all and go even closer. Her eyes follow me as I near. My instinct screaming at me, my mom's worried voice in my head. Maybe my dad, cautioning me from beyond. *Kit, what are you doing?*

At the base of the oak tree, near the open ground, I sink onto my knees. Before I second-guess myself, I climb into the hole, the smell of damp earth around me, sickly sweet, sharp, my palms pressed against the cold, crumbling dirt. For an instant, it's like I'm slipping into a grave, and my courage wavers. But I have to help, to free her from the twisted roots binding her. Her wrists are scarred pink with thick ridged bracelets of tissue, like she's been entombed for a long time.

How did she get here? How did she breathe under the ground?

She looks like she could be my age, but it's hard to tell. Beneath what looks like it might have once been a white nightgown, the girl's chest heaves. I study her, the details. Inky hair tangles around her body, matted, wet and soiled with root-rotted dead leaves. I can't tear my eyes away from her. Maybe because she looks otherworldly, so beautiful that it hurts a little.

I reach across to get at the knots pinning her down, and her eyes go wary, like I might harm her, like she's a wild animal caught in a trap, but she doesn't move, allowing me to free her. I pull at the knots—careful to not use my bad arm much. The slippery roots come undone from one of her wrists. Her hand flails, limp, weak. Her dark eyes big, bottomless, needy.

Hunger. The realization surges at the sympathetic part of me and holds tight. She's hungry. A starving thing. How long has she been here? Buried alive? I can't understand it. My brain will not compute. But here she is. Here I am.

The strange girl's strange eyes cut to my arm, the blood running down it, dripping from my skin.

She hisses, snatching my wrist with her free hand in a surprising surge of strength. The spell she's cast snaps, breaking my shock and stupor. I wrench my arm away, shrink back. Was she going to try to drink my blood?

When her eyes connect with mine again, there is a lightning-quick flash of intensity, of enchantment, a cord connecting us, and it feels like I've met fate itself. I'm drawn to her, but in the way a moth is to a hot lightbulb before it sizzles itself to death. She looks too wild, dangerous. Maybe she's not just feral but rabid, and maybe . . . not even human?

But then she looks like a girl again, although still a hungry one, and I'm scrambling up out of the earth, my wound slick with blood. I don't look back to see if she's gotten her other wrist free. I imagine her coming after me, and fear chases me the whole way back to town, but the farther I get from her, the more my fear of her becomes fear for my mom, for this girl, too.

She was trapped in the woods. I don't need to be scared. I need to help her. Maybe there's a serial killer in Rosemont. Maybe there's someone taking people and . . . and . . .

I run and run, my mind spinning ideas, twisting them all up so nothing makes sense.

It's a whirlwind, but I end up at the police station, just on the edge of downtown, a place I've passed more than once now. There are a few people manning desks, but they're on phone calls. So there's no one to stop me as I barge into Sheriff Thompson's tiny office, leaving the door wide open behind me.

He glances up from his paperwork, brows raised. "Kit."

"I found something," I pant. "A girl! A girl in the woods, buried alive." I can hear how unhinged I sound as I say it.

"What now?" His mustache tugs down. He leans back in his chair, unbothered. "Slow down a minute. You found someone?"

"She was in the ground," I say. *The ground opened and she was there.* But I can't say that, can I? "She was trapped. Maybe kidnapped or something. Her wrists . . ." I flutter my eyes closed, picturing the scarring. Picture my blood, dripping down onto the snow. When I look up, he's staring at me like I've lost my mind.

"Please," I plead with him. "She looks like she's starving. And my mom. I know she didn't leave me. What if she was taken, like this girl was?"

"Nobody is missing, and we were in the woods to retrieve a body—an accidental drowning—just yesterday. I'm sorry, but we've got quite a lot to deal with right now."

"You can't leave her there! You're supposed to help people!"

Sheriff Thompson's exhale is tinged with reluctance. "All right. Let's go have a look, okay? It's likely some kind of prank. Kids off school, bored, looking to fool with tourists."

He stands, smoothing his brown tie. "Let me get someone to drive us. Hang on."

I wait for him in the hallway, my back against the wall, fidgeting, then follow the sheriff to his car, where another man waits in the driver's seat. I sit in the back while we head to the woods by the river. I'm only now starting to feel cold, and I'm shivering.

Sheriff Thompson turns up the heat and apologizes from the front. "Sorry. By the time we get there, should be about warm."

"It's fine." I wipe my dirty, chilly fingers against my jeans, damp at the knees from where I fell. It's only minutes to the woods in the car, but it feels like forever. There's blood seeping through my sweatshirt, sticking it to my skin.

I lead the sheriff and deputy to where they should park, and we get out of the car. The men both eye the DO NOT TRESPASS sign, then me, but say nothing. Defiantly I lead them past the boundary and into the snowy woods. Past the trees I saw before, river flowing nearby. A squirrel here or there.

"It's maybe five minutes in," I say, "by a huge tree—I think it's an oak?" I try not to sound so uncertain. They look at each other. It's clear they're only humoring me anyway.

We walk in silence. I feel like they're probably having a quiet conversation behind me. Are they even supposed to walk *behind* me? What if there's someone dangerous here? There *is* someone dangerous here. Then, suddenly, I recognize this place. I was a little worried I wouldn't be able to find it again.

"Right up ahead," I say with relief, pointing. I can see part of the tree.

I put one foot in front of the other, holding my breath.

"Do you see her?" the one who drove us asks, slowing to barely a walk.

"No," I whisper, my heart thumping as I round the corner, pushing past the low branches to find the ground undisturbed. I would've sworn it was the same spot. But I can't see anything. I try to convince myself I got it wrong. The ground is solid, as if the hole never existed. Where the blood dripped from my arm onto the snow, it's white. The evidence is gone.

The girl is gone.

"There's no one here." Sheriff Thompson circles the tree, once, twice, looking up and around. Like he's looking for a bunny rabbit or something and not a girl in trouble. He shakes his head and motions for us to turn back. "Let's go."

"She was here," I say. "She was just here twenty minutes ago!"

"She ran off, then," he says easily, but he's still already heading the way we came, like he's strangely in a rush to leave the woods. "Got her prank in and ran before she got caught."

"It wasn't a prank!" I insist, panic rising in my throat. "She—her wrists—she was trapped."

They look at each other before Sheriff Thompson says, mustache cheating to one side as he twists his mouth, "You sure you're not overtired? Stressed?"

"I'm sure!" But am I sure? I search for an explanation. Like he said, maybe it was a prank. Or maybe . . . I'm losing my mind?

The ground opened up and a girl was inside.

"But I fell," I say, lifting my sleeve, showing them my arm, like if that's real, the girl must be. "My arm was bleeding."

"Nasty cut" is all the other man says, glancing at it. Then, "You'd better wash that up. Let's head back."

He mutters something to Sheriff Thompson, who shakes his head. I manage to walk back to where they left the car. Get in. Buckle up. The sheriff turns to look at me as we drive. "Why don't we give your grandma a call?"

My mouth is so dry, I can barely speak. Clearing my throat, I ask, "Am I in trouble?"

"No, you're not in trouble. It's probably what I said, just a harmless prank. Just some kids up to no good. Or . . ." He trails off.

Or I'm full of shit.

"I'm not lying," I insist. "I saw a girl and she was in trouble, hurt."

"I know," he says. "I believe that you thought you saw a girl."

Which isn't exactly the same thing as him actually believing I saw one. "I'm not lying."

Again they look at each other, and Sheriff Thompson exhales. I'm not sure if he's irritated that I dragged him out for nothing, worried about me (unlikely), or worried about upsetting Agatha (somehow more likely). But I don't care.

"I'll escort you home," he says. "Just to let your grandma know what's going on."

"I don't know if she's even home," I answer miserably. She didn't say when she'd be back from her meetings today.

When we get to the apartment, they follow me up. My hands shake as I unlock the door with the spare key.

"Uh." I look down awkwardly as we stand together just inside the living room. I'm dirty and damp, shaking with cold.

"You go on and clean up, get yourself warmed up," the sheriff says, taking pity on me. "We'll wait here for your grandmother. She should be home soon?"

I mumble agreement, but I don't really know when she'll be back. Maybe she won't be here for hours. Maybe they'll just leave and we'll forget all about this. But can I forget about it?

The two men wait on the couch while I grab clean clothes and then run into the bathroom. I shut the door and sink against it, twisting the lock.

Taking a few shaky breaths, I strip off my clothes, drop them onto the tiny white-and-green hexagon tiles. I grimace when I lift the fabric over my injured arm. My stomach turns violently as I stare at the gash. It doesn't matter that the injury is real; they still won't believe me about the girl. My credibility is in shreds. They already don't believe me about my mom not leaving me. They probably think I'm blowing everything out of proportion.

I step into the shower, my mind battling itself. It couldn't have been a prank. It couldn't have been. I make the water as hot as I can stand, to warm my skin, to disinfect what just happened, the nasty cut oozing blood. Plus, I touched her, someone living under the ground. Sleeping under it? Dying? Was she a ghost? A vampire? A being from the Unseelie Court, slipped out of one of my favorite novels?

Or just an illusion. Desperately I wash away the dirt, the blood still dripping from me.

I blink, and it goes black, oily.

I stare harder, and it's red again. *Keep it together. Breathe.*

My hand trembles as I shut off the water. I dry myself with Agatha's bleached-white fluffy bath towels but avoid my arm. Instead I blot at it with the black tank I had on under my sweatshirt, which probably negates the sterile shower, but blood won't ruin it.

A knock on the door. "Kit?" Agatha's voice. She's home, damn it.

"I'll be out in a minute," I say, dreading having to go out there and nod along while the sheriff tells Agatha I was the victim of a sick prank. Or that I imagined something. Maybe not in those words, but won't he be thinking it? Did I imagine it?

When I find a first aid kit under the sink, I let out a sigh of gratitude. I goop a thick antiseptic paste over the cut and wind a bandage around my arm, then finally look at the mirror. I try to smile; it is ten kinds of alarming. There are smudges under my eyes. Soggy hair dripping onto my collarbone. A haunted look. Like I've seen a ghost. Or I am one.

I pull on clean undies, a cotton bralette, leggings. My fluffiest, coziest sweater, which falls over my wrists and half covers my hands. I run my fingers through my damp hair and take a deep breath, slow, in and out. Eyes shut, eyes open.

In just one breath, the pain in my arm is searing, bending me at the waist. I gasp, hanging on to the edge of the sink until the pain passes. What the hell? Furtively I push up my sleeve and unwrap my bandage to see why it would hurt so bad suddenly, imagining all sorts of horror, gangrene maybe. Maybe they'll believe me then. If my arm falls off.

When I peel away the last layer, sticky with antiseptic, I let out a strangled "Oh."

It's worse, in some ways, than what I dreaded.

The cut is gone. Like it was never there.

That's when I lose my breath. All my oxygen. All my resolve to stay strong.

That's when I start to scream.

"No!" I cry, fumbling with the front door, trying to unlock it so I can run. "Let me go!"

"It's okay, Kit," Agatha says firmly, trying to pull me back, pushing my hands down.

I want to run. I need to find my mom. Before she dies, like that girl must have—I saw a ghost, didn't I? That had to be what she was.

"She's dead," I try to explain, but I'm crying. Or there are other things haunting me, and the girl in the woods is just a manifestation of it. My arm hurts, but there's nothing there. A phantom pain.

"—hysterical." Sheriff Thompson's low voice. "Can't you give her—"

They are holding me still now, and I'm trying to tell them I'm afraid of the girl, afraid for my mom, afraid for me, but my words come out as a wail.

"Shh, Kit, shh. It's all right." Agatha's hands cup my chin. I can hardly see, can hardly think. I am so scared that I need to run, run away, but they won't let me.

The sheriff holds me tight, and she tips something bitter and green into my mouth. I choke and sputter on it. Before the lights go out and I slump in the man's arms, my last thought is:

This is what death feels like.

I'm moaning when the lamp flicks on. I remember everything. A long, low cry comes out of me, loosening my lungs.

"Shhh." Agatha's hands on my forehead. But they feel nothing like my mom's. I pull away from her, struggling to sit up. She says softly, "You slept for hours. It's Christmas Eve."

"The girl was buried alive," I try to tell her, though my words come out all loose and jumbled, like I'm stoned. "I'm not lying."

She gives me a little smile, placating me. "I believe you."

I shake my head, tell her in between short, difficult breaths, "We have to save my mom, before she ends up like that."

"She won't," Agatha says. "Come now, one more, then. It'll help you rest."

That sharp taste against my lips again. I slap at her hands, choke against it, but it goes down too easily. I have no more fight left in me.

I surrender to a dark and heavy rest, but I find no peace.

I dream of things with sharp teeth, things covered in blood. I dream I'm chasing my mom through a woods, dark and twisty; she is always too far for me to reach, no matter how fast I go. Then suddenly I trip, and I'm down a rabbit hole, like Alice, the earth capturing me, putting me in a prison with bars made out of bones. Something touches my face. Something licks at it.

The girl from the ground smiles, her beautiful, terrible eyes locked on mine.

She reaches for me.

I shoot straight up in bed, gasping. I watch the freezing rain hitting the window. It must be the next day. It looks like morning.

It takes me a while to ground myself. To remember what happened.

Agatha sedated me because I was freaking out. And the two cops witnessed it, but I can't seem to find any embarrassment. I don't even care.

I'm still here, chest still heaving from the dream. From the reality.

My mom's bed is still empty.

Unfortunately, I didn't sleep through Christmas Day dinner. I stab at mashed potatoes and a chocolate-pecan pie from the diner, hating this holiday-ish meal we weren't even supposed to have, and hating ten million times more that I am having it without my mom. The roses from the beautiful bouquets stink up the air. I would rather have eaten in the guest room, alone. Would rather be anywhere other than sitting here, pretending my heart isn't torn in half.

After I woke up, for hours today I tried reaching out to our neighbors at home, to my mom's friends, and Agatha has done at least some minimal questioning here. There's still no sign of my mom. Nothing but that cryptic text she didn't send, couldn't have sent.

Agatha's voice shatters my thoughts, "Kit, tomorrow—"

I interrupt, "I have to look for my mom tomorrow. Can I borrow your car? I could check around town easier."

"I'm afraid not. I'll need it for prior engagements," she says, shaking her head without even a hesitation. "I was going to say that tomorrow I have several meetings I can't get out of, but we might have dinner after."

"You have a lot of meetings," I observe, trying not to sound upset. My mom is more important than any meeting.

"I'm on several boards, and the Ladies of Rosemont, among other things. But later this week you may use the car, if she's not back yet. In the meantime, perhaps we can see more of Rosemont together."

"I think I've seen it all," I answer sharply.

I don't mean for it to come out so harsh, but my mom is missing. Who cares about fucking Rosemont? But Agatha's face now makes me wish I hadn't said anything.

"Sorry," I mutter. "I'm just upset."

"Yes." She takes a sip of wine. I notice a mottled purple

band of bruising around her wrist. Half to herself, she says a small "I understand."

"Aren't you worried, too?" I search her face.

She sighs, slowly nodding. "I'm more upset that you're so upset. I believe she'll be in touch soon. It has to be a misunderstanding, that's all. I know she loves you and she's doing what she thinks is best."

"Leaving me isn't best," I say flatly.

I wait for her to respond but she doesn't, and we spend the rest of the meal in silence. When we're both finally done, I follow her to the kitchen and help her load the dishwasher as a peace offering. None of this is her fault. I know that. I disappear to the quiet of the guest room and flop onto the bed. I can hardly bear to be around even myself right now.

Bear. I hold tight to the image of his face in my mind, his hand in mine. I find his name in my phone and with jittery fingers type, *Hi.*

I squeeze my eyes closed, until I feel my phone buzz in my hand. A text. It worked.

flip phone. k if I call u

Flip phone, really? I type *yeah* and hit send.

I get comfortable on the bed, answer on the first ring. "Hey."

"Hey." His voice is soft. "I, uh, I heard about your mom."

"Wow, news does travel fast here," I say with more snark than intended.

"Sorry, yeah. So, I guess she's not back yet?"

"She didn't leave me," I say, and I can hear the defensiveness in my voice. "She sent a text message, but it sounded nothing like her."

"What do you mean?" he asks.

"I mean, I *know* her. She wouldn't ditch me here. It doesn't matter how stressed she was, or how hard things were. She wouldn't do that to me, especially after . . . everything." I choke down a sob. "I can't believe she would actually send that. I *don't* believe it."

A short silence. Then he asks, tentatively, "So . . . you think it was planted?"

I exhale through pursed lips. "I can't prove it, but yeah, in my gut, yeah. Who could have sent it, though? And why? I'm terrified she's in danger."

"But the police? What are they saying?"

I scoff, replying harshly, "They think she left town."

"I'll be honest, I've heard rumors that she left," he admits, and that stings to hear. He goes on gently, "But I believe you. I'll help you look around, if you want. But how can I help now?"

I come up empty. "I don't know. Distract me, I guess?"

"We could hang out tomorrow . . . but probably not here. I'd have you over, but my mom is in the middle of renovating the whole first floor—it's her latest hobby," he says. "The house is a disaster—we couldn't even have family over for Christmas be-cause of it—and I've been strictly forbidden to have guests over. Because the *horror* of anyone seeing it in less than a pristine con-dition. It's making me really regret not moving out a few months ago, like I was thinking. I'm just mad you can't meet my cat."

"What's its name again?" I ask, wading through my mem-ory, my spirits already lifted. "HoHo?"

Bear laughs. "Twinkie. HoHo is a ridiculous name."

"*You're* ridiculous." I laugh back, the reaction chasing my fear away. Bear chasing it away.

We talk until two in the morning, long after Agatha has gone to bed. We talk until I can't keep my eyes open, until my battery is drained. I fall asleep with one hand pressed against my dad's pages. I dream of him.

Before I even open my eyes in the morning, I can hear Agatha laughing somewhere in the apartment. Probably on her kitchen phone, cord twirled around her wrist.

I touch my arm again, just to make sure. My cut is gone, as if it were never there. But that doesn't mean it wasn't real. I try not to think about the girl, or rather, the *imaginary* girl. I had to have made it up, the way they think I did. I *want* to have made it up. But what does it mean if I'm hallucinating? Is reality so difficult that I'm starting to dream things up in the daylight to cope?

Get up, Kit. Get up, I tell myself.

I rise slowly, my senses relighting reluctantly, my body firing like an old furnace, lit with one goal, one truth, one prayer: my mom will come back to me. That's all that matters, isn't it?

My cell phone rings on the nightstand. I'm still, frozen. Because what if it's the police? What if it's news? What if it's bad? But I recognize the name that pops up.

"Kit?" A friendly, warm voice, like heated honey, on the other end. "Good morning."

I sink back against the pillow. "Bear. I'm glad you called."

My relief is so obvious that it's almost embarrassing, and we spoke for hours last night. I'd know him at once, just by his voice. I've heard the hoarse sound of it when he's spoken for too long, heard his laugh, heard his hope for me, my mom, our situation. Glad he called? I'm *thrilled*.

"I thought I'd see if you want to hang out, maybe watch movies," he says. "Get your mind off things. I can sweeten the deal with sweets, literally."

"I'd love that." I let out a breath of gratitude. "You want to come here?"

"Great. I'll be there in an hour or so? Around ten?"

"Yeah, but tell me you're not gonna walk," I say. "It's, like, sleeting."

Mom, are you outside in this weather? Fear is a fist squeezed around my throat.

"I'll get a ride, but it's kind of you to worry."

After we hang up, I clear my mind of everything and climb out of bed. On the way to the kitchen I hear Agatha's voice, a one-sided conversation. I step softly, listening to her.

"It's terribly sad, isn't it?" she's saying. "People always speak of fathers leaving their children, but mothers do it, too. I don't know what Sally was thinking. Kit is taking it very hard."

Rage rises up in me, and she turns, sees me. Her voice fades out, and she quickly finds an excuse to hang up.

"Kit," Agatha starts, coming after me as I march away. "Wait."

"What?" I spin back to face her, almost colliding with her near the couch, and I notice she's limping for some reason.

Agatha stops. Today she's wearing a pair of neat jeans, a crisp oversized white button-down, and a pearl necklace—chic but casual, the way rich people seem to just throw things on and look pulled together.

"I'm sorry you had to hear that," she says. "I know it must hurt."

I'm so angry that it's hard to keep my voice steady. She really thinks my mom left me. "She didn't leave," I say firmly.

Her face is full of pity, and it only makes me angrier. "She left you that message, Kit," she says. "See reason. People leave the ones they love—"

"You hardly know her!" I yell, making even myself cringe.

She shifts her gaze to me, eyes sharpening. "That may be so, but keep in mind that it's not for lack of desire. If you knew—"

"Knew what?" I snap. I snap at my poor old grandmother. Only, she's not poor or old. And she's saying all the wrong things.

With a sigh, Agatha lays both hands on the back of the couch, as if to anchor herself. "Kit, I wrote to you many times. Your parents hid my letters, and even after your father—well, your mother refused to let me speak with you."

The words leave me silent for a long minute. I shake my head, pushing away the doubt she's planted in my heart. "I don't believe you."

"It's true," she says calmly. "I was only able to finally convince her after I threatened to contact you myself with the aid of a private investigator. I promised that if you met me, if we had this one visit, I would leave you alone forever. And I would put you in my will."

It can't be true. "No," I say. "She wouldn't do that. She doesn't even care about money."

"For you, of course she does," Agatha answers, gesturing. "She wants you taken care of. But she did everything she could to keep us apart. Finally, though, she agreed—under strict conditions. We would pretend it was the first time I was writing. I would never, ever mention our hostility to one another. I think she blamed me for your father—or thought I blamed her and acted defensively. If it weren't for her, he never would have left Rosemont."

"What do you mean?" Inside my chest, my heart hammers. My mind reels.

"He was fine until she came here; he was a normal teenager. But she convinced him to leave, to abandon his family and choose her instead."

"That's a lie," I say, tightening my fists at my sides. "She would never do that."

"Yes," Agatha says, nodding. "She did."

"My mom was never here before," I argue, louder. I watched her take in Rosemont firsthand. It was all new to her, all charming and unfamiliar. She wasn't here. She wasn't!

Agatha's face creases in pity. "I'm sorry, Kit. I can't imagine how you must be feeling, finding out these things. First your father, then your mother lying to you and leaving. It would upset anyone."

My mouth falls open but no words come out as I stand frozen, both livid and stunned. Like she stuck an arrow into my chest. Like she pulled the rug from beneath my feet. Like she took the one person I have left in this world to trust, and shattered that trust. But I don't believe her. I don't! I can't. I sputter, outraged, "But—"

"But maybe you didn't know her as well as you thought," she finishes. The words come out of her mouth easily, but they sting me like a slap. "Your life—*their lives*—were built on lies," Agatha says. "I wish I didn't have to be the one to break your childhood illusions, but this is where we are."

On the tip of my tongue: *Fuck off, old lady.*

Except as I open my mouth to say it, my feet already itching to run to the guest room, grab my stuff, and go, I hesitate. Why don't I just take a bus home? Because I know my mom is still in Rosemont. I can feel her here, and I can't leave her behind. I can't. Isn't her heart tethered to mine?

"In the meantime," Agatha continues, "she left you in my care, and I *do* care about you. I want to get to know you better, and I want you to know me, to know our family. I have so much to give you. You have a legacy to fulfill."

"I don't understand why my mom would want this," I say. "If what you're saying is true, *why?* Why not just tell me the truth? Not only her but my dad, too. He never spoke the word 'Rosemont' my whole life. He never spoke of you." Maybe it's a mean thing to say. But it's true. It's all true. I stare at her accusingly. "I don't know what to believe anymore. You don't even have his books."

"That doesn't mean—" She tightens her lips, holding back what she might've said. "I see. You've made me out to be some kind of villain in his story, and I don't think that's fair."

"Are you saying *he's* the villain? My mom is?" My voice shakes with fury. It feels like she's turning them against me, unreasonable thought or no. I stare at her resentfully, waiting.

"Not at all." Her eyes search mine, and my anger deflates

a little. She goes on, quieter, "I loved him very much, and I hate that we have to have this talk. Please don't judge me too harshly. I may not always say the right thing, but I'm sorry to see you upset. I wanted you here to celebrate you, us, our family. I wanted to teach you and help you grow into the woman I know you can be. That's all I want."

I have nothing to say. I stand silently, and she finally moves past me, limping still, and lifts her fancy bag from the console table next to a potted orchid.

"I have an early lunch and a get-together today and then a last-minute meeting," Agatha says briskly. "I won't be home until late."

I remember Bear. I suppose I should have asked before inviting him. Tightly I ask, "Is it okay if I have a friend over?"

"Charlotte?" she says, suddenly happy. Charlotte is probably the only person she knows under thirty.

"No. Barrett," I say. Agatha doesn't seem like the type to appreciate cute nicknames. "I met him the day we got here. He took me to see the roses?"

"That's fine," she answers. "I'm glad you're staying in today, instead of looking around in this weather. Your mother would not want you to catch cold asking after her."

I look out the window, at the sleet driving into the glass. Defensively I turn back to Agatha. "I'm not *not* going out because of the weather. I may go out later."

Back to the woods? I wonder the question, shuddering. I don't want to see the girl again. But I won't, I stubbornly tell myself. She doesn't exist.

Agatha studies my face for a moment, sighs. Probably

worried that I'll have another hallucination. Or just disappointed that I'm not as obedient as she'd like. "There's a sturdier winter coat than yours in the small closet, if you wish to borrow it. If you must go out, at least dress warmly."

I bite back a snarky comment. Of course I will. But if she was actually worried, she'd let me take her car. Or she would go with me. But no. There are meetings. And she really, truly thinks my mom left.

Agatha tilts her head. "I can see how upset you still are. Maybe we disagree on the circumstances of why she left, but I know your mother is fine. Don't you, in your heart?"

Without answering, I turn away, before I start to cry. Because no, I don't know. I only hope. Just like I hope my mom didn't lie to me. Just like I hope she's still in Rosemont, somewhere I can find her. But maybe I'm wrong. Maybe I'm wrong about a lot of things.

Agatha makes her way out the door. As it closes, her words ring through my mind again.

She's lying; she has to be. Or maybe the truth isn't always easy to see in hindsight. Agatha is simply mistaken. There's no way this is real, any of what she said. I won't let it be.

CHAPTER NINE

I squeeze Bear the second he walks in, my arms shaking. "I'm happy you came."

"And I'm happy you invited me," he says, laughing, and I can tell that he's surprised by how excited I am. Bear's dimple creases, and it makes me want to laugh. His mood is contagious, smoothing out my worries. "We're going out of town to visit my crusty old aunt tonight, and I could use some company I actually like today."

I shake my head affectionately as I take his jacket and toss it onto one of the chairs. When I turn back, he's frowning.

"You look upset. Everything okay? I mean besides the obvious?"

I manage to nod. What else would I say? *Agatha just told me either a huge bombshell or a major lie? I found a girl in the woods and then she disappeared?* I shake out my arm; it suddenly stings.

But there's nothing there now, is there? I don't even have a bandage on. No scar, not even a scratch.

He holds out a white paper bag. "Cookie? I've had at least two already."

The smell wafts over to me, and my mouth waters as I accept the bag and pull one out. I take a bite and shut my eyes as I chew, placing the flavors. Something caramel-like, a hint of vanilla and browned butter. It might be the best cookie in the world. "Wow."

"Belinda made them, from the diner." He takes the bag back and pulls another one out, then sits on the couch, enjoying himself. "Anyway, how are you? No news today?"

I shake my head. "No," I say, emotion catching up to me. Because his expression is so soft and warm and sweet, and I'm afraid of what is happening. "There's nothing. No trace." When I say the last two words, I lose it. I join him on the couch and bury my head in my knees, and the tears come. Bear's arms around me flood me with relief as he pulls me into his chest and lets me cry on him.

He's like a cozy blanket, even though nothing about his frame is soft. He's all lanky, long boy with wiry muscles underneath.

"Sorry." I hiccup, trying to slow my breathing. "I'm embarrassed."

"Don't be." His touch on my back speaks. *I care about you. I'm sorry.*

Shaking my head, I slump my forehead back against my knees, hurting deep inside. "I don't understand where she could be. Did someone take her? Did she fall and get hurt? Is she lying in a ditch somewhere?" Or in a hole in the woods? I hate asking the questions, out loud or even to myself. I hate thinking them. Turning to him, rubbing my eyes, I say, "My mom is missing, and nobody is worried. They all think she left me."

He wraps me in his arms again then, and I'm glad for his warmth. Into my hair, he whispers, "Well, I believe you. And I'm here, however long you have to wait."

Bitterly I bury myself against him. I want to leave this town behind like a bad dream. Instead I'm here, stuck in limbo. In hell. Eventually I collect myself, rising with creaking, aching joints, and go into the kitchen. I make hot chocolate with Agatha's tinned Dutch cocoa and organic half-and-half and a lot of sugar. I find a bag of chips I don't remember seeing before. It crosses my mind that not only has Agatha been keeping the kitchen stocked for me but she's also been doing my laundry. The thought is uncomfortable. I'm even more uncomfortable that I didn't notice until now.

I carry the food in on a tray to the living room and set it down on the coffee table. "What movie do you want to watch?" I ask.

"You can pick," he replies easily.

Without any streaming service, I realize we'll have to rely on the DVDs that Agatha has. I rifle through the drawer of the TV cabinet and find *Stardust*, one of my favorites. It's odd finding it in Agatha's possession, just like it was odd seeing her eat pizza and play poker.

"I've never seen that," Bear says, tossing back a handful of chips.

"It's great. The book, too." I slip it into the DVD player and settle back next to him, pull a soft throw over us. I rest my feet on the coffee table, and he hauls me closer, so I lean my head against his shoulder. We fit together like a puzzle, easy, uncomplicated. We stay like that until the movie ends, and then we put in another. I try to pay attention, try not to think about my parents. Try not to think about the girl in the ground. My arm stings, and I tighten up. *It didn't happen. It's not real. . . .*

"You all right?" Bear asks.

I want to tell him about what I saw; I wish I could. But what if I'm losing my mind?

"I mean, no. But, yeah." I turn my face into his shirt, inhale his scent, chocolate and salty butter and a faint cologne I love. One that reminds me of pine needles and a sharp wind and a little bit of sweat and clean soap.

With the arm he has wrapped around me, he trails his fingers along my shoulder absentmindedly. Like he has to touch me, like he can't help it.

I tip my chin up, look into those warm brown eyes, and we share a breath.

My lips part and I wait, for a sign. Count the seconds.

Bear leans down, and presses his lips . . . to my forehead.

I force my eyes down, face hot, disappointed. Before I say something embarrassing, I take another cookie, despite his teasing that now *I'm* eating them all. My stomach hurts, actually, and it's not just me feeling the sting of rejection after that forehead kiss. Which was sweet and all, but not what I expected.

Not what I wanted.

Suddenly everything within me hurts, my heart most of all.

My belly turns over. Chills run down my back, and I shiver. I reach up and touch my forehead, and I'm hot, clammy.

"Kit . . ." Bear sits up sharply. "Your face is, um, *green.*"

I leap up from the couch, a sour taste filling my mouth, and run to the bathroom. I make it there just in time to vomit into the toilet, avoiding Agatha's immaculate tiles.

I feel his hand, tentative and soft, on my back. Another holding my hair from my face.

"No." I wave him away, self-conscious. "Gross. I don't want you to see me—"

"I don't give a shit about that, come on. You're really sick. Jesus."

As I heave, I choke on the strange earthy taste. I open my eyes, and a cold sweat runs down my neck as I stare, horrified, at a pile of wet, rotten roses.

But when I look up at Bear, he isn't shocked or upset, only concerned. When I look down again, the roses are gone.

My mouth tastes of perfume. Of terror. Of all my fears uprooted and made manifest. I brushed my teeth three times, but I can still taste those roses pushing up my raw throat.

Even when I return to the living room, to Bear, my heart is racing. Because why? Because what the fuck? Because what is happening to me? Why am I seeing things?

It's so far past not right that I can't make sense of it. Where is Agatha with her bitter sedative now? I don't want it . . . but maybe I need it.

My hands twitch, and I look up to find Bear watching me, frowning. Apprehensive. "Should I stay, or—"

"No," I say thickly. I clear my burning throat when I answer again, trying to sound upbeat because I know he has to go do a family thing. "No, I'll be okay. Promise."

"Can I wait until Agatha gets back at least?"

"That might be a while," I say, shaking my head. "I'll be okay."

"All right," he says, but he frowns, concerned. He pulls me into a hug. "Keep me posted, okay? No matter what, you'll let me know before you leave, right? When you find her?"

I love that he says "when" and not "if."

"Of course," I tell him, then add, "I hope it's soon."

"I know." His expression is understanding. "Me too. But, I'll miss you, you know?"

"I'll miss you, too." I say it, and I feel it, but I don't want to think about missing anyone. Not my mom. Not my dad. Not Bear, who I'll be sad about not seeing again. I don't know if I would want to come back to Rosemont after this. Actually, I know I wouldn't, I admit, pushing aside any guilt. "I wish I had something to give you. Something to remember me by."

For some reason it feels like if I do give him a present, it means I'm going to find my mom soon, that I'll be leaving. But there's nothing here of mine. Only what I brought with me.

"One second," I say, and get up and run to the guest room, rummage through my bag. I have to find something, anything. "Goodbye" means luck. "Goodbye" means my mom returns. Maybe tomorrow. Maybe if I mean it enough, maybe if I want it enough, it will come true. I'll find her, or she'll just come down the road, ready to pick me up, to take me from here. To take me home.

I skip over my velvet scarf, the stone. I find what I'm looking for, what I didn't know I was looking for. On the back, I scribble my email and a message:

Thanks for the cookies . . . and everything. Love, Kit.

I return to the living room, and Bear's standing by the couch, waiting with his coat on.

"Here." I place the old photo of the girl with the flowers in his hand. "I've had this forever. I found it in an antique store once when my mom was hunting for house stuff. I liked her expression. Usually old pictures are so serious, you know? But she's mischievous, you can tell."

"You like collecting things, don't you?" His smile wavers. "I don't think I have anything to give you back."

"That's okay," I say. I wasn't expecting him to give me anything.

"No, wait, hold on." He hunts in his pockets. Pulls a handful of loose coins out and picks through it. A fluff of lint. A cough drop wrapper. A crumpled receipt. A skinny strip of black ribbon, bow still on it, ends of the ribbon torn and ragged, as if he ripped it away from something.

"Don't you throw anything away?" I tease.

"I know," he laughs. "But . . ." He lifts my left wrist, tugs up the sleeve, the way he did when he wrote his number. His eyes are pinned to mine when he ties the ribbon on me. He does it without looking, fingers deft and warm. I shiver at his touch.

There *is* something between us. I can't be the only one who feels it.

"It's a little silly," he says. "But it's yours."

"I like silly," I reassure him. "I'll keep it on."

"Someday I'll give you a real present. I'll mail it." Bear smiles with the promise. "But look, I'd better go before the snow comes back. I don't have a ride home. You should rest. Hydrate."

He encircles me again, and I finally pull away, though I'd rather not. "I'll walk you down," I tell him.

Bear motions me ahead with a chivalrous sweep of his arm, and I duck my head in an exaggerated thank-you as he grabs my hand to hold it while we make our way downstairs. I love that. He smiles like he knows, squeezing it gently.

But still, that forehead kiss, damn. Was he being romantic? Or . . . brotherly?

In the foyer, Bear pauses at the building's exterior door, the gray sky not exactly welcoming but at least better than it was. I hold my breath, waiting for him to say "See you later," but he understands. I need this goodbye to be for real. He looks back once as he walks away. His smile sort of breaks my heart.

When he leaves, I realize I'm *alone*, alone. And I feel sick. My body aching, my stomach cramping, not just period pains but worse. But what happened? Why did I think I threw up flowers? And why can I still taste them, when I didn't? Nausea blooms in me again, almost violently, and I take a deep breath, pushing it down. I finger the ribbon on my wrist, and with each step back to Agatha's apartment, tell myself: *I will not throw up roses. I will not throw up roses. I will not throw up anything. But especially not roses.*

CHAPTER TEN

Wrapped in a blanket on the couch, still warm from Bear, I get a new text. It's from Leo back home.

I'm so sorry, Kit. I hope she's ok, Leo's text says. *Nobody's seen her here.*

I picture his black curls, his azure-blue eyes, the way we eased from friends into more than friends and then back to just friends again, with no drama. So far nobody besides him and Brenna has reached out, but at some point, Agatha will have to call my school, unless my mom is back soon. Break is over in a week.

Please, God, let her be back by then.

I type, *Thanks. Wish we could just get back home already. Miss you guys.*

To my relief, the text actually does send right away.

I'm still cocooned on the couch when Agatha returns. Her hat is wet, and her cheeks pink.

"Hello," she says pleasantly as she puts her coat away, like we didn't argue right before she left.

"Hi," I say cautiously.

She moves past me, and I peek over the couch to watch her start to tidy the already spotless kitchen, benign smile on her face. It's like nothing happened. At least to her.

"Kit?" she calls, breaking the silence. "Have you eaten?"

My stomach turns. I can't eat after the roses. But maybe that would get the taste out of my mouth. I move from my cozy spot and into the kitchen.

"We can order in," Agatha says. "What would you like?"

I shake my head. "I'll just have cereal."

I ignore her disappointed face and grab a box of organic knockoff Cinnamon Toast Crunch from the cupboard. I pour out a bowl and add milk, and force it down at the island, avoiding her eyes.

Her tone is more somber when she breaks the silence again. "I forgot to mention, I'll be gone most of tomorrow—some meetings early in the morning, and then a wake and funeral, so I won't be able to loan you the car yet. I'm sorry."

I look up. Funeral. Right. Tomorrow is Wednesday. "I heard about that from Charlotte," I say. "I forgot it was tomorrow, but I'd like to go. I met the girl's sister Daphne the other day."

Agatha pauses. She looks me over with something like pride. "Do you have an outfit for it?"

"I'll go check," I say, pushing away from the island. I dump the last of my cinnamon-flecked milk into the sink and leave the bowl in the dishwasher.

In the bedroom, I frown at the mess spilling from my suit-case, realizing that I actually don't have anything appropriate for a funeral. Agatha comes in after a minute, takes one look at the clothes strewn around, which I stubbornly refuse to put into the dresser because I still plan to leave the second my mom returns. I've already packed her stuff. Everything except for her purse, which she took with her.

Or someone took.

"I'll give you a credit card to go shopping," Agatha says, tak-ing the mess in stride. "Most stores are open until six or seven. You can get a dress for the funeral and anything else you need. I noticed your sock had a hole."

Ugh. I knew it.

She leaves the room and returns, handing me a platinum card. It occurs to me again that I don't know where her money comes from, what she used to do. What my grandfather did.

"Thanks," I say, trying to sound grateful. I hate that we ar-gued. But I'm still upset.

"Tonight, afterward, perhaps we can spend time together and talk," she says, her face finally showing *something*. Some sign that she wasn't as unaffected by earlier as I thought.

"Okay," I say hesitantly. I don't want to hear more about my parents lying to me, but I do still have so many questions for Agatha. Even small, safe ones, about my dad, about his child-hood, about our family. We do need to talk.

I brush my teeth yet again, and thank myself for eating something, because the rotten taste is nearly gone, and I slip her credit card into my wallet. I'll pull myself together—leave

Agatha to do whatever it is she does. This necessary shopping errand will distract my racing heart. My raging heart. My broken heart.

"Here," she says as I'm pulling on my boots. I whirl around to see her holding out keys. Not her spare, which I already have, but for her car. I look at her blankly, and she says in a mild voice, "It's nasty out, and I'm staying in. You can drive downtown to get your things. I don't want you walking in this mess."

I take the keys and say, "Thank you." She does care at least.

Outside, the sky is growing dark, and sleet hits my skin. I bundle my coat around me and hurry to the parking lot to her white car. I climb in and sit back, and my heart sinks as I stare out the windshield. It's getting darker by the minute, and even though I finally have Agatha's car, where am I going to go now to search for my mom? I sigh at the missed opportunity, but I've already been to every business within walking distance, as well as the woods. Memory of the tree and the girl echoes. I shudder, turning the key in the ignition. I don't want to go back to the woods, not at night. Not alone. This will just have to be a damn errand after all.

I drive the short distance to a boutique I went into the other day, looking for my mother. It's still open, but from the moment I step inside, I know it's all wrong for what I need—it's too trendy, too bright, not a dark-colored item in sight. The fresh roses on the counter are so harshly yellow that they're almost offensive to the eye. The racks up front are filled with crisp white dresses, and look out of place for winter. I stand there blinking at them, until I remember the damn festival. I turn to leave, move past a pair of girls who look college age perusing the racks playfully. They're holding dresses up to each other, trying to decide which to get.

"Ohh, Miss Starling," the girl behind the counter says loudly, and I turn to see her looking up from the magazine she had her nose in. "Are you here to find your dress?"

The shoppers notice me then, and their eyes go big. They turn to each other in a fit of laughter, which doesn't feel like they're laughing at me, exactly—more like they know a joke I don't.

"No," I answer, and turn from the clerk, hurrying out of the shop, feeling unnerved.

I huddle against the cold and head down to the next boutique, and I'm luckier. I quickly manage to find a pair of black pants and a nice sweater. I remember what I wore to my dad's funeral: a black dress, shoved now into the back of my closet. I should burn it when we get home. *If* we get home.

I push aside the steady drum of fear, sling the clothes over my arm, and grab three pairs of cushy socks and a new pair of leggings as well. Mine are getting worn through at the knees. The freckled shopgirl watches me over a giant vase of soft-peach roses at the register, but apart from staring at me a little too long, she doesn't say anything other than the total and "Have a nice night," which suits me fine.

The weather has worsened by the time I step out of the shop, and I rush back into the car, shivering.

When I return to the apartment, I drop Agatha's car keys into the dish and slip out of the wet coat, shaking snow out of my hair. I should have bought a new hat.

My phone dings with a new text from Bear. *I'm bored already. My aunt insists we stay overnight, maybe 2. Send help.*

I smile and text back, *lol sorry*. I add a heart on the end.

"Agatha?" I call, heading into the kitchen area. I smell the food before I see the take-out boxes on the counter, and my mouth waters. My appetite is back at least. I flip one open to see tacos—some vegetarian ones, too. I will eat the hell out of those. But first, comfies. I'll need an elastic waistband.

Agatha's door is shut when I head to the guest room to change. I drop my shopping bag onto the bed. Then I look up, stop short.

A creamy-white dress is hanging on the wardrobe. "Agatha?" I call, loudly this time, staring at it.

There's the sound of her door opening, and her footsteps as she enters the room behind me. "Yes?" she says.

I don't bother turning around. I point to the dress. "What's this?"

Looking back now, I catch how her painted mouth cracks into a smile. "It's your dress," she says. "For Crowning Day! Only now I don't have to ship it. Isn't that wonderful? I didn't think it would be ready so quickly."

I stare at her, expression blank. I can't believe she'd think I'd go to a celebration. "I'm not going to the stupid festival."

Her pursed lips make it clear how she feels. "Kit, the festival is important to our family. It means something to our town."

"This isn't my town," I say firmly. I square my shoulders even as I look again at the dress, helplessly. I don't know what I thought—that I would find my mom before the celebration and be gone? That they wouldn't have it—they'd cancel it because she's missing? It's in six damn days.

Agatha lets out a hefty sigh, and she reaches up to touch the milky silk. "It's a lovely dress. I think it will fit you perfectly—Vivienne truly outdid herself. This is exquisite work. Look at the buttons."

She turns the dress around to show me the row of buttons running up the back, and I frown.

"It looks like a wedding dress," I say.

"Well," she sighs, "if you don't love it, I suppose you could wear Juliet's. She was younger than you on her Crowning Day, but you're smaller than she was. Unless you'd rather wear mine."

"I'd rather gnaw off my arm," I grind out, my anger rising along with my frustration. She's not *listening*. I'd like to yank the dress down and chuck it out into the hall to prove my point. I raise my voice. "My mom is missing. Who gives a shit about a festival?"

"Well, you said you'd like to go—"

"That was before my mom disappeared!" I yell as I whirl around and stomp toward the door. Why does she not get it? "I'm going to find her before the stupid festival, and we're going home, and we're never, ever, ever coming back here!"

"Kit, please." Agatha follows me around the room. "Please. If your mother isn't back by then, won't you please still come and wear the dress? It would mean so much—"

"I don't understand what's so important about all this." I pause and turn near the foot of my mom's bed, stubbornly cross my arms, but I glance again at the dress. It's got a simple straight line to it, from the slightly empire waist to where it brushes the floor. The silk gleams. It really is beautiful.

"You're my only grandchild." Agatha's voice is timid in a way I've never heard it. She squeezes her hands together, as though she's holding herself back from reaching for me, and she unexpectedly looks old, vulnerable. "You're the last Starling, the only hope I have left."

"Hope for what?" Frustration and confusion make my reply come out harsher than I mean it to, but she's also freaking me out.

Agatha seems to go smaller. She sniffs, like she might cry. "Every mother has hopes for their children and grandchildren. You're all I have. You're it," she says, and her eyes are so full of need that I turn away from her, unsettled.

Agatha is halfway out the door when I call her back.

"Fine," I say. I'll go. I'll wear a pretty dress and smile and eat something fried on a stick. That's not a lot. I hate that I'm thinking about going. Only, refusing to go seems like a pointless hill to die on. I'll go to the festival, and then everyone can finally shut up about it. "If you stop badgering me about it, I'll go. One day, not all three. And I'm not socializing."

"You'll barely need to speak to anyone," she says, brightening.

"My mom will be back by then, or I'll find her," I add. "I know you don't think so. But I will. Then we're leaving."

"I know you're a very determined girl," she says, leaving the room, shutting the door before I can respond, before we can talk as we planned—not that I want to now. As soon as I'm alone, I regret saying I'd go to Crowning Day.

More than that, though, I regret coming to Rosemont in the first place. If we hadn't come here, my mom would still be with me, wouldn't she? The starlings at my dad's funeral—that moment felt like they were mourning. But now, coupled with the starlings as we entered town, altogether it seems like a warning. We never should have come to Rosemont. I've lost my dad. And now my mom is gone, too. What am I supposed to do—just go on?

Turning back to the dress, I reach out to feel the silk under my fingers, imagining wearing it, a crown of dried old flowers on my head. But the image shakes me, and I drop my hand.

Mom. Mom. Mom. I sit on the bed and close my eyes. I try to see her, try to call to her. *Please be okay. Please be okay.*

Instead I get a glimpse of my dad. Just a flash. A smile. Encouraging. I hold on to the memory of his face. It lasts through the night.

Of course Agatha is gone in the morning, but the wake isn't until five, so I have some time. I'm thankful for the bright sky today. At least I can walk around and won't freeze my ass off. I skip breakfast and get ready instead. Bear's still gone, of course. He won't be back until tomorrow. I frown. I'm not going to the woods alone. I don't want to see things by myself. No, I decide. I'll ask him to help me search when he gets home.

But maybe I don't have to walk around. Maybe I can start where I stand.

I grab my bag and lock up as I leave the apartment. But I don't leave the fifth floor. Instead I knock on Agatha's neighbors' doors.

"Have you seen her?" I pull out a flyer I've folded carefully in my bag. "My mom?"

"No." A crotchety old lady frowns. "Police already came by and asked."

I slump where I stand. I guess that was at least something they did. I don't let it stop me, though. I continue on, door-to-door, neighbor-to-neighbor. Most of them are super nice, but a lot aren't even home, or they don't answer. Nobody says anything weird, but I find myself holding my breath until each interaction is through.

I trudge down the last stretch of steps and into the foyer, just in case someone is getting mail or coming in. But there's nobody. What a pointless hour of my life.

My stomach rumbles, and I look across the street at the diner. I'll stop in, at least, for a hot breakfast. I'm so sick of cold cereal.

I push out the door and cross the street to Harold's and settle myself into a seat at the counter. Not long after I place my order, Belinda sets a plate of French toast in front of me. I eat half without hardly breathing. I glance up to where you can see the kitchen, listening to her sing as she grabs plates off the warming rack, her cheeks rosy.

When she returns, she pauses at the counter, gives me extra napkins. "How is it?"

"Great," I say truthfully. "And your voice is fantastic."

She smiles, flattered. "Don't mind me. Just dreaming about being in the movies. I'd love to be another Marilyn. Obviously." She looks down at herself pointedly.

"I can see that." She's her own version of it, but there's something in her, a hunger, a longing. I recognized that same thing in Miles's eyes. "You know Miles Jones, the florist?"

"Not well, but yes." She smiles. "I buy myself lilies every Friday. Why are you asking?"

"Maybe you guys could start a singing group. Miles loves music, too, musicals." *And you both seem like you could use a friend,* I want to say, but instead add, "I don't mean to butt in or anything. Just crossed my mind."

She laughs brightly. "It's not a bad idea. We could make our own little Broadway or Hollywood."

"Why don't you go to actual Hollywood?" I ask, before realizing it's a little rude and presumptuous to imply she could just up and leave her life and move across the country.

Belinda's eyes darken with something I can't name, but she doesn't seem offended by my asking. "I don't know. My life here is good; I like being a waitress." She ends this statement sort of defiantly, as if I'd judge her for it. "I have security here, and the tips are great. Besides." She shrugs. "I half run this place now. You know I make all the baked goods? I'm pretty much living the dream. One dream, I guess. The movie-star thing is just one I think about when I'm feeling brave. Sometimes I wish I could go, but . . . Rosemont is my home. Truthfully, there's nowhere else I'd rather be."

Something in her voice sets off warning bells. Or maybe it's the intense look that's come into her eyes.

"What—" I start, but she interrupts.

"It's okay, kiddo. You'll be okay, and I'm praying for your mom." She stares at me a moment, shrugs, but her smile is kind, and she blinks, her face relaxing.

"Thanks," I say, letting loose my tight breath. I can tell she's being sincere. For a minute there she seemed off.

I reach into my wallet and shove aside the hundred I forgot about, and that I don't even want, but there's no way she'd take it. I pull out a twenty-dollar bill and lay it on the counter before she doesn't let me pay at all. Then I head back to the apartment.

The rest of the morning zips by quickly, and it's late afternoon when Agatha finally pops her head into the guest room, where I'm trying in vain to call the sheriff for any updates, but my phone keeps dropping the call.

"I'm home, going to get ready now," she says, lifting one hand.

I sigh, glancing at the time. It's already three. I put down the phone and go to the bathroom. There I take a scalding shower and put on lip balm, mascara, a pearly highlighter to give me more cheekbone definition, a dusting of powder. My signature winged eyeliner because that's about all the technique I've mastered, despite Brenna's forcing me to study YouTube tutorials with her. It feels so ridiculous to put on makeup, knowing there's a dead girl in a casket just blocks away, knowing my mom is missing, knowing how I've been enveloped in strangeness since I arrived here, but the routine steadies my hand. When I leave the bathroom, Agatha's door is open, and I can hear her in the living room, puttering around.

In the guest room, I rip the tags off the new clothes. I slide the pants and soft sweater on over my clean skin. "Agatha?" I call, and walk out of the bedroom, into the living room, where she is waiting. "I'm ready," I say.

She glances at my outfit, lifting one brow, as though to say, *I told you to buy a dress.* But she only nods, approving enough. Then we go, the car filled with tension, a far contrast to the last time we drove together, when I was filled with a tentative hope.

I beg her silently not to bring up anything I don't want to hear. We will save our talk for tonight, maybe, since we didn't get to it last night. Right now, I'm at my limit. I will leap out of the car if I have to. She's not going fast; it wouldn't hurt too much. The road whirs by and I gauge the distance. *Duck and roll, Kit. Duck and roll.*

The funeral home stands, grand and stately, and people are gathered outside in the cold all the way out to the street. Agatha parks in the lot, and the sun hides behind clouds, then disappears entirely as we cross to join the other mourners. Snowflakes start falling and collect in everyone's hair like ashes. I glimpse Molly, standing with her parents, but otherwise don't see anyone I recognize. It seems the whole of Rosemont is here, though, so I'm not sure how I could go about finding a familiar face. It takes us nearly an hour to even make it into the building.

Inside it's welcoming, with a warm fire crackling in the fireplace, and despite the amount of people, we move quickly through the lobby into the viewing room. I look up at the front, where I don't want to look, where the girl lies. But her casket is closed, flowers neatly heaped atop. Roses, of course, but other kinds of flowers also, whites and pinks. My breath catches in my throat, sorrow climbing to tangle up with it in a dreadful dance. Sixteen, dead. I've already outlived her by a year.

When we finally get up to the slow-moving receiving line, I grasp Daphne's hand, whisper my apology. She looks confused, a glassy-eyed version of the girl I met only days ago, circles under her eyes. She gives me a faint nod. Her dad has a warm, surprisingly gentle grip, but Daphne's mother doesn't reach out and take my hand or Agatha's.

Instead she stares at both of us with something like loathing, pale eyes hard.

"How dare you show your face," she hisses.

"I'm sorry—" Agatha drops her hand. "I don't know why—"

As I stare at her, the woman turns and her glare pierces me. "What use are you?" She turns back to Agatha. "What's the point if this sort of thing still happens? My daughter *died*. I will never forgive you Starlings. Never."

A cold wave of fear hits me, and Agatha stiffens, pulling me from the line, whispers snagging in the air. I don't take my hand from hers, though it feels unnatural, and I can only listen to the low chatter as we make our way to the back of the room, her limping at my side. I hear our name, something about our family. But there is more I make out.

"Poor girl."

"Should never have gone to the river."

"Drowned, how tragic."

"Such a sad, sad accident."

Hard eyes follow us as we hurry into the lobby and then outside, away from the people. Their words, the ones they keep repeating: "Accident. . . . Drowned. . . . Shock."

But something about it all feels like a lie.

Except for Daphne's mother. Except for that closed casket. Those feel real.

CHAPTER ELEVEN

Agatha's hands are tight on the steering wheel. I open my mouth a half dozen times but shut it again. The silence hurts. I keep waiting for her to say something. To explain what everyone seemed to understand at the funeral home except me.

Once we're back in the quiet apartment, I break the silence.

"Agatha—" My throat is dry, and I clear it before trying again. "Agatha—"

"I'm going to get out of this dress and make some tea. You get comfortable. Then we'll talk," she says simply. "It's long overdue anyhow."

Apprehension fills me. Slowly I retreat to the guest room so I can change into my new leggings, throw on a sweatshirt. In the hall after I'm done, I pause, my hand on her doorknob, when I hear voices. A man? The door jerks open, and she walks out into the hall.

"Oh," she says, her cheeks flushed when she looks up, startled.

"Is someone here?" I ask. "I thought I heard a man." I'd almost forgotten that deep voice. The night my mom vanished I heard it in Agatha's room. A man. Chills run over my skin, and suspiciously I crane my head to look behind her.

"No, no." She pushes gently past me, still wearing her funeral clothing: a black sheath, pearls, black heels. The ring on her hand catches the light. "There's no one."

"You didn't change," I note, confused.

"I know. I'm sorry, but I have to go. Something came up."

"What?" We were going to talk. The wake . . . everything. I need to understand. "But—"

"I have to. I'm . . . Someone needs me now," she says abruptly. "It may be late, before I'm home. Tomorrow we'll talk about everything. I promise."

I open my mouth to protest, and she repeats, "Tomorrow, Kit. A long and important conversation cannot be rushed. I'm sorry, but there's nothing to be done about it now." Her hands shake as she picks up her bag. I catch a faint red mark on the side of her neck, a scrape. "Order a pizza for supper if you like. Tell them to put it on my account."

Then she walks out the door, her gait uneven.

I stand there, not moving, for too long, thinking over everything. Then I fall onto the couch and ruminate over it some more.

An hour ticks by. And I'm still no closer to understanding. Everyone is obsessed with our family, but what did Daphne's mom mean at the funeral by not forgiving us Starlings? If nothing else, Agatha was flustered, but why? And where is my mom? And what happened to Corinne? And the girl I hallucinated in the woods? Is it me? Or . . .

Black sheep. It reverberates, along with words like "honor." Like "legacy."

My dad didn't want the Starling legacy. Could it be for more reasons than Agatha told me? I close my eyes in frustration and lean my head back, exhausted by the way my mind is spinning. What am I missing here?

Why can't I shake the feeling that it's something very, very important?

I come aware slowly, head fuzzy, throat dry. I sit up on the couch, rub my heavy eyes. I fell asleep. I blink around the dark apartment. Force myself up to my feet, unsteady from the nap.

"Agatha?" I call, but she's not back yet. I glance at the time in the kitchen. Quarter after eleven. Where the hell is she? I wander back to the couch to see my phone blinking a notification.

I pick it up, yawning. I missed a text from Bear, hours ago. My heart leaps at the sight of his name.

> *Dad not feeling good, we decided not to stay. Heading home now. Wanna get dessert? meet at Harold's for pie later? Coffee?*

But it's not the thought of a late-night date that intrigues me. I slept hard—maybe my mind worked something out in the hours I stopped overthinking. Suddenly, I feel like I know what I should do.

I need answers, and I'm going to have to find them for myself. But maybe I can bring him along, for company, for courage.

Starling House. The words blow against my neck like a gentle breeze, almost like a real voice urging me on. A scent I almost recall, a word on the tip of my tongue that I lose right away. I shake my head out of the lingering haze. *Focus, Kit.*

I don't waste time texting. Instead I call him, even though it's late. It'll be easier to explain.

"Hey," I say hurriedly. "Sorry to call so late."

"I'm still up," his warm, sweet voice, like melted chocolate, answers. "Can't sleep. Do you—"

"I want to see you," I interrupt. "But I have something I need to do."

"Yeah?"

"Can you meet me at Starling House?" I ask.

"Of course," he says, no questions asked. I love that about him.

When I hang up the phone, I already feel a little better.

I leave immediately, but Bear is standing outside when I get to Starling House. Makes sense. He lives on this block.

"Hi." He smiles, waiting for me on the sidewalk, silhouetted in the dark. "What are we—"

"Shhh," I say, snagging his hand and leading him around to the back garden. "We have to be quiet," I whisper.

To his credit, he doesn't argue or ask questions. He watches me while I stare at the back of the house from the shadows of the evergreen shrubs in the garden. I can only imagine how it would look in the height of summer, vines twining up, flowers and herbs everywhere. Now it's covered in snow and we're about to break in. At my side, Bear isn't even flustered. He nods, trusting me to do what I need to do. I'm not even sure why I'm here, but I have to trust myself.

I search the ground, try to find something hard beneath the snow. A stone. I pick it up, meeting Bear's eyes.

"I'm going inside," I say, then wait a beat. Letting him have a chance to leave, to talk me out of it. "I need to look around."

His eyes go wide, but he nods. I take a breath and hesitate, glancing at the stone. I look back up at Bear, and he encourages me with a second nod. Without another breath, I throw the stone through the back door's window.

It's so loud that I expect all of Rosemont's lights to flick on, the cops to be here in an instant. A dog barks but that's it. I breathe until my heart slows to a human pace before I cross the grass, reach in, and unlatch the back door, careful not to cut myself on the jagged glass.

An alarm. I think of it too late, but there is none that I can hear. Gratitude floods me, but I still stall at the door. Am I really doing this?

"Come on," Bear whispers at my side. He takes me by the hand and leads me over the threshold and inside.

"You act like you've done this before," I whisper back, stepping over the broken glass, the stone.

"What? Break in?" He smiles crookedly, easing the door shut behind us. "Nah, this is the pinnacle of my illegal activities. You?"

I bite my lip. "Nothing too bad."

"What are we looking for, exactly?" Bear asks finally. "You're being pretty vague."

"I *feel* vague," I answer unhelpfully as we walk down the dark hall. "I don't know what I'm looking for. But Agatha, she's hiding something. She keeps saying stuff to me, about our family, except she's leaving things out. Something told me to come here. Instinct, I guess."

Or foolishness.

With the moonlight streaming in, I catch how Bear opens his mouth as if he might say something, then after a second just nods yet again, like he's trying to be sympathetic but doesn't quite understand.

"Anyway, I'm sorry for dragging you out in the cold to break into a house when I don't even have a clear reason," I apologize, guilt catching up to me. "Pie would have been more fun."

"I don't care about that," he says. "I want to help. Just think of it this way, it's your family's house. Part of your birthright. And nobody is going to care if you're here. Tell yourself, 'This is my house. This is my house.'"

This is *my house,* I think, gesturing him forward. We'll go upstairs. People hide stuff in their bedrooms, don't they? Maybe I can find something there.

We walk side by side, hand in hand, then pause at the main staircase.

"We'll go up here first," I say with more confidence. "Just look for anything unusual, I guess."

That's also entirely unhelpful, but I truly think we'll find *something.* Or at least, I hope we will. This house, it pulses with energy, whispers not with a voice but with a hundred of them, buzzing in the shadows. It pulls at my nervous system, my atoms, my marrow. I can't imagine living here. I don't think I would ever be able to sleep.

We break apart to search the bedrooms separately. Bear takes the yellow, and I head straight to the blue. I step into the room, breathing in hope that I won't just find something to clarify any of this mess but something of my dad's, too. Yet other than a bed, a dresser whose drawers are all empty, and a chair in the corner, all personal possessions have been removed, just as the room was last time. There is nothing here, at least not in this room.

I leave and head into the largest bedroom, the green, and freeze when I see that it has a new addition—a dress on a model form. Black as night, a thick, rich fabric, lace dripping from the sleeves, a tiny waist. A placard near the roped-off dress tells me it was hers. Franny's.

The longer I look at it, the worse I feel. Dread, bubbling up inside my chest. Bear comes to stand next to me and reaches out to touch the dress.

I gently elbow him, pointing out the sign. "No touching."

"Kit, we are literally breaking and entering." His smile is naughty.

I shake my head in affection. "Come on," I say. "Let's look downstairs."

The kitchen search is fruitless, but when he heads to the doorway of the portrait room, I tug him forward. "Gift shop first. This room last."

He follows good-naturedly, not questioning me. It's childish, but I'm dreading seeing Franny again, and defeat is inching its way into my heart. I reassure myself that there must be *some-thing* here to lead me to answers. A map? A secret chest?

"What about secret passageways?" I ask, thinking of my dad's books. "Anything like that here?"

"If I knew, do you think I'd tell you?" he teases as he opens the glass doors to the gift shop.

I look up at him, failing to keep my face straight. "I mean, yeah. I think you would."

When Bear laughs, his dimple comes into full view. "You're so right," he says.

I follow him into the huge high-ceilinged gift shop, which is as generic and strange as I expected. Roses and starlings stamped on soap and enamel coffee mugs, replica eighteenth-century earrings I can picture paired with a gown, like the one upstairs. But nothing helpful. I turn to go back the way we came, and something on the wall in the hallway draws my eye this time. But the moonlight isn't bright enough for me to see the details. I turn on the flashlight on my phone to see better.

It's a framed piece of embroidery, black thread against a linen background the pale color of milky coffee. At the top center, a starling, wings outstretched against two outlined roses on either side, head pointed down, a ribbon curling under it and through each rose. Written in the center below the bird is one word: "forever."

Thorns border the entire piece, names threaded into it, the family tree. Frances—Franny—is the root, the start of our tree. Then it goes on and on, down and down, and across. I touch the glass, tracing names along the branches, and my fingers slow as a striking, sudden understanding hits me: my father is glaringly missing, along with all the other men.

I continue searching down to the bottom, and a cold chill floods my chest.

Embroidered in cursive, the black sharper, newer, is *Katherine Wilder–Juliet Starling*.

Me.

"What is this?" I whisper.

"Huh," Bear says as I struggle to make sense of what I'm seeing. "I haven't seen that before, but I haven't been here since junior year. Was it here the first time you came?"

"We didn't come down this hall." I bite my lip. "I wasn't feeling good and we left."

"Probably someone made it for a gift to the family, once you arrived," he says.

It looks old—antique, at least the linen itself—but I only shrug, my throat thick. I don't like seeing my name here. But I don't know why. I turn first, heading into the portrait room, and Bear follows close behind.

From above the fireplace, Franny's green eyes seem to glow triumphantly, and the silk of her emerald dress shines right off the canvas, lace falling against her white arms, the glint of a ring on her finger. My breath catches as I step closer. It's Agatha's ring, I think. I didn't notice it last time.

I stare up at Franny's cold face, force myself not to recoil. What am I so afraid of? She can't step out from the painting and get me. She's just my great-great-great-whatever-grandma. Her high pile of red curls looks slightly faded, powdered. "She's young here," I finally say.

"Yeah," Bear says. "Probably around our age. I've always thought she was so beautiful." His comment sounds offhanded, but then his cheeks flush because I know he means me, too. I look like her. She looks like me.

Holding my breath, I inch closer to him, waiting for him to catch my eye, but he is looking down, clearly embarrassed. While I continue the search, I pause to cheat a glance his way, but he studies a bookcase on one wall, intent on scanning the shelves. The moment has passed. Disappointment settles deep in my bones, mostly because now I realize. Other than a few books and some vases, a footed pedestal bowl in silver, there's nothing in here. What was I expecting? An arrow pointing me to something? To the big fat answer I need?

The painting seems to smirk, like Franny *knows*.

On impulse, I reach up to the frame and try to lift it from the wall, as though there's a secret safe behind it or something, but it doesn't budge.

I touch the mantel under it, run my fingers along the wood, along that missing corner at the end, my stomach turning as I touch it. What could have happened to the corner? I swallow the lump in my throat, push aside the uneasy feeling, and look around one last time, determined not to give up. Have I missed anything? I look from the ceiling to the floor, an idea sparking. Trapdoors and childish dreams aside, I have to at least check.

"Um, Kit?" Bear says as I go down on one knee, peel back the rug. I scan the wood with the flashlight, and stop suddenly, staring at a dark-colored stain on the floorboards, spread out, like—

"Blood," I whisper, my heart pounding.

He reaches down to touch it, runs his fingers along the grain. "It could be wine," he says, but reservation tinges his voice.

"A lot of wine," I say. Why would I think blood?

Bear helps me put the rug back down, and I stand up—too fast. I pause, light-headed, and his arms wrap around me as I sink back to the floor.

"Whoa, you okay?" he asks, not letting go. "You're not going to get sick again, are you?"

My stomach turns at the thought of the roses I thought I threw up, but I shake my head to reassure him. "No. Sorry," I say. "I just got dizzy for a second. I feel better now."

It's a lie. I'm still dizzy, and he seems to know it. We stay on the floor, sitting on the rug, hiding the faded stain of a secret, and I rest my head in my hands as he strokes my hair. We need to get out of here, as soon as this dizziness passes.

I shake my head, exhaustion and frustration hitting me. "I don't get it."

"What?"

"I don't know," I say. "I have this terrible feeling that I can't put my finger on. Not just about this house but about Rosemont."

There's a beat of silence before he speaks. "Rosemont was founded on terrible."

"Terrible?" I ask, looking up at him.

"I thought Agatha would tell you," he says, hesitating.

"Oh." I remember the story. "Yeah. She said people starved."

His face gives him away. There's more to the story.

"What?" I say. "That's not it?"

"Not exactly. It's not really a secret. I just . . . don't want to overstep."

My heart seems to stall in my chest, like I'm on the edge of a cliff, about to jump off. I look up at Bear's face. "Tell me," I say. "I want to know the rest of the story."

He lets out a breath. "A long time ago, when Rosemont was first settled . . ." He hesitates, and I prod him. He lets out a huff of a laugh, then grows serious, running his fingers through his messy hair. "It's not a pretty story, Kit."

"I don't care. I don't need pretty," I say. I just want to know what everyone's hiding.

"Okay, well, the first years were hard for the early settlers," he says. "There weren't resources here; food was hard to come by, for one. Indigenous people wouldn't settle in the area, and they actually tried to warn the settlers to go elsewhere. But they didn't listen. They managed for a couple of winters, and then, uh, the third was especially harsh. Nobody was prepared for the cold, or how long it would last. There wasn't enough food. People starved to death, as you already know. Others resorted to . . . cannibalism."

My stomach flips upside down. I stare at him, unable to process the information.

"Who . . ." I don't finish the sentence. I can't.

His answer is somber. "First their own family members. Those who'd died from starvation or cold. But then they killed their own friends, their husbands, and wives. Even children. They killed them for food willfully. There was talk that they were acting crazed." He pauses, then adds, "It, uh, created a lot of bad feelings."

I stare at him, let what he just said sink in. "Understatement?"

Bear gives me a pained smile. "It's hard to get past something so gruesome. The history books don't talk about it, but generation by generation the families here are handed down the truth. It left a stain on this place. We don't always notice the feeling, we're so used to it. But maybe it's easier to see from your eyes. Anyway, Franny stopped all of that. She brought in money and food. Among other things. So, you can see why people would respect your family so much."

I let out a breath. "Yeah. Agatha told me some sanitized version." I shake my head. "But she left out the cannibalism thing. That can't explain everything, though. It feels like there's more."

Bear stays silent—but I can't tell . . . Does that mean he doesn't know anything else?

"I'm not even sure why we came here," I say. "I feel stupid for dragging you out. I'm sorry."

"I'm not." Bear's eyes search my face, and he tucks a loose hair behind my ear, the pad of his thumb brushing my earlobe. "Kit . . ."

"Yeah?"

"You're beautiful," he finally says.

Everything leaves my mind except for him in front of me. His eyes dart to my mouth, and his fingers trace my face. I draw my fingers to the nape of his neck, feel his warm skin, the curls that need a trim.

"Kit." He leans in, and I lean in, lips parted.

We breathe each other in.

And then we meet in the middle, stretching time and space to finally press our lips together. A kiss that feels like it lasts forever, but is over in the blink of an eye. And then it starts up again, and again. His mouth moving from mine to brush my skin, to taste my jaw, run down my throat. My breath hitches.

We are in the middle of the portrait room, still on the floor, my ancestors looking down at us, and his lips are on my neck, chills running down my skin. No. We are in a fairy-tale land, this would be our castle, he would be my prince. There is nobody else in the world right now.

I pull his face back to mine, kiss him harder this time, until we're breathless with it, until my lips feel bruised. Until we finally break apart, because things are getting too intense. Now I'm almost too shy to look at him again.

Bear makes me feel . . . something.

He catches my hand on his shoulder, pulls it around his neck again, takes the other and does the same. "Kit, I—" He swallows. Now he's the one to look shy, look away. He stills, and asks, focusing his eyes over my shoulder, "What's that?"

I look but he's already crawling forward to the fireplace. A corner of something sticks out, something I missed. He reaches in and pulls down what looks like crumpled-up papers.

"Someone there?" a man's voice calls from deeper in the house, and we jolt to our feet. I look around wildly.

The window, Bear mouths. He shoves the papers inside his coat and zips it up, then grabs my hand tightly.

We run over, push aside the draperies. I pray it's not stuck, and let loose a quick breath of relief when, together, we manage to shove up the old glass pane. A blast of cold air strikes my face as I climb over the sill, Bear following me out into the garden.

The stars shining down on us, cool air hitting our skin as we run, relieved not to get caught. Hearts pounding. Alive.

I look at him, and we laugh as we slip into the night.

CHAPTER TWELVE

We run, hands clasped, all the way back to the apartment, silent the whole way. I can't stop thinking about everything . . . the kiss. The cannibalism. The papers from the fireplace.

In the foyer I breathlessly ask, "Can I see those papers?"

"Of course." Bear pulls them away from his chest and hesitates a moment before he hands them to me.

"They look like someone ripped them from a book or something," I murmur, staring at the torn edges along one side, the other smooth. I unfold the pages and peer at the slanted handwriting on the first, and suck in a sharp breath.

> *1st January 1784*
> *Franny Black Starling*

Shocked, I look up. "Bear. These are hers. Franny's." This is as close to a buried treasure as I've ever gotten, this fragile paper beneath my fingers. "Why would someone hide these in the fireplace?"

His eyes widen, his mouth falling open. Silence. His face holds not a question but an answer.

"What?" I search his eyes, his expression. I've seen that look. Like he was going to say something, but now I think I misunderstood it before. "What do you know?"

His reluctance is palpable, almost painful. Finally he says, "Agatha isn't home, right? Maybe there's something in the apartment you can find. Something that will give you answers."

"Bear, do you know something about my family that I should know?" I ask helplessly.

When he doesn't answer, I squeeze his hand tighter, urgent. "What's going on? Why are you being weird?"

"I know things . . . about your family. Everyone does," he says carefully. "But nobody knows more than Agatha. You need to talk to her."

"So, it's not just about that winter?" I press, trying to wade through the confusion and make a connection. I scan the papers in my hand, but the words jumble together. Impatiently I look up at a living, breathing person who might help me understand. "There's more?"

He doesn't answer, but I can see it in his eyes. That's a yes.

"I don't understand why you can't tell me," I say, but I'm not really angry. I'm hurt, frustrated. I feel so alone in this.

He tugs me close. "Kit," he sighs against my neck, then brushes his lips there. "I wish I could explain everything. Please don't hate me."

"I don't hate you." I lean up and kiss him, and get lost in it. The world stops being so confusing while his lips are against mine. I sink into him and sigh.

Bear finally pulls away. "I'm sorry," he says. "I should get home. You want to get lunch tomorrow maybe?"

"Yeah." My arm stings suddenly, and I twist my mouth to the side, considering. "Then we can look for my mom? I want to go to the woods."

As much as I've tried to convince myself that the girl I found wasn't real, I can't help it. I need to look again. I need to try to find her. Somehow I can't help thinking that if I figure out the girl, I can figure out my mom. What if someone in the woods is holding her just the same way?

His eyes flicker with hesitation. Again. He nods, though. "Okay."

The woods are dangerous. He said that one day, even if I don't quite get why. A girl drowned in the river. Another was buried alive, maybe. But he still said yes.

We say goodbye, and I watch him move back outside in the cold, and I go on, through the door and up the stairs, each step away from him more difficult than the last. I want to run back. I want to demand that he tell me what Agatha is hiding, what he knows about our family. But I don't.

I use my keys to open the door, and lock it behind me with shaking hands.

What I *do* know is this: Agatha lied to me about the history. Or at least, lied by omission.

Maybe she didn't want to talk about the cannibalism. But a

lie is a lie is a lie. Then there's the stuff she said about my mom. That can't be true.

I don't even take off my coat. Praying there's something in these pages to give me some answers, I unfold and smooth them out on the living room floor and sit cross-legged, bending over them to read. I start from the first line, carefully making out Franny's old-fashioned script.

1st January 1784
Franny Black Starling

It is January, the first of the New Year. Today I am ten
and seven, though it feels like I have just been birthed,
am brand new, my whole life spread out before me.

Somehow it's even stranger knowing she was my age when she wrote this. And it was right around the same time of year, I realize. Today is December 27. Or, I note, peering at the time, it's after midnight. It's the twenty-eighth now. I go on.

This morning I walked to where I know the beast
waits. Where I have felt him before, in the river. I
sank into the icy water, and I called for him, with
my need. I yearned for answers, for an answer from
him. The spark of him, grown stronger these last four
months as blood spilled from throats, as children cried
from hunger, as lives were stolen by fierce creatures
I cannot lay a name to, and by neighbors whose faces

I've known my whole life. On the banks of this river I have met the moon on moon-full nights, where I have pulled wild herbs from the ground, where I have sewn my wishes onto linen and written my fears into cotton and set them both afire.

I said words to call him, words that seemed to grow in my bones before I knew how to speak.

When he appeared, he came to me half-formed, barely corporeal. Not a shadow, not a man, not the beast I so expected.

"What manner of witch are you?" a voice came.

"A weak one, compared to how I so desire," I told him. "Yet I could be stronger if you lend me your strength."

When he asked me to what end, and why he should, I told him I would give him my own in turn, if he would end this torment. This hunger. This brutality. The attacks.

He told me I would trade one death for another, but I could see I had intrigued him.

I laughed, though it was a bitter sound. He seemed to shine before my eyes, to change a bit from that sound alone.

He told me he was hungry, and how he needed to feed.

"I will feed you," I promised. "I will give you all of myself, willingly. I will bind my blood to yours. I will do this, if you in turn give me you. If you in turn grant us fortune. Not just my kin but my people."

He asked how I knew he could do it. I think he smiled when he said it, if a form without form can smile. He is ancient. I've known him since I was a babe. Heard his whisper at night, felt the way the river called to me as I played in it as a child. Knew he was looking for something.

I answered that I knew he could, that I knew power when I saw it, and I knew I could increase it.

I asked of him ease, comfort, prosperity. That we have enough game and berries, enough food in every garden, enough crops no matter the drought, that our axes fall easily, that we avoid war, and famine, and always, ever, hunger. That our purses never empty, that our fortune never ceases. I asked also for safety. That the creatures be bound and no longer terrorize us.

"And in return, I will be with you in the dark. I will sleep beside you as a bride, and be yours."

"I am hungry. Your fealty will not change it," he said.

"Then feed on me. It is not truly blood that you seek. We both know that."

He stared for a long time, then nodded his agreement. I gave him his name, and we took hands. We surrendered to each other.

This is how it begins. And how it ends.

I stare at the letters, jumbling together on the page. Fascinated and also terrified. Also confused. What in the actual hell is she talking about?

This can't be real. A beast? Magic? And what did she perform? Some sort of spell?

I turn the page over and read on.

5 January 1784
Franny Black Starling

I waited.

I waited and waited for what felt like centuries. 'Twas probably less. When he finally came to me, there was no pretense.

Wife, he calls me already, yet I'm no bride, not like how I always expected, back when Maman and my papa and my brothers were alive. There was no ceremony, at least not one ordained by God. There was no feast afterward, though he did feed me. He put a ring on my finger. However, he does not promise me eternity. We both know I shall not last forever.

Yet, he shall.
He shall.

27 June 1785
Franny Black Starling

So much has happened, yet I suppose I should begin somewhere near where I left off prior. We buried our dead before the ground froze, before the yule last year. What remained of them—bones and broken promises. What is left of their souls? I fear they've been consumed, too. We did not put a headstone, not for any of them, or bury them in the cemetery. Nobody wants to remember. At times I look around at the faces of the people around me and ask myself, Who is more the monsters? Them, or the ones lurking in shadows? The one who holds me when I wake screaming?

That spring, the stems began rising from the ground, taller and taller, harder to ignore, until the leaves uncurled. Then, in whispered hushed tones: roses.

There are hundreds of them now, this summer, more than a year later. Life grows from death. They bloom all colors, all seasons, yet it is the blood-red ones that catch the eyes the most. That leave the most unsettled feeling upon my skin. They are the deep, dark red of spilled blood. We all know what that shade looks like, have all seen it, spattered against the snow. 'Tis not a color one forgets.

The roses have lasted through the scorch of last summer, even when it did not rain for three weeks. Still, they bloomed hardily, as did all our gardens. Folks are using the petals, the oils, to make beauty, to turn to coins for their pockets.

Some do not speak of the roses at all. They still do not know what to say.

They are very much like that with me as well.

Mostly they love me, I believe. For what I've done, for how I have saved them.

A few, though, they look at me with disgust, because I lie with him, because I do so willingly. A few look at me with fear. They know I could hurt them, could punish them for what they have done, the bad ones. That I could make him.

Sometimes I pretend he does punish them. He smiles at me, as if he knows what I am thinking. He admires that part of me. He likes most when I am all myself and all of him at once. When we are one. When we share each other. I give myself to him, and he takes all of me.

'Tis frightening to me, a bit. How much I enjoy doing the same to him.

Sometimes I simply stop caring about it all. I put on my plumed hat, and I eat my rich food, and I drink champagne, and I feel the eyes of the adoring on me. His eyes on me. His secrets in my ear, telling me his fear, telling me the truths inside his soul. His lips upon mine.

What more is there?

There are more pages beyond this, but I can hardly grasp what I've already read.

I skim the handful of entries, recounting tales of masked balls, and new windfalls, of husbands, friends, births of children, names that blur together. But one keeps standing out. Jack.

Who the hell is Jack? Or . . . I ask myself . . . *what* is he?

I gather the pages together. Even touching them makes me feel uneasy. I gently fold them into my bag, then get up, finally pull off my coat and toss it onto a chair. Then I go to Agatha's room. I open her door and peek inside.

I've never been in her room. It smells like her perfume. I step in cautiously, looking around, taking the details in. It's bland, really, compared to the rest of the apartment, as if she keeps all the interesting things in the living room. Here is pale cream and faded blues and delicate floral prints that don't seem like her. I peer into the en suite bathroom—it's filled with expensive moisturizers and her white towels, the shimmery shell-pink tiles managing to bounce light around the dim room.

I move on to the closet. There are rows of shoes, suede and leather, and even a pair of barely worn sneakers; her purses; all her clothing, from casual to extravagant. The thought of going through her drawers is nauseating, but I do it.

I open each drawer, rifle through fabrics. It feels wrong. I should leave her room and forget all of it, pass off Franny's pages as storytelling, as fantasy, as folklore. Wait for tomorrow, when Agatha will tell me something that makes so much sense I'll wonder how I ever worried enough to go snooping through someone's private property—and look what I did at Starling House! It will probably be laughably simple. Our family saved the town from a terrible winter of starvation. From cannibals. There is more, something bad like that, maybe, but not as bad as my mind is coming up with.

My fingers skim over something cool and smooth. Glass.

I pull out a small frame, tucked in between silk.

An antique framed poem of sorts, or maybe a song?

Bring them to the river, flowers in their hair—
The monster loves a bride bound in roses.
They give themselves to him, all their daughters fair
And dark and in between—they bend below the golden
    man,
Sleep within his lair. They wash his hands of blood.
They give themselves to him, all their daughters fair
And dark and in between—their bond is in this blood,
Forever, they do swear.

My heartbeat rises with each line until I feel it in my throat. On my walk with Bear to see the roses, when I saw the sisters in their yard, dancing. They were singing it.

"Shh," the mother scolded, "he'll hear you." I swallow, re-reading the lines. Maybe she wasn't talking about their dad at all.

Monsters don't exist, I tell myself, my heart clipping at a dangerous pace.

"There you are," a voice says at the closet door, and I jerk my head up, caught. Agatha stares down at me, at the poem in my hands.

"I . . ." I stumble over an explanation. "I found this."

"I see." Agatha cracks a slightly amused smile.

Her eyes shine. I picture gingerbread houses and witches with kind faces who lure children in. Lies and sweets. Ovens and bones.

A sudden and unexplainable fear strikes me in the chest. I hardly know her.

"Why don't we go sit and talk in the living room," she says.

She walks out before I can answer. I follow her, the frame gripped in my sweaty grasp. When she reaches her chair in the living room, she gestures at me. Says, "Sit."

"I'd rather stand," I say defiantly. I don't know who this woman really is, do I? I stare at her. "And I don't want tea. I want to get this over with."

"Suit yourself, then," Agatha says as she reclines. She studies me for a moment. "I want to start by apologizing to you," she finally says. "What I'm about to tell you may be difficult to hear, but I want you to know you can ask me anything."

"Really?" I laugh, the sound brittle. "Because you've been so forthright?" The sarcasm is sharp, precise. I'm so angry—so scared suddenly—I could cry.

One of her brows pitches upward. "I've imagined this conversation for seventeen years, yet it's difficult to put it into words."

"Because it's so bad?" I ask quietly. I swallow, the lines of the song echoing in my mind. "I read about the monster . . . but that can't be real, right? I mean, it's symbolic—"

"It's real," she replies, voice clear, unwavering.

Shock steals my words, and she continues, "There are many monsters in Rosemont, or there were, in the past. There is one who remains, who is feared above all. He can take any shape, any that would beckon you nearer, or frighten you, depending on his mood. You probably haven't read *The Wizard of Oz*—"

"Yes, I have," I snap. *My dad was an avid reader, in case you forgot. He taught me well.*

I fix my eyes on the roses on the coffee table and resist a terrible childlike urge to knock them over.

Agatha inclines her head, approving. "Well, the beast here creates illusions, as the Wizard of Oz did. For my sister he was a horned man, like Pan. To me, he's most often a beautiful man with golden hair, but he doesn't always appear in a human form. Sometimes he can be most monstrous."

I don't want to imagine what else this creature can look like. I'm already picturing a half beast with horns and a lute, a wreath of ivy on his head. Was that what Pan looked like? I clear my mind of muddled recollections of Greek deities.

Agatha continues. "He goes by many names. He even answers to a scream, though his name, for all intents and purposes, is 'Jack.'"

Jack. My heartbeat picks up, Franny's pages starting to make sense. Sort of. "But—" I whisper.

"He's been entwined with our family for centuries, ever since that terrible winter."

Blanching, I say, "The cannibalism. I heard about that."

"You've never known starvation," she says at my expression. "Nor have I. But you're right to be disgusted. People starved to death, resorted to brutality, and that wasn't the worst of it. There's something about this place . . ." She trails off.

"What?"

"Rosemont is unlike any other place I've heard of. The very land seems to be corrupt, although I don't think it's alone in its natural curiosities. I've heard there are other places that exist as we do, pockets of unique locations within nature that, given the right circumstances, can create monstrosities."

Monsters. "So, he just . . . was?" I ask.

"Was, is, will always be. Jack is a part of nature, as much a part of Rosemont as the river, the woods, the sky."

"You said he was always here?" I say, trying to make sense of it. "But it sounds like Rosemont came first."

"You cannot separate them. This couldn't have happened just anywhere. Jack is Rosemont. Rosemont *is* Jack," Agatha insists, and then goes on, "That year, it's almost as if Rosemont itself caused the brutal winter, as though it were punishing the people for living here, which in turn caused the starvation. But there were also other ancient creatures that grew *from* him, weaker versions, nuisances, mostly. However, some of them were truly dangerous. Many think these creatures made the people go mad, making them face their biggest fears or bringing up the demons inside them. There were beasts who would suck the marrow from your bones; ones who would strip you of all your flesh; ones who would trap you with their kind faces and gentle voices, only to cause you more pain than you'd ever imagined, not in your worst nightmares."

I gulp, picturing it.

"They made killing and eating humans nearly into a sport," Agatha explains. "During those awful days one might be attacked by a creature in the woods—or their own neighbor. It continued for weeks, until Franny Black Starling united with Jack to stop the atrocities. They were joined in a magical marriage, a trade, and she got the promise that the people in Rosemont would be safe. The monsters would be prohibited from harming humans, bound forever."

The girl in the ground flashes in my mind. She was literally bound. I open my mouth, stunned, but Agatha takes my silence as the cue to go on.

"Not only that, but she made sure Rosemont would prosper. We've never starved since then. No one goes without. There is always work, our roses provide, our businesses expand, even in the worst economic crisis. And we stay safe. For her sacrifice, she saved us all."

With a wary hesitation, pushing everything else aside for the moment, I recall Franny's entries. "But you said a trade," I say. "What kind of a trade?"

"It's not so bad." Something in Agatha's quiet voice makes me think: the bruises around her wrist; her broken pinkie; her limping; those late-night meetings. Was she with *him* those times? The echo of a man's voice coming from her room . . . Has he been here? Jack in this apartment?

My lips part but no words come.

"The rules are simple," she goes on. "The contract includes her descendants. We are each, in turn, his brides. The women in our line. And there are only two women left in our line."

"No," I gasp, realizing what she's implying. "I know where this is going, and there's no way in hell I'm going to sleep with a monster in the woods to keep this town rich."

Agatha shakes her head urgently. "Oh, no, no. He doesn't want us like that," she says. "The idea is absurd. Yes, Franny was his bride, in the truest sense of the word, but he doesn't want *us* like that. He feeds on pain and fear, that's all."

"That's all?" My words come out in a shriek. "No. No way. I'm not having anything to do with this."

"It is your bloodline," she continues, pleading almost, "your legacy to fulfill, and Crowning Day is imminent. You see, that's when a Starling officially joins herself with him. It has taken place at different times over the years, whenever Jack chose. The town celebrates with three days of a festival. The bride walks into the river on the evening of the first day, and after some time, wades back out. We go to him that first time, wearing a white dress, a wreath of flowers in our hair." Her voice gets dreamy, as if it's a romantic memory she's clinging to, not some terrible tradition that sounds more like bringing lambs to slaughter. "This year," she says, "it is on January first."

All the strange whispers, the town's preparations. I'm supposed to give myself to a monster, and they are all anticipating it, relishing it. And no one told me, not even Bear. Not Miles. Not Charlotte. Not anyone I thought of as a friend. A hollow aching fills me. In four days they expect me to walk into the river and sacrifice myself.

"So this is why my dad left." I don't say it as a question, because it isn't. "He wanted to protect me."

"It was never an ideal situation, Kit." Agatha's sigh is heavy. "Your father would've rather told you I was dead than come to terms with the truth. He wanted nothing to do with me or our family, and I've spent many lonely years with that. It hasn't been easy, you know." Pain crosses her face. "Forgive me if I over-simplified our falling-out."

In this instant I hate Agatha and her cold heart. "You lured me and my mom here to basically ruin my life."

"Oh, Kit. You'll have a lovely life here." She looks at me with sincerity. "I wish you'd see how much of an honor this is, to be us, to be a Starling. Jack won't hurt you, not—not really, and we save so many. I'll be proud of you on your Crowning Day, not fearful for you."

I think of the funeral, Daphne's mother's rage, the resentment on her face. Her dead daughter lying feet away from us. "Did he kill that girl?"

Agatha looks away, moving her chin just enough to be considered an affirmation. Twirls the black stone on her bony finger.

I lower my voice to keep from shouting. "How could he even do that? Isn't the whole point to protect people? How could you *let* him?"

"I can't imagine why, after all I've told you so far, you'd think controlling him was even possible. Jack gets what he wants. He always has and he always will. He acted out, for some reason, but I know that once you're his, he'll be satiated." As if I'm not shaking my head wildly, she goes on, "What else to know? Hmm. It's been so long since I had to explain to anyone. You'll be able to sense when he's near. You'll feel it in your bones."

"*That's* why my body aches?" I ask, surprised, almost glad to realize there is a reason for it. "But why?"

"There is something so unnatural about him, your body can't help but feel it," she answers, ignoring my horrified face. "Additionally, we have somewhat of an immunity against injuries. It's not that we don't get hurt as easily; we just heal faster. That is a gift from him, in fact."

My wound healing so quickly after I fell in the woods. I wipe my arm on my side, imagining the blood running from it. I don't want anything from him, or from Franny. Even my blood feels dirty now, because of my ancestor trading away my life like it was nothing. For her, I suppose it was nothing. A vague concept. A far-off thing. Yes, she saved people. But she also damned her entire family. It feels terrible, disgusting. My DNA poisoned.

"What about my mom?" I ask. "She was having those headaches. Does this stuff have anything to do with her?"

"This has to do with *you*, Kit," she answers, in a circular way, tone almost reprimanding me. "With us. Starlings."

"I don't believe you," I say. "Do you know where she is? Is she involved somehow?"

Agatha shakes her head, managing to look offended. "Of course not, to either question. You'll just have to trust me."

"Trust you?" I shout, not caring who in the building may hear us, may wake from their sleep to hear me yelling. "I don't even know you. You're not on my side."

"We're on the same side, Kit." She sighs, like I'm being dramatic. Ridiculous. "Yes, this is a burden as well as a blessing given to us. But I know you can meet the challenge."

"No," I say, seething. "I don't want your burdens or your blessings. I'm not part of this alliance."

"You think that," she says mildly. "And you may imply that we are selfish and greedy all you like. The fact is, our bloodline has kept Rosemont safer since that bargain was struck. It's not just that our alliance keeps us safe from other beings here; it keeps *him* away from innocents." She amends, looking only vaguely sheepish, "Most of the time."

"I don't want to do this," I say finally. "I won't."

"Oh, Kit." Agatha's eyes are pinned on me, not with anger or any sort of fight. But a clear, clear knowing. "You must."

I don't reply. The silence thickens. I spin and stomp away to the guest room, the frame still in my hand. I drop it onto the dresser. Contemplate chucking it against the wall, but I have no energy to clean up a bunch of broken glass.

I lie down on the bed and thrust my hand under the pillow, touch my dad's pages for luck, for courage. Touch Bear's ribbon, still looped around my wrist, the hurt I feel compounded. He didn't tell me. Nobody did. But the clues were there all along.

Fear squeezes my breath away. I close my eyes, try to slow my breathing and get some sleep, to get a few hours before the sun rises.

A storm begins to pick up outside, the snow falling against the window, chilling the room. The wind howls and I shiver.

I wonder if somewhere, wherever *he* is, if he thinks of me.

CHAPTER THIRTEEN

My dreams are a jumble of twisted thoughts, someone laughing.
I'm at Starling House, and Frances is stepping from her portrait, dancing in a shining room full of people dressed in silks
and satins. Nobody can see me, but I stand transfixed, watching
her red curls bouncing as she spins, grinning, a flute of champagne bubbling in her hand. Someone dark and faceless—some
thing—tugging her over and nuzzling her neck, biting her, and
Frances throwing her head back and laughing. Now I'm standing on the snowy riverbank, and someone is crying. A girl before me, knee-deep in the river, slim and tall, long hair like
her sister's, but dark. Her eyes gouged out, blood running like
tears from the silver-dollar-sized sockets. Daphne's dead little
sister.

Sobbing, I back away, but she only shakes her head. Holds
out her hands to me, asking for my help, or maybe telling

me something, showing me. Palms up. Every other finger bitten off.

I startle awake, gasping for breath, covers askew. I inhale slowly, staring around the room. A new notification on my phone blinks. I stare at the text, frowning.

Bear. Damn it. I ignore his cheerful morning greeting. I don't know if "angry" is the right word, but I'm something at him. He couldn't have warned me? Couldn't have told me the truth? *But he did warn me,* the reasonable part reminds me. He told me Agatha had secrets. He found the pages for me. Maybe there were hints all along that I missed. Maybe he wanted to tell me.

That's not enough, though.

I get out of bed and throw on rumpled clothes that need washing. I don't need to look or smell pretty for what I'm doing today. As terrifying as the prospect is, I'm going to the woods to find answers. There was a girl in the ground—is she one of the creatures that were bound? How could she not be? Even as I stared into her eyes, I had the thought, *Not human.*

Jack already broke one promise—he killed Daphne's sister. Fairy-tale logic worms its way into my brain as I pull on my boots. Is my mom trapped under the ground, taken as insurance, until I become the bride? Rosemont *is* Jack. The earth itself is corrupt, Agatha said. It could have swallowed her until I do what it wants. What Jack wants.

After a moment's consideration, I grab a steak knife from Agatha's knife block. Just in case I need to protect myself. I slip it into my coat pocket.

When my phone rings, I jump, body tensed into tight coils. Another ring, and I ignore it. It's only when I'm stepping out the door that I finally text Bear, hoping he'll leave me alone for a bit. I'm still too hurt to talk.

I'm not going to lunch today. I stab the letters into the keypad. *Agatha told me the truth about Crowning Day.*

I hit send, and it actually sends successfully.

I run my hands through my hair, my nerves burning with fatigue. It must have been nearly two a.m. before I fell asleep. My eyes are swollen, the lingering fear about the truth making my body stiff.

Bear's reply takes a while. I imagine him typing in every single letter on his stupid flip phone. *Shit. Sorry. I know how hard this must be. And it's not fair of us. Why should u care?*

"I do care," I say to the silent hallway, picturing the people I've met here. Belinda. Miles. Charlotte. Even Daphne and Molly. Agatha, though I'm conflicted about her. Still, as much as I hate her right now, I don't want her hurt. I don't want people to die.

I'm not heartless, you know, I send. Then add, *I'm going to look for my mom. In the woods.*

Bear's response comes right away. *I'll help you.*

I leave him on read. I know he's sorry he didn't tell me—and would I have believed him? But I'm still too upset. I leave the apartment while Agatha is doing whatever she's doing, glad I don't have to see her. As I walk, I pass flyers for my mom, her face staring out, quite a few less than what I put up, some already ripped off, or maybe blown away, but something in me doubts that. I push on angrily as I pass a couple smiling on the sidewalk, holding hands. Pass little children playing in the snow. Pass liars and people pretending that their ancestors didn't gobble each other up for dinner. I slow when I reach Miles and Belinda, standing outside the flower shop, laughing together, a bucket of tools at their feet.

"Hey, Kit. Want to help us? We got to talking, and we're taking you up on your idea. I have a spare room we're going to use." Miles points to the windows above his shop.

Belinda adds, apple cheeks rosy, "For the musical theatre group."

"If you can count two members as a group." His dark eyes sparkle as he looks at me, his dove-gray herringbone scarf blowing in the wind.

"Two members *for now*," she adjusts.

"That's great," I say. "I'd love to help, but I've got something to do, sorry." I hide behind a smile, so they don't worry. But why do I care if I worry them? Don't they know about Jack, too? Doesn't everyone?

"No problem." Miles takes the bucket, smiling, and Belinda holds up a hammer in a wave, and they disappear inside, friendly arguing about a used piano. I press on. The morning sun is pink and bright, as if in apology for the shitty weather last night, but I still hurry to the woods.

It takes me a good fifteen minutes to reach the tree line, where I stop. Bear's form is illuminated in gold as he stands, hands shoved into his coat pockets, waiting for me on this side of the privacy chain.

"Hey." He tries to smile, but it's weak. "Kit, I'm so sorry."

I regard him, the copper-brown shine of his hair. His regretful eyes. "What are you doing here?"

"I said I'd help you," he says hoarsely. "I know you're mad . . . and I don't blame you."

I bite on my lip to keep from crying. The emotions pouring over me outweigh everything else. "Bear, what the *fuck*? You couldn't have said something this whole time?"

I stare accusingly for a moment, then push past him.

"Kit, I'm sorry," he says, heartfelt, serious. I keep walking but he's at my heels. "Look, I wanted to tell you, but it didn't seem my place to say. Starlings are powerful, and I didn't want to piss Agatha off—"

"So you weren't going to tell me *anything*?" It hurts to say it, hurts when I whirl around, to see the way he hangs his head.

"I'm sorry. I feel like such an asshole. I didn't want to lie to you. I wanted to tell you everything." He reaches out and threads his fingers into mine. "And I want to help you with your mom. If you want to look for her—"

"I don't want your pity. I can do this on my own," I say. I glance over my shoulder, through the trees. Try not to shiver. "I'll go look alone."

I don't say I've already been in the woods alone. I never told him about the girl. I realize now that he would've just acted like she didn't exist. Everyone made me think I was losing my grip on reality, but I know she was there. Only, who—*what*—is she? It seems far too coincidental that my mom disappeared and I found the girl a day later. Plus, Jack lives in there.

I lift my chin bravely, or maybe I'm just playing at being brave. "I'm going to find my mom, and today I'm starting here.

I don't care how many scary forests I have to search, or doors I have to knock on; I'm going to find her. Then we're leaving this horrible place and never coming back. I'm not going to be the next Starling girl to go into the river."

"I'll help you," Bear insists. "I meant what I said before." He looks down at me, wounded, desperate. "That's why I'm here. Let me help you. Let me make it up to you."

I stare back at him, measuring his offer against the fact that he knew about everything and didn't tell me. A car drives down the nearest road. Someone slams their door. A dog barks somewhere far away.

"Okay," I say finally. And he smiles in relief, slings his hand into mine again.

I blow out a breath, trying to steel my nerves. I'm exhausted from last night. I hardly slept. Sheepishly I pull the steak knife from my pocket. "I brought this, just in case."

Bear nods. "Good idea."

I push aside the embarrassment. I do feel better for it. "Right," I say. "I thought I'd look again where I found this girl." I explain about finding her, and he listens, wide-eyed, but doesn't challenge me about her existence. I let go of his hand and walk on, kicking the private-property sign as I pass it. "So, let's go. If you don't mind trespassing again for me."

He gives me a hesitant smile. "This is your family's property."

I shut my eyes. Of course it is. When I open them, he's gazing at me, face so full of apology, so kind, I almost want to curl up right there, safe, cared for.

"I'm sorry again," he says, and his tender embrace enfolds me, his chin resting on the top of my head. "If you're this certain your mom is somewhere in Rosemont, that you need to look for her, I trust your judgment. We're going to get you home safe. I know we will."

"Thanks," I say, fighting back tears. I take a breath for courage, and nod. "Let's go."

We duck under the chain and walk into the woods silently. I'm afraid, I can't deny it, but when I glance up at Bear, there's something in his eyes that tells me he is, too. He knows about Jack, at least a vague concept, like all the rest of the people in town. He knows this is dangerous. He must care about me an awful lot to be walking by my side. I silently forgive Bear again for not telling me every awful detail about Rosemont.

I take his hand and hold it tighter, and together we walk deeper into the woods, over the snow-covered ground. Though the sky is blue, the day beautiful, there's no peace to be found here, like there was the first time I came. Everything is quiet, a stillness that feels like a warning.

I lead Bear to the site where I found the girl, and stop at the tree, wary. I was only here twice before, but the landscape is seared in my memory. The ground is still closed, as it was when I brought the cops. Only, now I know I was right all along.

"This is where I found her," I say. "The girl."

I kneel down and run my gloved hands along the ground, as if I could find a seam in the earth. I press my palms against the snow, squeezing my eyes tight, trying to feel my mother, as if the very idea of her being buried alive isn't unfathomable.

A rustle in the branches. I look up, and it's the girl from the ground. She stares at me, from the trees, and I stand slowly, jab Bear with my elbow to draw his attention to her. As soon as he looks up, she gets a wild look in her eyes and darts away, disappearing into the shadows. He swears quietly, looking shaken.

I let out a sharp exhalation. "Did you see her?"

"Partly." Bear grimaces.

It's a relief to know I didn't hallucinate her, even though seeing her again was nothing short of shocking. She's real.

"Are you okay?" Bear asks, pulling me out of my head. "You're shaking. Do you want to go back?"

"No." That's the last thing I want to do. I scan the ground, reach up and run my hands along the tree, like I can somehow find a hidden button to open the earth. "I'm fine. We've barely even started."

"You're stubborn," he says affectionately, gathering me to him. The light shines on his curls, his skin. His warm eyes go warmer as he grips my hand, anchoring me.

"My mother would do the same for me," I say, and I know I'm right.

"I love how sure you are about her," he says.

I tip my face up to him, my throat clenching as I say, "My mom is the only thing in my life that I'm sure of."

"And I know she feels the same way about you, Kit." Bear kisses me gently, brushing my hair off my face. "Isn't that what her tattoo is for?" he asks. "To remind her of how much she loves you?"

I think of the ink winding up her arm, the flowers—not roses, thank goodness, but the kind of blooms that look like they fell off a children's fantasy book, an old fairy tale, some ancient blessing. "I've planted you here." My mom scooped me up and laid me against her chest when I was little, right after

184

she'd gotten her tattoo done. "And now I've planted you *here,* on my arm. And even though the flowers stop at my shoulder, they go on and on in my heart, just like you, baby."

But as I sink against him, our past conversations run through my mind, and I know something's wrong. He leans down to kiss me, his warm mouth on mine, and I stiffen, pulling away.

"Bear." My voice sounds funny. "I never told you about my mom's tattoo."

"Sure you did, on the phone." He nudges me, smiling.

Time stalls. I don't want to entertain the idea that he's lying. It's impossible. Roses blooming all year long are impossible. Monsters living in the woods are impossible. But I know.

We lock eyes. "No," I say finally. A whisper. "I didn't."

His hand on my hair stills, the other wrapped around my waist.

There's a flash of something across his face. A split second of disappointment. Then something else. Something almost like glee.

He leans down again and whispers into my ear, "Finally. You got it."

The words strike like lightning, and my heart is beating in my throat. I push away from him as he erupts into laughter, delighted. I can't breathe deep enough. I can't—

"My darling," he says, his voice different, deeper, and slightly accented. "Did you even have an inkling? I had hoped to play a little longer, but I admit that the charade was getting old."

I'm speechless with shock, and then Bear is shimmering. By the time I blink, he isn't Bear anymore. I stumble back and almost fall into the snow. I want to run, but I already know I can't run from him. I stare at this stranger in horror. Except I know that voice. I've heard it twice before, coming from Agatha's room.

He looks like a young man—but there's something eternal about him, like he's a golden god—even his eyes have changed from chocolate brown to amber. He's bare-chested, the white background of snow contrasting his glowing honey-skin. He's bare-footed, too, with loose, dark trousers—and dangerously beautiful, his long hair blowing back in the wind, crown of rose thorns on his head. All sleek muscle, he's lean and powerful. I don't want to think of what he could do to me.

"No," I say, shaking my head. I don't want it to be true. "No. No."

"It's always been me." Then, in a satisfied whisper, "I'm the one who has her. Your mother."

My mother. I stare at him, shock overwhelming me. Then anger stings like a white-hot poker. I want to stab him with it. This is Jack. And he's got my mom? "*You* took her?"

His smile is cocky, and it unleashes something in me. I fly at him, rake my nails down his pretty face.

His eyes flash hot as he takes my wrists, holds me from attacking him again. "Good for you, Kit. I wasn't sure you had it in you. Words are one thing. I'm pleased to see you have some violence in your heart."

"If you hurt my mom, I'll rip off your face!" My scream cuts across the woods.

Another laugh. "Oh, but it's you I want to hurt." His voice a whisper once more. "To hurt and to heal and to have."

"You think I'm going to let you own me?"

"But you would own me as well." I shudder as he draws me closer, his words against my neck a dark promise. "You would have me as well."

"Like her?" I say in revulsion. "Franny? If it weren't for her—"

"If it weren't for her"—his fingers tighten—"you would not exist."

"Better to not exist than belong to you."

His mouth tugs into a frown. He has the audacity to look almost hurt, and I see Bear in his eyes, just for a moment. I hate that he makes me think that.

Jack shakes his head, a patient smile stretching his full lips. "You will be my bride, Kit," he says. "You cannot fight destiny. Besides, you promised Agatha you would go to your Crowning."

The truth hits me. "You . . . you always called her 'Agatha.' Everyone else says 'Mrs. Starling' or my 'grandma.' But you used her first name."

He smiles again. "Little bread crumbs, darling. I know how you like fairy tales."

"Tell me where my mom is," I demand.

He only laughs, which fills me with rage, and I rip my arms out of his grasp, suddenly remembering the knife in my pocket. I pull it out clumsily and swing it toward his beautiful lying face. I want to hurt him.

I stick the blade into his throat.

It's silent in the woods, in my mind. I stare. At the blade in his neck, then at his eyes. His face. His smile.

He pulls the knife out, cocking his brows as he drops it to the snow. "Good try, anyway." There's no blood. He isn't even scratched.

"I'm sorry," I whisper, backing away, suddenly terrified.

"You don't mean it." His arms encircle me and hold me in place. "A knife, really? You should not have done that. Did you really think you'd hurt me?"

My legs ache, and I realize I'm shaking with fear. For a second I thought maybe I could kill him. A rumble against my body. He's laughing at me, and it's terrifying.

"Please. I'm sorry," I say.

"No, you're not," he says, thumb swiping a stray lock of hair from my forehead. His touch is gentle, but his eyes are on fire. "And perhaps you need to be taught a lesson. No. Why don't we play a little game instead?"

"A game?" I ask. "Hasn't this all been a game to you?"

He clicks his tongue and lets me go. I stumble as he wanders in a circle. Then he stops, leans his bare back against a tree trunk, folding his arms casually. "Call it a game, call it a deal, call it mercy. If you can find your mother before you come to me on Crowning Day, she may leave Rosemont, alive. See, I can be generous. You can trust me."

My heart is going to pound itself out of my chest. "Why would you let me find her?" I ask in disbelief.

A wicked smile touches his wicked mouth. "Amusement."

"Like how you helped me at Starling House? Why did you give me those pages?"

"Oh, Kit." A shadow of a smirk. "Do you think there's

anything she could have written that I wouldn't already know? Or anything I could've let you have that would've spoiled my fun?"

I don't know what to say to that.

He clasps his hands together. "So. You want to feel brave? You want to win a little? I'll give you a fighting chance. I like watching you try."

I'm not naïve enough to believe him this time. "You'd probably rather see me fail."

He laughs at that.

"And if I don't find her by Crowning Day, then what?" I challenge.

He pushes off the tree and moves close again, too close. "It will be a Crowning to remember, when I kill the mother of my bride!"

My knees go weak. It was one thing to know he had her, but this isn't a threat. It's a promise, a cruel and certain one. He will kill her.

"Please, no. Please." I cry, like I did on his chest before. Like I cried in my bed, face shoved against my pillow so my mom wouldn't hear after my dad ended his life. Like I want to cry every day. And I do now, emptying out before the very one who would spill me. "Please, I'll do anything. Don't do this."

"But we've barely gotten started," he murmurs, running his lips along my arm, laughing as I weep against him. Because this is the game we are playing now.

The game is this: he hurts me, and I cry.

"Why are you doing this?" I whisper.

He kisses my forehead tenderly. "Because I can."

Then he is gone, his laughter on the air. My hands clutching emptiness.

"No!" I scream. Then I'm on my knees, crying. *Mom, Mom, Mom. Please don't hurt her, please don't.*

But there is nothing, no reply; all of Rosemont is quiet. This whole town is a curse. But I can't just lie down here and give up. He has my mom, at least I know that, and she's alive. He didn't have to take her. He only did it to hurt me.

I look down, repulsed at the sight of the ribbon he tied around my wrist, but when I go to rip it off, the ribbon disintegrates into dust beneath my fingers, blows away. An illusion? A lie.

I take my phone out, pull up my texts. There's nothing. All our conversations, gone. Were they ever there? Illusions.

Just like Bear.

I walk and I walk, and I scream my mom's name, the river raging to my right, boots covered in snow, my toes freezing. I know it's only in my mind, but swear I hear my mom call my name once, twice, then fade away into nothing.

I weave in and out around the trees, moving along this gloomy, lonely place. "Mom," I call, to no answer. I try again, again. "Sally," I call.

Still nothing. I even try "Mama" and "Mommy," my voice cracking with longing. She never answers. I scream his name, both of them. *Bear. Jack.* Nobody answers. But I'm sure he can hear me. I remember what Agatha told me about the pain in my body being a warning. I can't believe I didn't connect it before. I test my body, but I feel nothing.

When a form moves from the shadows, my heart jolts. Those eyes, that face. Her hair like wet seaweed tangled about her, that same dirty sheath blending into her milk-pale limbs.

The girl from the ground. Has she been watching the whole time? How exactly does she fit into all this? I hold my breath, watching her with equal parts fear and curiosity.

She takes another few light steps toward me, her dirty bare feet graceful, like a ballerina's. Those thickly-pink-scarred wrists. Intense deep-gray eyes pinned on me.

"Stop," I say, and my voice sounds quiet and meek, but I wave the knife at her in warning. "Don't come any closer. What are you?"

She cocks her head and blinks. I swear she blurs at the edges. "You know what I am."

"A monster," I whisper.

Barely tipping her head in agreement, her gaze hardens as she says, "And I know you. I know your name. I know your blood. Your kin, the one who had me bound."

I don't trust my trembling hand. My fingers grip the handle of the knife like it's a lifeline. "You mean Franny," I say as I stare at her in wonder—and wariness. Now I know it's true. She is ancient, just like him. "I thought *he* bound your kind."

Her eyes seem to go darker. "It was her fault," she says. "There were several others caught before me. I could hear them underground, their cries. I still can."

I quiver, remembering her haunted look when I found her; she still has it. "All the others are still trapped? Could you help them?" I ask.

"I wouldn't even if I could," she says darkly.

Even as I realize that I wouldn't *want* the others to be released, I lower the knife, deliberately, purposefully. I clear my throat and say, "I'm sorry they did that to you, but *I'm* not your enemy. I only want to fight Jack. You knew him. You could see through the disguise?"

"Any fool could have," she says, shrugging through her insult. Then she pauses, studying me. "He has your mother."

"Yes." She must have heard us.

"That's good for me, then," she says.

"What?" My voice goes sharp. I tighten my grip around the hilt of the knife, weigh the expression on her face. The breath between us is taut, something strong and curious and deadly. "What do you mean?"

"I *mean*," she begins, "you are an enemy of my enemy. I will help you find your mother, but in return I want something from you."

I didn't ask for her help, but I'm intrigued. It's stupid of me to trust her, but it doesn't mean I'll let my guard down.

"Like what?" I hate how wimpy I sound, but even now, something about the terrible hunger on her face makes my heart squeeze.

"I want you to kill him."

My heart thumps. Kill Jack?

"But I tried," I say, picturing that blade in his throat. "Sort of. I don't think he can be killed. Isn't he immortal?"

Immortal like you, starving to death for centuries, buried alive.

"Everything can be killed. It's just a matter of knowing how." She says it like she's reassuring herself of this, more than reassuring me. "There must be a way. And if anyone can do it, it would be a Starling." The girl studies me for a moment and turns away.

"But *how*?" I press. Stabbing him didn't even make a scratch. "And why a Starling? What difference does it make?"

"Let me think," she says, not answering me. And without turning back, she starts walking.

I hurry to follow her down to the river, where she pauses, staring out at it.

"What are you doing?" I ask.

"Trying to catch his scent. He lives here."

"I know it's near the river, his lair—"

"He lives beneath it," she interrupts, then adds impatiently, "Beneath the river."

"Like the way you were under the tree?"

Her eyes darken, two black coals in her white face, and I'm sorry I reminded her of being imprisoned. "He lives within it, beneath it," she says. "He becomes the river itself. It doesn't matter; we can't get in because he won't have the entrance in plain sight. It's magic, girl. The fact is, he could hide your mother in your own bedroom and you wouldn't know it."

"Well, why not try the obvious first?" I say. "Let's go closer. I'll jump in."

She shakes her head. "Only brides go into his waters, or those unfortunate enough to break his fast. Do you think he just lets anyone in at any time? It will be locked. We need the key."

I can feel my forehead wrinkle in confusion, frustration, too. "What key?"

"There is a key, to open his lair. *She* used it."

"A key." I blink, mind racing. Franny had a key? "Well, then Agatha might have it, but even if she does . . ." I trail off. She'd never give it to me, would she? I feel beaten already.

"I assume you have a way to figure it out. You're a Starling, aren't you?"

I clamp my lips shut, before I start crying in frustration. She moves forward, and I follow, watching her feet ease into the snow, only now really realizing how dangerous it is for her to walk in the snow like that, because of frostbite. Her arms are bare. Her legs. Her pale throat. "Aren't you cold?" I ask, motioning to the scrap of fabric she's wearing, maybe a nightgown. She walks. She speaks and thinks. Surely her body has sensation. Doesn't she get cold?

The monster girl shakes her head, snowflakes on her black hair.

"Do you need clothes?"

"Shhh," she says, sharp. Chin pointed up, like a dog, looking for a scent. She points to the left. "First we will go to places here, where I know she was with him. Where she might have hidden a key."

"Franny?" I ask. "Why would she hide it?"

"She was not the sharing sort."

"How do you know?"

"Stop asking ridiculous questions and start using your eyes; this key will be hard to find," she scolds, then turns back. "Why are you so slow?"

"I'm cold," I whisper. "And I'm scared."

The girl studies me with curiosity, face going softer. "Nothing is going to happen to you. Not today."

It brings little comfort, but I stop, pull in a deep breath, and follow her deeper into the woods.

CHAPTER FOURTEEN

When I get back to the apartment, snow-caked and freezing, Agatha's not home, but I find a note, scrawled in her elegant hand. *Had to go out. Lasagna in freezer. Vegetarian.*

In the shower, I let the hot water warm my icy skin, and it's not until the bathroom fogs up that I feel warm again. But disappointment is a bitter chill. We didn't find anything in the woods.

I will win, I repeat to myself. I will find my mom before I'm supposed to go into the river on Crowning Day and we will get out of here, and leave Rosemont behind. That's all that matters. I have three days. Isn't that plenty of time? People in movies change the world in a single day. They beat the bad guys by chance. Don't I just need to get lucky? Isn't the universe on my side?

As I wash my hair, my wrinkled fingers running through

it, I let the steam envelop me, the water rinsing away my fear. It does seem to help, but my body still aches. I step out of the shower and wrap my hair in a towel, turning to the mirror, and my heart stalls in my chest.

There's a handprint on the foggy glass. Fine long fingertips splayed out.

It's his. I know it.

I hear the tinny, faraway echo of his laugh.

While I wipe the mirror clean, I half convince myself I'm too angry to be afraid. I also should have known from the pain, but I'm so tired that I didn't connect it.

I get dressed in my warmest clothes and go into the living room, after grabbing Franny's pages to reread, to get my mind off Jack. Why did I think he would be like a vampire or something? Unable to come inside uninvited? Obviously he's been here before, he's been with Agatha, he's been with me as Bear. I push aside the twisted feeling in my gut and flip through the pages, starting at the beginning. Everything is more clear than the last time I tried to read. It makes sense now, or at least most of it does. I learn more about her life, or as much as I can in limited entries—they all read as though she's holding something back. But she writes of being the guest of honor at every party, of having lace shipped from Belgium, and new gowns and hats stuffed full of feathers and flowers. Of having lovers, and then slipping out of their beds at night to meet Jack.

She writes like she loves him, and my stomach turns, imagining it. But there's nothing I can find about how to possibly beat him. If she loved him, why would she write how to beat him?

The door opens, and I turn to see Agatha, a layer of snow still settled on her pale hair.

"Hello," she says as she closes the door.

I set the pages on the coffee table, noting how her eyes zero in on them.

"Agatha, did you know?" I ask, instead of saying hello. My words are fire and ice. "That he took my mom?"

For a moment, only a moment, she manages to look guilty. Then she says, "It's only temporary. Just to keep you from leaving." She explains it so calmly, as if it's no big deal. "I managed to get you here almost at the date he'd chosen. He had to figure out how to get you to stay a bit longer. But don't worry, he's assured me that she's safe, and he'll release her when the time is right. He's promised."

I gape at her, my heart pounding. "Are you serious? You believe him?" I want to scream. I am half fear, half rage. "He hurts people! He kills people!" I yell.

Agatha's mouth tightens. She holds my gaze for a breath before looking away.

After a moment, she swallows, and nods. "He's not hurting her," she says quietly. "He hasn't hurt her."

"Are you trying to make me feel better? Or yourself?" I snap.

"It wasn't easy, not telling you. He didn't want me to."

"You still should have told me. Instead, he did."

Her body goes still. "You saw Jack?"

"Yes." It's one syllable that says so much. She doesn't say anything else, so I go on, telling her about what happened, about the big, horrible reveal, about the threat he made against my mom.

"So," I say finally, "how do I get to her? What do you know about a key?"

Confusion shadows her face when she glances back at me. "What key?"

"*The* key," I repeat, sharper. I ball up my fists, holding myself back from grabbing Agatha and shaking the answer out of her. Trying to remain patient, I clarify, "The key to get into his lair. I know Franny had one, so you must. Where is it?"

She finally shrugs off her fine wool coat, looking utterly bewildered. "I've never heard of such a thing. I don't use a key. He lets me in."

Why would Franny need one, then? "You walk into the river, and bam, you're there?" I ask.

"It's not so . . . simple as that, but yes." She flings her hand. "He calls me, I go to him, he lets me in. Or he comes here."

I've come to know when she's lying. . . . I think? And right now, it feels like she's telling me the truth. But the girl was so certain that Franny had a key. And I have far more reason to trust her than I do Agatha. Or, more accurately, I have more reason to distrust Agatha.

"If I had it, I could get into his lair." I falter, whisper to myself, "Then I could get my mom out."

Agatha shoots me a pitying look. "Did you eat?" she asks, changing the subject. She moves past me, heading to the kitchen.

"No." I wave away her question, getting up and following her. "What do you know about Franny before?" Maybe if I know more about her, I reason, I can find out more about Jack.

"Before Jack?" She pivots, facing me, considering. "Well, it's said she lost both parents, as well as two siblings. They died before everything in Rosemont started happening. Sometime after *that*, she summoned Jack from the river."

The pages said as much. "But how?" Frustration and interest war in me. I sit at the island and lean my elbows on the counter. "Her entries don't go into that much detail, but it sounds like she did a spell or something."

"I don't know." Agatha plucks a tea bag from her golden tin and plops it into her mug. "Tea?" she asks, and when I shake my head, she goes on, "But she was a legend, the root of us. He is the other root."

"But they didn't have children together."

"No," Agatha answers. "But part of him lingers in our veins, because love is stronger than blood, and what they had was imprinted on us forever. It will never die."

"Not in my veins. Not in me," I challenge. "I have no love for him."

"Oh, Kit." She sighs. "I take it you broke the window at Starling House." It catches me off guard and I look at her in surprise. She points over to Franny's pages on the coffee table. "I didn't realize that you'd found those, but I knew someone had broken in, and they must have been there. I'm a member of the board, of course. The house will be closed to fix the damage."

"Yeah," I say, frowning. "They were hidden in the fireplace. Franny wrote them. They were ripped from a book."

Agatha nods. "A missing book. The last person to have it was Juliet," she muses, head down as she rummages through a drawer. Then she stops. "She didn't like Franny. I never quite understood why." From where I'm sitting, I can just make out the humorous curve of a smile, and it sends me over the edge.

"Are you kidding?" I nearly yell. "Franny damned us all. She ruined our family." I could spit fire, just thinking about how little I want to be like Franny.

He kissed me in her house, her portrait staring down at us. I shudder at the thought, and the kettle cries on cue.

Agatha pours water into her cup, steam clouding her face.

"Is there a way to kill him?" I ask abruptly.

"Oh, Kit," Agatha says. Then she places the kettle back on the stove and turns to look at me. "Do you think you're the first to think of that?" Her voice goes far away, thin and wispy. "I had a sister. Junie decided she didn't want to do it anymore, didn't want her young daughter, Amy, to have to go to her own Crowning. So, she took a knife and drew it across his throat while he slept. Do you know what he did?"

"I'm guessing something bad," I say.

"Jack told me how he made a mirror, an illusion. Instead of him, it was her own throat she cut, and then he killed Amy as well. It was a lesson to the few of the Starlings left." She sips her peppermint tea, eyes pinned on me over the rim of the cup.

"I'm sorry," I say, "but he said if I find my mom before Crowning Day, he'll let her go."

"I hope you can—"

"And if I *don't*, he'll kill her," I say, cutting her off.

Agatha's face suddenly looks every minute her age. "I hope that's not the case," she says. "I only want you to understand that he's strong, and we've been entwined with him for so long.

You keep asking questions, but I don't know how to tell you, there may not be an answer you want at the end of this path."

"I have to save her. I'm not going to *accept* any other answer," I reply, grinding my teeth. I have to save myself, too. I have to get us out of Rosemont, and away from Jack. But it's not Jack I envision. It's a boy my traitor heart beats faster for, damn this human body of mine. Anything that would beckon you closer, Agatha said. A teddy-bear boy with melted-chocolate eyes, a dimpled smile, a sweet laugh, a writer like me. Everything about him was curated to get my defenses down. I hate how easy it was. He was the wolf in plain sight. And I fell for it. "I don't know why I'm even talking to you about this," I say bitterly. "You've known he has her, and you never told me. For all I know, this is fun for you."

"Please." She frowns, clearly offended. "That's not true at all. I don't want you or your mother harmed."

"Then why all the secrets? If it's not so bad, why lie?"

She shakes her head. "Because I can't risk losing you like your father. We need you."

"But why does it have to be me?" I ask. "Why do you even care if I have my Crowning? Can't you just keep doing what you've been doing?"

"Do you think I'll live forever?" Agatha asks with a pained smile. "This is a *legacy*. It must be passed down, and when there are no more Starlings to pass it down to, then there will be nothing to keep the people here safe. That is the deal. We are integral to it."

I understand, I think, but I can't help narrowing the focus. It's my life, too. "Do you even care that he'll hurt me?"

A sigh. "I would never want you to hurt. I love you; you're my blood."

"If you love someone, you don't feed them to the wolves." I choke on my words and look down, embarrassed.

Agatha hesitates, then stands up and motions for me to follow her. "Come."

Reluctantly I rise, and I trail her back to the living room.

"Do you know what I have?" Agatha asks.

I shake my head cautiously as she moves to the shelves. She pulls down a linen photo album and takes a seat on the floral couch. "In the middle," she says, offering the book to me.

Sitting as far from her on the couch as I can, I open the album, doing my best not to get stuck on the family pictures covering the pages. As I turn the pages, though, my eyes catch on Starling woman after Starling woman—standing against the house, carrying babies, holding roses.

I freeze when I get to a piece of lined paper, my name written in childish handwriting, vines drawn along the border.

"Your father sent it to me," she says.

Flushing, I read it over to myself. I don't remember writing it.

Spring is flowers, and when everything is blooming
Fresh, a flash, green and quick, and I think I hear
Birdsong, and I think I hear my own song since winter
Took over, made cold drifts out of my throat, made smoke
Out of my voice.
Spring is here, and I think I am watching not only things
Being born, but also, somehow, myself
Being born, too.

I look up at Agatha. "But I mean, I was, like, nine," I say. "That's so embarrassing."

"Not at all. I kept it all these years, didn't I?" she says.

"Maybe because that's all he gave you?" I guess. "I don't see anything else of mine around here. Why did you show this to me?"

Her cool blue eyes assess me. "I kept it not only because it was good but mostly because he wrote on the back. It was the one and only time your father wrote me."

Agatha reaches to pull the page out of the sleeve and turns it over, handing it to me. I almost don't want to take it from her, but I do, and when she sees my face, she just nods. I hold the paper to my chest. I'll read it when I'm alone.

"How old was Juliet when she started going to Jack?" I ask.

Something passes across her face before she answers. "She was thirteen."

"That's young," I say, aching somewhere deep inside, even though I never knew my aunt. "She must have been scared. He hurts you in the lair."

"He survives on pain and fear." Agatha busies herself, avoiding me, tidying the coffee table.

"I'd rather die than let him hurt someone I love," I finally whisper. "You're a coward."

She looks at me like I've slapped her.

I stand up from the couch and collect Franny's pages, and without saying good night I head back to the guest room, my dad's letter against my heart. With a long exhale, I sink onto the bed and look down, and I'm crying when I see his handwriting.

I dreamt of you last night, my dad wrote to her.

In my dream, I told you about my daughter, and you cried happy tears. It was enough for you, just knowing. Maybe I'm a fool. Maybe a selfish coward, like you said before I left. I know you're angry, you're angry still. I'm angry, too, and I'm sad that I couldn't say goodbye to Dad before he died. I heard about it only by chance. I know it was my choice to leave, but I miss him. I miss you, too.

I wish you could see her, but of course that's impossible. You will never leave Rosemont, and I'll never bring her there. I have killed off all my past, and I will keep her safe from you all.

She's the light of my life, as stubborn and funny and creative as any soul I've ever met, so much like Juliet, too, that sometimes it hurts. She has Juliet's sweet tooth and she wants to be a writer, like me, can you believe it? You can see it, maybe here in this little poem she wrote for school. She's going to do great things.

I just wanted you to know that she exists. That she's the reason I can never see you. That she strengthened by a million any resolve I had to leave Rosemont.

In any case, Mom, I hope you're safe. After everything, after how it's poisoned you. I wish you well.

I do love you, you know. We're happy here, me and my beautiful wife and our wonderful girl, in our cozy run-down house, with books and pens

and art everywhere. Like a dream come true, most
days. I hardly think of the sadness that was. I think
sometimes it will never touch me again.

Daniel

The tears slide down my face, slow, a trail of grief that never ceases, a loss that doesn't ease up.

How I wish I could go back to him, one time, just once. Take him by the hands and tell him something, anything, that would make him stay. Not quite a year ago, I found another piece of paper, something he had scratched a pen into. *I will never escape my monsters.* The context changes when I consider it now. He was in so much pain, for so long.

I love you, I love you. I squeeze my eyes shut. He escaped Rosemont. He protected me.

Well, he to tried anyway.

Even though I should sleep—even though I am exhausted— I turn to Franny again and the pages she left, searching. I read and reread them, time melding together, and the desperation eats away at me until my phone dings.

You up? Brenna's text says. *We're all thinkin of you.*

Hanging in there, I guess, I respond. Then I add, *love you.*

Just letting myself type the words hits at something in me, hard. I should have said it before, should not have pulled away from her friendship, or Leo's, when I got too messed up. Should have said it to my mom more. Should have told my dad a million times.

Once, when I was little, the three of us had been driving

in the country, and he stopped the car and hoisted me onto his shoulders to watch the starlings flit from the farmer's trees to the silo to the sky and back. I was delighted, my mom's old thirty-five-millimeter camera clicking as she captured the birds in flight.

"I wish I could fly," I said.

My dad pulled my hands down, bringing my ear closer to his mouth, and said, "There's a fairy tale I'll find for you to read, about a girl whose brothers turn into swans. You'll like it."

"It would be better if they were starlings." I pouted.

After a moment, he said softly, "No. Starlings are bad birds. Farmers hate them."

Bitterness rolled off him in waves, didn't it? Or is this my memory placing emotions where there weren't any? Still. Why did he keep the name "Starling"?

I know now that Agatha would have found me no matter what, even if my last name were different. Jack would have known, wouldn't he?

Before I forget to breathe, I shove away the sadness, the bad thoughts. I muster up my courage. I'm not ready to lie down and stop fighting. I'm going back to the woods. I'm going to find the key, find my mom. And somehow I'm going to beat Jack.

"What they had was imprinted on us forever. It will never die," Agatha said.

It will die, I vow silently. I'm going to be the one to kill it.

When I know Agatha is showering, I let myself into her bed-room, in case she's lying about the key, in case she has it hidden here. I tiptoe to her dresser. Fate is on my side when I find a jewelry box. I lift the wooden lid to find a wedding ring that, somehow, I've never even noticed, though it's impressive enough in size and shine. And the black ring. Close up, for the first time, I notice that the stone is carved with a starling bird.

I pluck up the ring, run my fingers along the cool stone. It's heavier than I expected.

I'm not sure why, but I slip it on, and it's too big. It easily spins around my finger, sort of the way Agatha twirls it when she's fidgety, and if I weren't careful, if my hand were tipped downward instead of up, it would fall off completely.

I place it back in the box, then search around for a key, checking the tiny drawers, lifting the velvet compartments. There are diamond studs. Ropes of pearls.

But no key.

Disappointment twines its fingers around my heart and squeezes. It would have been too easy, finding the key here. I'm just a girl standing in a dark bedroom that doesn't belong to me.

In the conjoined bathroom, the shower turns off. Agatha will be out soon.

I close the jewelry box lid and leave her room.

But I haven't given up. I've barely even started. Tomorrow I'll go back to the woods, find the girl, search for the key some more.

"Hold on, Mom," I whisper. "Keep holding on."

In my dreams, she answers. *I will.*

CHAPTER FIFTEEN

*"Hello?" I say the next morning as I step into the woods. Some-*how, I know the girl could hear me if she wanted. Light streams, golden, through the trees, and it's quiet; only the faintest breeze ruffles my hair.

Then someone moves from the trees. I glimpse her foot first, slippered in a satin shoe, for some reason more shocking than when it was bare. The dainty shoe so feminine, tied with ribbon, a clean stocking beneath, the curve of her rounded calf covered in a fine cream fabric as she lifts her skirts to step over a log.

There she stands. Hair hanging down to her knees, but this time combed out in dark, polished waves. Her face, her eyes, her rose-stained lips.

"Oh . . ." My words drop off as I am struck, astonished by how she looks.

Her gown has a corset bodice that comes to a V before

floating out into a wide skirt. The sleeves are tight to the elbows, then bell out, and end in snow-white lace trim. The silk is blue, as blue as the ink of my mom's tattoo. It makes the girl's skin look like fresh cream. It's as though she stepped out of an antique book. Something in my throat catches as I gaze at her face again. She appears human, almost comfortable in this form, like a version of herself she might have lived in another timeline. But I instinctively know this isn't her only form.

I try not to stare, and fumble out, "It's pretty."

You're pretty, I almost say, surprised by it. Distressed by it.

Her skin is nearly translucent, eyes too big, flashing black, metallic gray, lilac. They're too strange in her strange face. And she's filled out, curves coming in remarkably fast, probably from whatever it is she's eating, which I try not to linger on. She's not eating humans, I feel sure of that. But what does someone like her eat?

It all suits her, this aesthetic, this dress. Didn't I think she was beautiful before?

A mild smirk. "I'm thrilled you approve."

"Whatever," I say, self-conscious somehow, and look away.

She starts moving through the woods, and I follow her for a time. I finally break the silence. "So, um, do you have a name?"

"I'm called 'Sabelle.'"

I continue to trail her, sounding her name in my mind, a variation of the more familiar "Isobel," emphasis on the second syllable. *Sa-BELL. Sa-BELL.*

"Right here," she says, and I look up. She's gesturing to a flat clearing deeper in the woods, impatiently, waiting for me to catch up. "Her home was just there."

I follow her and stop next to her in the clearing. There's nothing here now, not even the old foundational bones of a home. "So, why are we here? I see nothing."

But I don't *sense* nothing. A shiver runs though me, standing on this ground. I look down and murmur, half to myself, "Maybe she buried it."

"She did like burying things." Her eyes heat in resentment. Then she sighs. "But no, I don't believe it's been buried."

"Do you even know what the key looks like?" I ask, doubt tinging my voice. I can't help but imagine it as a huge old-fashioned skeleton key. "Maybe I should check Starling House."

"I hardly think it could be so simple. She would have hidden it," Sabelle says. "Besides, I cannot leave the woods unless *he* unbinds me fully."

"Oh." I frown, nearly tripping over a branch, but she reaches out reflexively to catch me. Her fingers circle my arm, and I almost feel the touch of her through the coat covering me. Rattled, I say, "Maybe Jack has the key."

She lifts her gaze off me and steps away, creating distance between us. "No," she says. "But he may as well, for how difficult this could prove to be." Irritation laces her words together. "I'm helping you, but I don't actually believe we will find the key. I may have seen some things, but I haven't seen us holding it or even opening the door."

"We have to," I say desperately. But then I pause, staring at her. "What do you mean, you've seen some things? You can see the future?" I ask warily.

"Pieces of it," she says. "Not just the future, but any moment in time may come to me. Small, jagged moments, as though they are made of glass. I cannot turn it off or on." She walks forward, calling back to me, "Time, and the events within it, shifts like water. It changes shape. It cannot be contained or studied, not as you might hope."

"That's how you know about the key." I gaze at her in wonder. "And everything else."

She turns to face me, and rolls her eyes suddenly, looking so natural as a human that I'm taken aback. "I've also lived, you realize. I know things not only because of this ability but because I *saw* them."

"Franny and Jack?"

"Not only them. The people! I lived through the killings, and the feedings, and I was there when we were being hunted down ourselves!" she cries, impassioned, eyes wide. "I saw things that would curdle your blood."

I shiver and swallow back the image.

Before I can speak, she shakes her head, the loose ringlet hanging by her cheekbone swinging. "I don't know where the key is, but I know there is one, and that he won't let you in without it. Unless he wants you, in which case you may as well be wearing a wedding gown."

"No," I say firmly, but what can I do? I feel helpless.

She glances at me sideways. "You'll be his bride. I can see you going to him," she says. Then her voice goes curious. "But you'll wear a black dress—not white as the others have—when you are joined."

I tremor at the thought of the white silk dress hanging in the guest room wardrobe, of what it means, but I stubbornly set my shoulders. "You're wrong."

"So you say." But there's pity in her voice. "Come along. It's not here."

Desperation drives me forward, and I follow after her faster as she slips through a knot of trees. "Where are we going now?" I ask, irritated.

"I am letting my instinct lead me," she says. "I already told you, I know only that the key exists. It's likely somewhere that was important to *her*. She spent most of her time here, in these woods, at least in the early days. So, this is where we focus our search. But if you're so curious—I *have* seen another thing. A woman."

"What?" I can feel my heart pound. "My mom?"

Shrugging, she says, "Perhaps it's her. I don't know for certain. But I saw you leaving Rosemont, and someone else was driving. You went past me as I set the roses on fire."

I stare at her, afraid to believe it. "You saw me leaving?" It had to be my mom driving, it had to be. I would never leave without her. But then, Sabelle also saw me going to Jack, going into the river? How can both visions be true? How can either be?

"Wait a minute," I say, my mind catching on something else. "How could you go to the roses? You just said you're bound to the woods, so he'd have to release you for that to happen. And why would you set the roses on fire?"

Her eyes glitter. "I'd like to set this whole town on fire."

"Ohhh-*kay*." I try not to sound surprised. I suppose I shouldn't be. "Why, though?"

"This place was never meant for humans. It was never meant to exist as it is."

I walk quicker, taking that in. "You know he'll be angry at you for helping me," I eventually say. "You're not afraid of him?"

"You saw what he did to me. I was kept trapped while centuries passed, simply because his bride didn't want any others of my kind kept free—and I didn't even feed upon humans like the others did! What worse can he do? Kill me?" She laughs harshly, then adds, "Besides, he's not here now. He cannot see us or hear us."

"I'm afraid he's everywhere," I confess, but I feel no physical pain now. I have to assume he's not near. "And you're risking getting caught again, or worse, if he catches you . . . Do you *want* to die?"

"Do you?" It doesn't quite feel like a threat but like a challenge.

I answer, quietly, "No."

She stops walking, and her blue skirts swing forward, sweeping the snow. Her face draws my gaze upward, the annoyance gone from her eyes, and she looks at me, head tipped to the side. Again I see pity. "Are you certain?"

"Why?" I can hear the defensive tone in my voice. "I don't want to die. I want to stop hurting. My heart . . ." My voice cracks, utterly human. All my anger is gone and only raw truth is left. "Is broken. I lost someone I loved."

"He could take your pain away for you, if you wanted. He could make you forget."

The suggestion rests on my skin. He could do that, I bet. He could do a lot of things. It would be trading one pain for another, though. The death of my memories.

We stand quietly while I collect myself. "I hate him," I say.

"Everyone hates him," she replies simply. "He even hates himself. He's why she died."

"Franny?" I ask. When she nods, I open my mouth to ask what she means, but Sabelle has already turned away, lifting her face to the bright sky, to the sun, looking like she's searching for a moment of peace. Then she exhales, motioning me on. She walks, humming a strange, eerily beautiful melody, and I follow, my helpless, all-too-human hands in my pockets, the stupid kitchen knife in one.

"Come on." She slows, turning back to me. The smile isn't as unnatural on her face as I'd have thought. "It will be all right."

"Will it?" I ask faintly.

"Yes." She sounds so sure that it leaves me silent.

She's a walking contradiction, and half of what she says makes no sense. I'll go to Jack but I'll leave Rosemont. We won't find the key but everything will be all right. How can all this be true?

Her words hang in the air, and I swallow, nervous because she's right next to me, but neither of us shies away. Her shoulder touching mine now. I swear her pinkie finger grazes mine, but my hands are too numb for me to be sure. I turn my head to meet her inkwell eyes, we share a long breath.

But the spell breaks, and we split apart again. Onward.

Back in the apartment, in the guest room, I drop onto the bed. I close my eyes in relief, and then they fly open again when the door creaks. I didn't shut it all the way.

Agatha knocks once and pushes it open. "Here." Her voice

is soft as she steps forward and hands me a brown leather book wrapped in a cord. "I should have given it to you before. I don't know if there's anything in it to help you. I haven't read it all. But it's yours, rightfully."

I stare down at the book. One word is stamped on the cover.

STARLING

"What is it?" I ask, slipping the cord down. But even as I ask, I realize, my breath catching. I flip through the yellowed pages. The first several are torn out, but I recognize the paper itself. I look back at Agatha, stunned. She said it was missing. Another lie.

"It's a diary, for the Starling women. Franny started it." Agatha's lips pinch to the side. "I don't recall there being anything very compelling, not in the pages I've read."

Not in the pages she's read? "Why haven't you read it all?" I ask in surprise.

"Because." Her voice is hesitant, her body turned away from me. I count the buttons on the back of her sweater. Three, mother-of-pearl. "It wouldn't change anything to know."

I let that sit for a moment. I don't say anything about her lying about it. I just wait until she walks out of the room, then turn back to the book.

After the torn-out pages come Celine and Elizabeth—both Franny's daughters, though they barely write a page each, and nothing from either girl is very interesting. Not a single mention of Jack or their Crownings. I'm glad when I turn to the fourth entry and see how long it is. Eagerly I begin to read.

April 26, 1820
Sylvie Frances Esperanza Starling

*The whole first floor of the house is strung with
flowers, roses from floor to ceiling. Perhaps I
exaggerate a bit—as Rose says I tend to do—but
the scent is heavenly. As I write this in the drawing
room, Frances's portrait hangs above the fireplace,
and it seems almost as though she is here with me.
I never met her, yet I often think of her, of what it
must have been like, then. Most people do not discuss
those times, but they bow and curtsy to me on the
street as we drive by in the carriage, or go out for
a stroll. Last week, Mama took us for new dresses,
and the seamstress was so honored, she could hardly
stop stammering. She was old enough to remember
what it was like before. Mama filled her purse with
extra coins—far more than we owed for six new
spring party dresses—and the woman kissed her
cheeks when we left.*

*My Crowning was two days ago—hence the
new dresses, and all the flowers decorating the
house. Papa threw a party beforehand, and our
whole family was there, all gay and laughing,
toasting in not just my honor but my mama's, my
grandmama's. I wore the creamiest white dress, and
new gloves and slippers. Mama tied ribbons in my
hair and told me what to do. I walked into the river
just as the others did, and I wore Mama's pearls*

and Frances's ring, the one Jack gave her. It's beautiful!

But, oh, I forgot to mention what I found out. You see, the rumor Rose whispered to me that evening, and that someone had whispered to her, was that Frances was buried with the starling ring when she died in that tragic accident. However, somehow the next morning it showed up in Mama's nursery, and when the nursemaid didn't string it up on a necklace immediately for our infant mother, the nursemaid was struck by a carriage and run over.

It sounds terrible, and there is something about it that makes my throat ache. By that time, my grandfather George had already died, too, and Mama was left an orphan. It was horrible, both deaths were, and it makes me quite sad to think of poor Mama left all alone, her life starting with such tragic events.

Though that's dreadful, I do not mean to say such things in here, to fill these pages with ugliness. What would Frances think? I am quite ashamed now and should just as soon cross these words out!

And so, I shall fill the rest with loveliness, about our glorious binding. How when I went into the water, my fear dissipated at once, about how he was on the other side, and he took my hand and kissed it like ever such a fine gentleman. About how the leaves at the bottom of my teacup said good fortune this morning. About how the starlings outside the

*window sing right this very moment, chattering
as they swell and swoop among the treetops. About
how I'm hardly sore at all today, and in another
two I should recover quite nicely. About the pile of
satin and silk and fine muslin dresses on my bed.
About Rose, practicing piano in the next room.
About Papa looking so proud, and Mama's beautiful
smile as they placed the flowers on my head, the
pearls shining in the mirror. About all the good to
come, all the good that's been done.*

*Years ago, my grandmother saved Rosemont.
It is my honor to continue what she began.*

It turns my stomach, her devotion. But I go on, reading the words of the women and girls before me. Sometimes I don't want to connect with them, want to hate them all the way I hate Franny. Other moments, I feel a connection so deep that it pierces my heart. I flip through the diary, finding entries from my great-greats, their names merging before me. Maria-Louise, Aurora, Alma, Nanette, Josephine, Minnie, Clara, Coralie.

*December 11th, 1930
Hazel Frances Starling*

*Today it snowed for the first time all season, and
with the cold came death. They pulled little Bobby
Jakes from the river. We all know who did it. Jack
is hungrier than normal because he's used so much
energy on us the last few years. Not just because*

there's fewer Starlings for him to use but because he expels so much power. With the rest of the country hungry and out of work, Rosemont is thriving more than ever.

Some say Bobby's death is a fluke, that he probably fell in while trying to fish or something—he was not a tourist, though, and everyone is warned not to go to the river, so I don't think they're fooling anyone. I was there when they got him out, and his body was stripped of its flesh. No fish in our river would do that. We all know who would, but Mama won't admit it. I know for a fact, though, because Jack told me he did it. The worst part is that he doesn't even need flesh—it's the pain that feeds him. He smiled when I asked, and I hated him for a moment, but then he kissed my eyelids and promised he wouldn't again. I don't believe him, but I stayed with him for three days, to make sure he was well fed. Then when I got home, I couldn't get out of bed for another week. Paul was furious with me, but I can't help it. I'm just exhausted, too tired to fight with anyone. Not that I'd fight Jack.

Jack makes bad things happen. Grandma Josephine was killed young, when Mama was only two, along with her twin sister, Nanette. People still talk about them, that they were special. That Josephine could draw lightning from the sky and set your barn afire if you wronged her—or that he

would do it for her. Some people say he killed them.
That they did something wrong. I don't ask him.
The idea of it scares me. I only focus on the good, the
way he says he cares for us all, all the Starlings.

I think he only meant that affection for Franny.
The way he looks when he's thinking of Franny . . .
it makes me shiver. I suppose he used her for the
same reason he uses all. Because he's hungry. Because
we give him power, energy, because we increase
his magic. Other times? I suspect he's hungry for
something else, something nobody can give him. It
gives me a strange feeling—something like pity, I
suppose.

It's not all bad, with Jack. You get used to it,
even when you don't think you will. I've always
hated him. But sometimes, only secretly, to myself, I
think I love him, too.

I rub my eyes and continue reading through more entries, making sure I focus on each and every word, just so I don't miss anything important.

July 8th, 1952
Alice Frances Starling

I had the tiles laid today for the shop. It took a while
because I had to special order some, but it's well
worth it—to me, anyhow. It's all coming along, and
I think it will be absolutely wonderful. The painters

were there last week, and I've already started ordering. I know I don't have to work—Aunt Bea doesn't approve, and Mother said I could better use my energy for other things, like raising my children. I say I can do all of it, or at least I can try. I can't sit around waiting for him all the time, and I hate social functions. I'd rather be with my flowers and make people happy sometimes—which is funny because I feel like I'm always so angry. It seems to only get worse the older I get.

I used to envy the other girls in town, that nobody took me on dates much because the boys here were intimidated by Starling girls—they know they'll always have to share us. I wanted it so badly, just to have someone of my own, but even though I care for my husband, it's simply not enough. I love my little girls more than anything else, this newest already stirring in my belly, but it's still not enough. Sometimes I worry nothing will make me happy but to be free from Jack, but with every year gone by, I start to think it won't happen. Not because I don't think I know how but because I lack courage. For all my fire, I'm just a coward. But I have so much to lose now. How can I jeopardize everything and all those I love? I feel like I'm on fire, but maybe it's simply that I do not have enough fire to do anything about anything.

So for now, I suppose the shop—it's a dream I've made true, and if I have done nothing else, at least

I've done that. At least if I cannot stand against Jack, I've done something, built right into the shop. Just a quiet rebellion. Nobody will probably ever notice but me, or make sense of it if they do. Still, I feel better for it. Is that enough?

For today, it must be.

I've done something, built right into the shop. I drop the book and jump out of bed, adrenaline pushing me faster. Alice—Agatha's mother—is the one who built the flower shop! Why didn't Agatha ever say? *But it's not important,* I tell myself as I pull my shoes on. What's important is what Alice wrote.

I've done something, built right into the shop. Just a quiet rebellion. Nobody will probably ever notice but me. I race down the stairs and out onto the street. I saw one word in a tile that second day I went to the shop: "forever." There must be more. There has to be.

CHAPTER SIXTEEN

The cheery little bell rings as I enter the shop, and Miles looks up from his perch at the counter where he leans over a book, a frown on his face. He replaces it with a smile when he sees me, but it's a troubled one. He sets his pencil down and stands. "Hey, Kit."

"Hey," I say, the wet flower scent of the shop enveloping me. I slow my breathing, steady my excitement. I didn't even think before coming here.

I study Miles closer, frowning. "You look upset."

"No." His sigh is low, and he catches himself and stops. "We're having a shortage."

"Shortage?"

"The eternal roses," he explains. "It seems as though they're diseased."

"What?" I say in disbelief, forgetting for a moment why I'm here. The roses shouldn't be diseased. There should be no shortage. They're supposed to last forever, perfectly, aren't they? I look around, taking in the flowers. Lilies, pansies, peonies, Gerbera daisies, greenery. Roses, yes, a few buckets, but a tenth of what was here last time. My heart rate picks up and I turn back to him. "Why? Do you know anything about it?"

Miles pushes up his sleeves, face creased with worry. Today he's back in a suit, or a partial suit. Trousers and a vest, in dove gray, the buttons winking gold. "Probably less than you. Only that they're dying."

"They're dying?" I can feel my eyebrows rise in confusion. Jack made the roses as part of the contract, didn't he? Why would he let them die? "I don't get it," I say, almost to myself.

Miles inclines his head, sighing. "It's so strange. Usually you clip a rose, and three more will grow from that same spot within a day. Now they're dying on their own, and they're not growing back. It's only been a few days. Most people probably wouldn't even notice unless they saw them every day, but Calla—from the perfumery—and I agree, it's getting worse. Whatever it is, it's swift and unforgiving. I'm afraid we may lose our roses." His breath catches, his eyes shining with dread.

My heart sinks as I realize his unspoken fear. It's not only the financial ramifications of the roses dying, how bad that might be for him, for the town. It's bigger than that. If Jack takes the roses away, what else might he take from them? I bite my lip. As complicit as some of the people in Rosemont have been, not all of them deserve this. Not Miles.

Staring at his concerned face, I blurt out, "I swear I don't know anything about it. . . ." Helplessly I add, "I don't even know what to do here."

"I know. Sometimes I stand here and wonder how I even got to this moment. Sometimes I wonder why I'm still here. I'm sorry, Kit. I don't really understand all this, but I don't feel right about it. . . ." His voice falls away, so unsure, his eyes so sorry, I lose any resentment I might have held for him hiding things from me. He's an outsider in a way, too.

"It's okay," I say. "I can try to find out more about the roses. . . ."

Miles shakes his head. "We'll figure it out. Now, I know you didn't come here to talk about that."

"Oh," I say, returning to the present. Remembering why I came. Alice. "Well, I sort of was wondering if I could look at something that might help me find my mom."

My eyes travel the floor even as I say it.

"Miles." I bend lower, searching for words, and I see one. It says "lily." My pulse picks up. There might actually be something here! "Do you know you have words in your tiles?" I ask.

It's quiet for a long moment. I turn and look up at him.

"I do." His voice is faint. "I've been finding them for years."

"How many have you found?"

"Eight or nine, I think."

My heart does a flip, and something in me lights up. Alice called it a quiet rebellion. "Can I stay and look?"

"Absolutely you can," Miles says with a warm smile.

The shop is quiet, barely five customers between phone calls and drop-ins. I stalk around the room, collecting words in a note-pad Miles gave me, his pencil in my sweaty hand. So far, fifteen of them—many of them flower related, curiously enough. A few more than he knew were there.

"I've never actually gone looking for the words," he admits, "though I was curious initially when I came across them."

"It was my great-grandmother's shop," I tell him. Alice, who talked about being angry. Alice, who spoke about standing against Jack. She ended up staying, building this business and raising a family. But what's a quieter way to rebel than some tiles in a floor? Hidden. Tiny words on tiny tiles that nobody would notice or look for.

I crawl under a table full of metal buckets of greenery, and scan each tile individually, touching them, feeling for words I might miss with my eyes. "Found another!" I call, and triumphantly add it to my book: "rose." My legs tremble as I rise.

"And you think it's going to add up to something?"

I almost want to say, *Yes! I* know *words. My life was built around them. My father's life.* But I say the messier truth, "I'm not sure. I only hope it does."

He cocks one brow and says, "All right."

"You sure you don't mind me in here snooping?"

Miles chuckles. "I have nothing to hide, Kit, and if this makes you happy, take all the time you need. Just, for God's sake, don't knock over any of my babies, okay?"

I grin at him. "I won't."

At around five, he orders dinner for us from the diner, and by the way he teases on the phone, I can tell he's talking to Belinda. At six he turns his music way up—he says it's Eartha Kitt—and flips the CLOSED sign just as Belinda waltzes in, bags in hand, cheeks flushed.

"I've brought burgers, no whining!" she announces. "I brought wine, Miles. Kit, you're good with soda?" When I nod, she says, "Good. 'Cause I'm not cool enough to let you drink."

I smile. "That's fine."

"Come eat, Kit," Miles orders cheerfully, and I stand from where I've been crouched, along the back right wall. I ache, but not from Jack being nearby. I'm sure of that at least. I'm just tired.

"Here, kiddo." Belinda hands me a take-out box, a big *K* scrawled on top in what looks like lipstick but is probably just marker.

I flip open the container and peek under the toasted buttery bun to see what she's brought me: lettuce, tomato, fried cheese curds, good mustard, and a pile of golden fries on the side.

I smile gratefully, and Belinda winks at me and hands Miles his box—real burger for him.

As we eat, Miles tells her about the tiles.

"So, how many new ones have you found?" she asks.

"Fourteen, I think?" I dunk a fry in ketchup. "I have one more section to finish. Then I'm done."

"Do they say anything? Can you tell yet?" Belinda asks.

I look over the list of words. "Not yet."

"A puzzle?" She grins, wiping the edge of her mouth, some-how not smudging her lipstick at all. "We can make a night of it, try to figure out if it says anything."

"I'd love that," I say with a smile, balling up my napkin.

"I'm happy to help you," Belinda answers kindly. What she doesn't say I understand perfectly well anyway: she's on my side. I can trust her. I can trust them both.

Miles nudges me. "I will suggest that you let your grandma know you're here safe."

"I'll call her soon," I promise.

While Miles catches Belinda up about the rest, and I fill in all the details, I clear our food boxes and toss them into the garbage in the back room, eyeing the floor while I'm there. It's only plain white tiles, wall to wall. I call Agatha, but she doesn't answer, so I leave a message. Something—fear mingled with revulsion—ripples through me. She must be with Jack. She's made a choice, all these years. She knows what she's doing. I cast aside the memory of the bruises on her skin and tuck the phone into my pocket. It's almost dead.

When I get back to the front room, Belinda has tossed her apron over Miles's chair and is moving her hips gently to the music while he sings along, clearing out his register. I love them both in this moment, and I pick up where I left off, crawling along the baseboard.

The words are small, and the corners shadowy, even with the lights all on overhead. I pause when I find a new word and run my fingers along the bronze letters: "blood." A small breath escapes me. With the pulsing surety of it, I know now: there's a message hidden in this floor.

I inch forward until I can't go farther, a display cabinet tucked in the corner.

"Miles? Can I move this?"

"Not alone you can't." He closes his drawer and moves around the counter. "Not unless you want to hurt yourself."

"Unless you want to hurt yourself" repeats in my mind. I shake it out of my head, heart pierced.

Belinda joins me and Miles at the cabinet and helps us scoot it over, but only after we've carefully moved the baby plants atop it. In the corner where it stood, under a layer of dust, which I swipe at with my hand, I find another word: "him."

Goose bumps, the good kind.

"I think that's the last one. I've searched this entire room," I say as I rise, thrilled. I'm high on anticipation. I touched every single tile in this room, crawled around for hours, moved furniture and buckets of plants, spilling water on myself in the process. I'm sore and dirty and I don't remember if I brushed my teeth this morning, but I don't care. I've found something. We've found something.

"Miles, thank you," I say, and my voice breaks.

He wraps one arm around my shoulder and squeezes. "Hey. Thank me after we figure out if it's worth anything, if it might lead to your mom somehow."

"Even so. It's worth it to me," I tell him. "You didn't have to let me look."

"Yes," he says, his gaze loving as he continues, "I did. Besides, after five years I'm pretty curious."

"Come on." Belinda pulls me to a chair. "Come sit and we'll work on it together. I'm fairly good at fridge-magnet poetry, you know."

"I bet you are, Sylvia Plath," he jokes back.

"Shush, Miles." She taunts him cheerfully, "I know you're going to boast about your Scrabble skills. But this will be harder."

I laugh, and wipe at my eyes. "Okay. Twenty-four words, I think." I count them again. "Yeah."

"You found more in a few hours than I found in a few years."

"Fear makes you move faster," I tell him, almost as a joke. But it sobers us all. They know why I'm so driven. I care about Miles's shop, the roses, the people in town. But the heart of it, the heart of me, beats for my mom.

"Can you list them alphabetically, Kit?" Belinda asks. "That might help me."

"Sure." I'm good with alphabetical, from scanning author names on library shelves, from working at a bookstore. It takes me a minute; then I flip the list their way.

azalea
blood
bluebell
daffodil
daisy
forever
give
him
hyacinth
iris
is
lily
lupine
magnolia
our
peony
promise
rose

the
tulip
we
willow
yarrow
zinnia

"Hey, hold on," Miles says, looking up from the words. "Most of these are names of flowers, a few trees, but not all. So, if we eliminate those . . ."

"You're right." I study the list, pleased but surprised that it hadn't occurred to me yet, that maybe the message is hidden within a message.

I'm afraid to get excited, because there's a chance it's simply words in tiles, but I remind myself of Alice's passage, and begin to cross out the plants. We lean over the page, heads bowed.

"Hold on," I say, and jot down all the words twice, then rip two pages out of the notebook. "Here. We have our own set of words. So, we can each try putting them together in different orders. The flowers might be in there, or they might just be a distraction."

"Oh, I like a challenge." Belinda snatches one page up, then turns away from us.

"So competitive," Miles jokes before taking his own.

The three of us bend over our own papers, music in the background, Belinda tapping her pen to the beat. I move words around and around.

"I have something. Or, part of something," Miles says. Then

he reads, "'We promise him our blood. Roses are forever.'" He groans. "No, that's not right. *Are* isn't even on the list, and it's *rose*, not *roses*. This is a lot harder than it seems."

"Mine's not great, but I think I got closer," Belinda says with a smirk. But then her expression goes more solemn, lips pressing together as she seems to realize what she has unpuzzled. Her voice softens as she says, "We give him our blood promise forever."

"I think it's good to keep the flower names out," I say. "I think they're just to throw it off somehow."

They both agree, and I stare down at my paper, run Belinda's line through my mind again.

I read mine. "'We promise him our blood'? Then another line to use the rest of the non-flower words?" I stare at the lines I've jotted down, my hope plummeting. "But either way, this doesn't really help me. It's all so obvious."

My laugh is self-deprecating. So much for the quiet rebellion. I'm not any closer to finding my mom.

They look at each other, then back at me. Slowly Belinda says, "I think we're all just tired." Her reassurance is kind. "Even if you got the words in the correct order, it's still a puzzle—which isn't solved overnight. Sometimes the easiest ones look the hardest until you see them from a new angle. . . ."

Miles puts his hand on mine. "I agree. Maybe it's best you get home and get some sleep?"

I nod, try to smile. "Okay. Yeah, you're both right."

Belinda offers, "I'll drive you."

"I can walk," I say.

"No." She is firm. "I'll drive you. Miles, thanks, doll."

He hugs us both, and says to her, "Take the wine with you, Bel? I'm up to bed."

"Save it for next time," she says, and we wave goodbye as we walk out. He follows and locks the shop behind us.

The night air is cold and fresh, a change from the warm, wet floral of the shop, but it's cozy in Belinda's VW bug, a vintage model. There's a hula girl on her dash, which I've never seen in real life.

"Don't sweat it, okay?" she says as she pulls up in front of the apartment. "You'll figure it out. I believe in you, Kit. I wish none of this had happened to your family, to any of you, you know. We're rooting for you, Miles and I."

"Thanks." I stare out the window, my face reflecting back at me. "I'm rooting for me, too."

CHAPTER SEVENTEEN

I wake up the next morning with words in my mouth, in my head, dancing around. And the fact that my Crowning is only two days away. I can't just assume I got the lines right last night. I need to keep going, and I at least need to use all the words: blood, forever, give, him, is, our, promise, the, we. Otherwise it feels like I'm missing half of it. I roll over and reach for the notebook with the tile message, my eyes still blurry. I push myself up and scan the list again, scratch out a few attempts at unscrambling the words. It seems easier than it did last night—and before long I have something that runs chills down my body. It's not even much different from our attempts yesterday, but it clicks into place. Exactly like a puzzle piece would. This feels *right*. But I stare at it, trying to understand exactly what it means.

> *our blood is the promise*
> *we give him forever*

Not "we promise him our blood," but "our blood is the promise." Which isn't quite the same. It's also not as obvious, but what does it mean? I spilled my blood and it opened the ground. . . . Isn't that what let Sabelle out? If I bleed again, would it open the door to the lair?

But this says nothing about the lair. Nothing about a key.

All the first line says is "our blood is the promise," which could mean blood but could actually mean more of a metaphorical blood. Family. Kin. Starlings. So . . . what? I already know that our blood is promised to Jack, literally and figuratively. Why couldn't Alice have hidden something more helpful?

Frustrated, I throw the pen and notebook down and reach for the diary instead. I lean back into my pillow and draw my knees up, to rest the book against. Then I start again, picking up where I left off, falling back into the diary.

I flip past Alice to the next name, and I can't help it— I hesitate.

But only for a second.

July 17th, 1968
Agatha Frances Starling

Rosemont threw a parade for us this afternoon. Not because of any particular reason—my Crowning was a year ago already. Everyone clapping in the street and children stomping their feet with joy. I was nervous about being on the float, but Junie laughed at me and said, "Why be nervous! They love us." Her words eased my nerves. She was right.

I climbed onto the float, and I stood there waving like a princess, and it felt true. They do love us and him, because look at what we have. The skies have opened and showered us with fortune, only we all know it's Jack. There's been nothing but good lately—perfect weather and investments that have boomed, and the parade is only one small part of the thanks our family has received for our sacrifice. This is bigger than tokens pressed into our hands. This feels especially poignant, and I'm welling up with it.

I've had so many emotions already this weekend. This morning I was anxious, but Junie lent me her peach-colored taffeta from prom, and I only had to take it in about two inches in the waist and it was perfect! She wore some new, smart suit she has, and Barbara looked pretty, too, in a pale green tea dress, and Mother and Father dressed up, and Grandma Hazel, and Great-Grandma, too. We rode on that big, fluffy float decorated with paper starlings and strung all over with roses. I got to throw out candy and coins to everyone, and Father handed me a wad of five-dollar bills to pass out to the sweetest children! It was a real laugh, and just like that, my nerves settled into happiness.

I felt like he was watching, his eyes on me, and in my mind he was the Jack I love the most, all golden-skinned and hot to the touch, like warm honey, and his voice soft, like a whisper, when he says my name. Of course, he wasn't there, or if he was, he didn't show himself to me, nor to any of the other brides. But I know I'm his favorite. He hardly sees Mother anymore, nor either of my aunts. It makes me feel a little sad, jealous, to admit that part of me is dreading getting married and having a baby of my own. Because someday, he'll love my daughter more than me. But I know that's how it's meant to be. I know that Franny had to pass on the torch. I think of her often and wonder if she'd be proud, of him, of all of us, because look at what we've made from her sacrifices. Look at the lives we've changed. Mother reminds me all the time, how important what we're doing is. How could I ever wish it otherwise? We are lucky.

After the parade, we drank tea with the Ladies of Rosemont, and they all said I looked so pretty, and loved the chiffon cake I'd made—decorated with rose petals, of course! Mrs. Louis said she'd love for me to consider joining them, someday, when I'm married, and I was so flattered, I think I hardly said a word. Of course, then Junie replied later, all snide, that they'd be lucky to have a Starling, and not the other way around. But I'm surprised she cares at all. We know Junie isn't traditional like Mother or me, and it seems Barbara feels the same. She said she's never going to get married, and we laughed because obviously that's not true. But anyhow, when they left, Junie asked me to see him *instead—she had a headache and told me not to bother Mother about it—so of course I went. I kept the peach dress on. I thought he'd like that. I don't write in here about the times when I see him. I feel like they're for me and him, alone.*

Still, perhaps I'm feeling sad now that I'm home. Remember those emotions all over the place today? First nervous, then happy, then excited, and now, I suppose, I'm a touch melancholy. Now that it's quiet. He really hurt me tonight. However, I just remembered all those faces, all those children smiling at me, those bills wadded up in my hand, and the tokens people give us to bestow extra favor on their families, and I didn't say anything. I did not cry. Junie says the scar will fade, if not go away completely like they almost always do, and anyway, who cares about a thing like that? I worry a bit, when I think of him doing that to Barbara, or to Mother. I know that's senseless of me, though. It's our duty.

It has been a long night, and I have nothing left to say, so with these words, I part:

Good night, present me, future reader. I hope you ease into sleep tonight. Do not dream of monsters and frightening things. I know I won't. I hope I won't.

A million things run through my mind. Agatha didn't just drink the Kool-Aid; she injected it into her veins. I already knew that, but it's somehow shockingly painful to read it. She didn't inherit Alice's fire. She didn't rebel at all, and here she calls her own mother traditional. Bitterly, I can't help but think Jack broke Alice's spirit.

I flip the page, and the next entry is Juliet's.

February 5th, 1999
Juliet Frances Starling

This is supposed to be advice, I guess, for whoever comes after me. It's also a diary, so here's my confession: I don't want to do this anymore.

I remember what it was like for my mom after Junie was killed, how scared she was, and Aunt Barbara, who never even had kids. I knew he thought Barbara was thumbing her nose at him because of that, and how his temper was. Everyone knows if you push at Jack, he will take you down a peg . . . or ten. I wasn't old enough to go to him, but I remember how nervous everyone was. Now I think of all the things I'd rather do. Daniel and I talk when Mom isn't around, about getting out of here. We know they wouldn't understand; we know they'd all hate us for it. We have roles. Daniel's supposed to get married and continue the line with a daughter. I need to do the same (even though I'd rather do almost anything else than marry a man and have babies), and in the meantime, give myself to Jack, and I do. But I'm twenty now. I'm ready to live my life. It's been seven years. Seven years of going to him, seven years of pain. I can push through. I know I need to, but sometimes I just want to run.

I'm grateful for the fact that he's been easy on us, that there've been no unnatural deaths for years. It's just that I know it can change at any minute. When he's with me, I'm scared. I hate every moment. I think about how he appears for others, how he can be beautiful and gentle. But he's not usually like that with me. There's always time to think. I lie there and listen to him breathing. I don't leave until he tells me to go. Sometimes it's days. I don't leave.

I'm going to get out of Rosemont. I need to not care what people will think. Daniel tells me it's not selfish. He tells me to go now, that there've been dissenters before, even if just a few. Nobody speaks of them, of the dishonor. But we know it's been done. I'm just not ready yet. Because everyone says this place curses you. That bad things happen to Starlings who leave. But bad things happen here, too. I'm going to do it. Eventually.

I'll say it here, for the girls who will come after me: Stay quiet and obedient. Be grateful to him when he's kind. He so infrequently is. I still remember when he burned half my clothes because I talked back. Jack likes fire. I'm only glad he didn't do worse. He has to others.

So I'll say, when you get a chance, run. And

never look back. Or maybe just fight, like I'm not
brave enough to do. Sometimes I think it's not so
much that he's all that powerful or the contract is
all that ironclad. I think sometimes we let him
do it.

People say Franny loved him, that he loved her.
But I never want that kind of love.

I just want to be free.

"Good morning," a voice interrupts as I reach the last line. Agatha is standing at my door when I look up. Her eyes drop to the diary in my hands, then drift back up to my face. "I got your message last night. What were you doing at the florist?"

"Looking," I say, closing the diary. "Did you know there are words in the tiles?"

"Oh yes. I spent half my childhood there." She leans against the doorframe. "It was my parents' shop—well, my mother's, really."

I don't bother asking why she didn't keep it running herself. Instead I ask, "What does it mean? Why are the words there?"

Her voice is soft. "Whenever someone asked, she would say they meant nothing."

The tiles meant nothing? How can I believe that? Alice said she'd built in a quiet rebellion. They must mean *something*.

I run my hand along the diary's cover, and when I glance back up, Agatha's eyes are on the book again. She never read all the entries.

"Do you want to read it?" I ask.

Her hesitation stretches out, and then she tilts her head casually. Like it doesn't matter. "Maybe."

I climb out of the bed and hand it to her. For a brief moment I don't let go and we hold it together.

"I will give it back to you," she says. "It's just, I should read the whole thing, at least once."

I nod after a moment. Study her face, and say, "Okay. Tell me if anything clicks."

"I will." Her eyes hold the promise. I think I can believe it. Then she turns and leaves the room.

My stomach rumbles, and I know I can't put off eating any longer. I need the energy anyhow. I make myself a peanut-butter-and-brown-sugar sandwich and end up in the living room, near Agatha. While she reads, I play with the words again, refusing to abandon the idea that they're important. Even as I work on the puzzle, I can't help thinking that school's starting again in a couple of days. I wish I were there now. I miss the smells in the halls of Callins North. Miss the teachers—my favorites, but also cranky Mr. O'Brien the gym teacher—miss my friends and the school librarian and all the books. Miss doing homework. I'd take a million math tests right now, just to be back, knowing my mom was waiting for me to get home at the end of the day.

I swallow the lump in my throat as I go over the sheet of words, and look up when there's a knock on the apartment door. Agatha stands to answer it, leaving the diary on the chair where she was reading it. I can't see who she's speaking to, but my ears perk up when I hear the person murmur: ". . . two boys are missing . . . Tanner and Lee . . . seventeen . . . went snow-shoeing yesterday . . . haven't returned."

I strain to see the woman talking to Agatha, and she looks familiar—it's Charlotte's mom.

Agatha closes the door and turns.

"Did he take them?" I can't help but ask. "Are they dead?"

She looks up, and her face gives the answer. A suffocating weight of sadness lies over us both. But I'm also angry. I stare at her. "Why is he doing this?" I say, and I can hear the accusation in my voice.

"He—he—" she stammers, then shakes her head. "He's angry. At me. He knows I gave you the diary."

"But why would he care?"

"It's not that. It's enough that I tried to offer you informa-tion." Her mouth pinches. She says, "He's punishing me. I've made him angry. And he isn't exactly merciful."

"I sort of figured that out." I cover my face with my hands. "How come nobody outside of Rosemont knows about all this? People die here all the time."

"Not all the time," she says defensively.

"Three people in days!" I argue. "He killed that girl." Because he was so hungry, and Agatha just wasn't enough? "And now two more? He's breaking the contract because you did what? Pushed back on something? And what about other times? No-body's been curious about what goes on in this town?"

"Nobody outside of Rosemont seems to even notice Rose-mont," she says, her voice hollow. "I can only remember once, I believe it was the midseventies, when a young man new to town was asking questions." Agatha sits, gaze fixed as she remembers. "Jack didn't like that. Then the questions stopped."

"What happened to the guy?" I ask it warily. I can only imagine.

She meets my eyes. "Jack bit off his tongue and burned him alive. He can be quite brutal. Be glad he thinks of you with fondness."

I blanche. "He's terrible to me, too. Look what he's done."

"He's not all bad." Agatha touches her ring woefully, stroking the starling. But the way she says it is tinged with doubt. She doesn't even believe it. But I know she used to. What exactly has changed? "I believe he loves our family, as much as he can love."

"Well, what happens when there's no more of us? I'm the last of the line. What if I hadn't come back? What if I was dead or never existed?" I press. "What if I don't have kids?"

She lifts her hands, a small gesture. "The contract would be void then. All the other creatures would be freed. Rosemont would become a bloodbath."

"It already is!" I nearly scream. "Three people have been killed since I got here!" I want to pound my fists into something. "He's taking the roses away. Why didn't you tell Charlotte's mom about the boys?"

"I don't go around announcing when Jack does things. What he does is between him and us. That's always how it's been. The people here know what we do—vaguely—but they know nothing of the details. They only feel the consequences—rarely."

"But it's not fair," I say. "None of this is fair, especially not innocent people dying. That was part of the deal. Wasn't it? He gets a Starling, and no one else gets hurt. How can he just break the deal when it's convenient for him?"

I stare at her, waiting for an answer, and finally add, "You should tell someone where the boys are," not wanting to hate her. She tried to help me, and it ended up with two people dying. And what about Corinne? I hate him.

"I'll tell Sheriff Thompson where they are." Agatha looks back down at her hands. At that starling stone on her finger. Then, voice low, she adds, "What's left of them."

CHAPTER EIGHTEEN

I wait until Agatha disappears into her room an hour later before I slip out of the apartment.

I take the path past the park on my way to the woods and stop when I get to the roses. It's difficult to accept—more than half of the roses are dead, black, withered away, like old, burnt paper. I stare for a while and finally reach out to touch the crumpled petals. The dying ones seem to shrink in the beauty of the others, which are still fresh and fragrant beneath my mittens.

My hand drops to my side and I wonder again. Why?

As I slog through the woods, heading toward the river, I make out Sabelle, standing in the snow, her back to me. Snowflakes begin to fall, and when she turns, I see the white flecks catching in her black hair, on her lashes, on her full bottom lip.

But it's the dirt on her, the smudge on her cheek, the filth on her hands, that gets my attention. And when I get closer, I see the wild, pleased look in her eyes.

"What?" I ask when I reach her.

She steps forward triumphantly and holds out her hand. "Here. I have no use for it."

I stare down at what she's holding. It's a dagger, the carved handle inlaid with roses and leaves. The blade dull but probably once deadly. "Why?"

"It was hers."

"Franny's?"

Her lips turn up higher, and a mischievous look comes into her gaze. "Yes, her. She wasn't using it any longer. Had to break a few of her bones to get it out of her grasp, though—"

"Stop." I shake my head; images of a red-haired skeleton come to mind. Or would her hair be white now? Would she even have hair? "You dug it up? You grave-robbed?"

A sheepish little laugh, the glint in her eyes going wicked at the same time. I get a sudden flash of her dancing over Franny's grave, gleeful laugh slipping out of her lips.

I stare at the ground, where a mound of dirt has been replaced. "Why is she buried here? I would think she'd be in a big, fancy graveyard, along with the other Starlings."

"There is a place, a showpiece," she says. "But that grave is empty."

"Does anyone else know that?"

Sabelle snickers. "Only he knows. He's the reason she's there in the first place." My eyes go wide at that. When I don't laugh with her, she sighs and says, "I was looking for the key. I wondered if perhaps she had been buried with it." Before I can respond, she shakes her head. "I didn't find a key. Only this."

I look down at it in my mittened hands. I turn it over, reluctantly admiring its beauty. I try not to sound too disappointed when I realize it really is just a dagger. I don't want Sabelle to feel bad, that she robbed a grave for nothing. Then again, when I stare at her rosy glow, the way her eyes shine, it doesn't seem like it was difficult for her to do. I force myself to smile. "Thank you for looking. I wouldn't have thought of that."

"Keep it for protection," she says. "It will do more harm than that tiny little knife you had before."

Nodding, I agree, even though I know I can't hurt Jack with some ordinary dagger. Still, this feels inherently special. Franny was buried with it.

After tucking the dagger carefully into my coat, I nudge her forward, to walk with me closer to the river. The water is an inkwell spilled across a white carpet of snow.

"The roses are dying. In the park," I say. "Why do you think he's doing this?"

She cocks her head, tracing her fingers along an evergreen. "Perhaps he can sense that the link is dying."

My lips part as I stare at her, taking this new information in. Maybe the roses are because of me. "Dying? What do you mean? I didn't miss the Crowning."

"But you *want* to," she says thoughtfully. "And he knows it. That's what matters. It's a warning. He can give, but he can take away just as easily."

Jack killed those boys because Agatha didn't behave the way he wanted. And I'm pushing back.

She stares at me, letting me digest this. Her face is rounder now, a soft oval, lips smoothed out, hydrated, her hair hanging, clean somehow, apart from a little grave dirt. Today she wears a gray dress, far less elaborate than the blue one.

"Come on," she says, eyes dark and wide, like a bird, and she hooks her arm in mine. She turns from the river and heads deeper into the woods. "Tell me of your stories," she says.

"My stories?" The request surprises me. "How do you know I'm a writer?" I ask, and remember, she can see the future, maybe even read my thoughts. Shifting uncomfortably, I explain, "Um. I write fantasy, mostly. Like, made-up things . . ." I trail off.

"Does it bring you joy?" she asks.

"Yes," I answer after a long pause. But I don't want to talk about me. "You *know* things. I don't understand, though, how did Franny trap you, especially if you can see the future? Couldn't you just have outwitted her?"

"She didn't trap me." Sabelle's voice is heated with impatience. "*He* did. It was his powers that did me in—did us all in. And I already explained to you—I can't see everything."

"But was she really a witch?" I ask.

Sabelle steps over a big rock, walking toward the trees ahead of us. "She had some gifts, I'll say that."

"So, did my blood somehow release you?" I ask, mentally repeating everything that's happened, trying to understand. "You were trapped, and I bled. That's what opened the ground up, right?"

When she nods, I go on, considering all this. "Did you know it was going to happen? That you'd be freed? You must have."

Sabelle opens her mouth, then clamps her lips shut, facing forward.

"You just made a face like you were going to say something."

"It's nothing."

"Tell me, Sabelle."

She turns, eyes locked on mine, and her words ring with truth. "I knew your face, when the sky opened above me. It was one that haunted my thoughts for years. I knew you would be there, on the other side of freedom. I did not know why, or when, or who you were, exactly, except that you were a Starling. You had a face like hers, yet lovelier, kinder. But I knew. I waited for you."

I lose the words as quickly as they come to mind. Flustered, I watch her point to a tree whose naked branches graze the sky.

"This is where I live." I can just make out how the bases of some branches meet to form a hammock at the top, a space for her.

"Can I see it?" I ask, curiosity scratching at me. I want to see where she spends her time when she's not with me.

Without words, she helps me climb the tree, to far above the winter snow. I haven't climbed a tree in years, but she shows me all the places to put my feet, to grip with my hands so that I make it up safely. Once there, we sit in that space, wrapped inside the tree, among her possessions: a rough wooly blanket, a couple of smooth pebbles, the branch of a cedar tree, a water-logged book that I'm guessing is unreadable but that she probably found in the woods, a broken watch. I realize she's a collector, like me.

"I like looking at the sun, and the sky," she says, explaining.

I tip my face up, look into the tops of the tall giants around us.

With her at my side, the wind doesn't seem to touch me. I don't feel cold.

I don't know what I feel.

Sabelle reaches over and tugs off my mitten. Before I can question it, she slides her hand into mine. I don't even flinch.

"Kit." She traces my face.

I touch her wrist, feel the ridge beneath my fingertips. I take her hand and flip it, bring her wrist to my lips, barely brush them against her scar.

Her eyes dart to my mouth, and I know my answer. Her hands threaded through my hair is the answer; her shoulders under my palms; her sweet, cold mouth; her wet tongue twirling with my own. It doesn't feel wrong, the way it maybe should. It feels as easy as breathing, this kiss, her soft lips, and it wakes something in me, a deep-seated hunger for connection. I release my pain into her mouth, but my hands are gentle, not as soft as hers, though. Her touch is featherlight.

I am the one to pull away first, breath sharp and short. Fumbling over my words, in an oh-so-human way, I try to make sense of it. "I kissed you," I say stupidly. "We kissed."

She observes me with those dark silvery eyes of hers, unblinking. Could I pretend none of this happened? Then her fingers take mine again.

Surprised, unsettled, I look back to her. Wait a breath.

"Yes," she says, voice quiet. But I hear it. I feel it.

I'm the first to reach for her this time, but she takes over, takes me with her to nestle into the space where she must lay her body to rest. I guide her hand to my body, under my coat, sweater, T-shirt, against my skin. And beneath my touch, she sighs in unison with me. We catch each other's breath in our mouths.

She tastes like salt and sugar and darkness, and the promise of light just barely beneath it.

I shouldn't want to kiss her this much. But I do it anyway.

CHAPTER NINETEEN

It is dark by the time I sneak back into the apartment, quietly taking off my coat and boots, slipping the dagger into my bag where I left it in the living room, just in case I need it for anything. When I pass Agatha's room to get to mine, I stop at what sounds like a muffled cry.

Quietly I open her door and peek in, and on her bed, her back to me, hugging her pillow against her chest, Agatha is crying. Her arms are bare, hair hanging long, pale as straw. She's weeping, and then I hear my dad's name, a choked whimper into her pillow.

I back up quickly and close the door, feeling the weight of her agony in my chest as I go into the bathroom to shower before bed.

Her cries echo in my mind. That's the sorrow that will never escape me. It's true, sincere, and it cuts straight to the heart. She's not faking. She loved my dad, and I must believe that love has carried to me, no matter what she's done. Even if it didn't, if all this time she took us in only to hand me over to a monster, we shared a love for my dad, and once upon a time he must have loved her, too.

The grief goes to my core.

I'd like to comfort her, but I can't. If I go back and see her like that, if I open my mouth, I'm afraid all that will come out is a scream. There is too much hurt inside me. If I take on one drop more, I'm afraid I will overflow, flood this house, this town, this world. I'll become an empty ship, a vessel, a casket. What am I without this pain? With all this loss and fear and sadness? Poison that has run through my blood for centuries?

I gather it back inside me. If I share it, it'll hurt someone else.

I take off my clothes, shower quickly, washing grave dirt off my skin. When I've dried myself and wrapped a towel around my body, I ease open the door, listening.

Agatha's room is quiet now. I slip back into the guest room and get dressed in something warm. Then I climb into my bed, lay one hand on my dad's pages, the other holding the diary, as though somehow the answers will ease themselves into me if I keep contact. I close my eyes. Time is almost up; it feels like a ridiculous indulgence to even sleep. But I can't help it. Sleep finds me before I can escape it.

I dream of Franny, bleeding from the middle, pouring herself out at my feet, the charred flesh of her hands pulling at me, ripping a crown of flowers from my head. I scream with her. We scream together.

*I wake in the night, turn to my side, press myself against some-*thing warm. Someone.

My eyes snap open and my heart lurches.

Jack smiles, white teeth flashing in the dark. "Hello, my girl."

"You're not here," I say.

His laugh is amused, low. Agatha won't hear. And if she did, what would she do? Chase him out like a normal, raging grandmother? No, she'd maybe look in, troubled, shut my door. Walk away. She's been trying to help me, in her own small ways, but I don't think she'd fight him to his face.

"I *am* here, Kit. Can't you feel me?" His amber eyes shouldn't shine this bright. My bones ache. He says, "I missed you. I can't wait until you're mine."

"Liar. If that were true, why would you hurt me so much?"

"Because you still have fight in you. I want you broken." I stiffen as he drags his fingers along my bare arm.

"You want me afraid," I counter.

An indulgent smile. "Do you think me so terrible?"

"You kill innocent people," I whisper, trying not to shake under his touch.

"I do like acting out." A soft laugh, his startled honesty as he admits it. "There is too much to amuse me here. It would be better if I had a beautiful bride at my side to tame me."

"Why are you here? Just to fuck with me?"

"Oh, that mouth of yours." Jack bends his head, and for a horrible moment I think he's going to kiss me, but he just leans in to murmur against my cheek, fingers tightening on my wrist. "Though, at least you didn't try to strike me again."

"You know why I'm not trying to hurt you right now," I say.

"But, my darling"—his voice is soft; he sounds like Bear—"you hurt me every day."

He pulls away from me, draws his eyes down to the diary, left in the middle of the bed. My hand reaches for it possessively. "Not yours," I say.

His mouth curves into a smile. "Are we speaking of those pages or of you now?"

"Both." I want to hide from those amber eyes. "I want my mom. I swear to God, if you hurt her—"

"No." His hand hovers over my throat, cutting me off. "Don't forget who holds the power here." He inclines his golden head, breathes against my neck, inhales as he trails one cold finger against my collarbone. "It's nearly time. Do you think you'll find her by then? I would nibble her so slowly; her screams would flavor my meal from start to finish."

"Don't, don't. Please don't." I swallow back the bile that's burning up my throat.

Now he isn't a golden-skinned beauty. Fur brushes against my arm. Hot breath in my face, putrid and foul, then a mouth on my throat, his arms around me a vise, one I struggle against, trying to breathe, like he's a snake squeezing a doe to death. Long talons graze along my collarbone.

I cry, eyes shut as his claws gouge into my neck, piercing my skin. Not real. Not real. Just a nightmare.

"No," I choke. "Please, Jack. Bear, please. Don't."

"I'll see you soon, my love."

His laugh echoes around the room long after he disappears.

My blood seeps onto my pillow, the bite of his nails still gouging into me.

When he's gone, I lie frozen, almost paralyzed with fright. Everything hurts. I don't get up until the blood has crusted over, don't look into the mirror until the five holes in my neck have turned green at the edges. I walk, hollow-eyed, to the living room as the sun rises. When Agatha comes out of her room, she sees me on the couch, stops. "Kit?"

I look up into her face. I say the word I never thought I'd say to her, something breaking in my voice, a pleading in my soul, "Grandma."

Then she is beside me, and I throw my arms around her, forgetting for a moment all the things between us, all the things pushing us apart. Our history, my prejudice, my resentment, her deceit. For a moment, I need her. I let myself need her.

She's the only human I have right now. And when she rocks me a little, first hesitantly, then more confidently, it's as though she's remembering something she'd forgotten.

Agatha dabs at my wound with antiseptic, her mouth a grim line. "You know, my great-grandmother Coralie could have cured this with her eyes closed. She had a knack for medicine, for mixing up just the right thing to heal you, and she always helped the pain ease."

"Well, too bad she's not here, then." I wince.

"Hurt?"

"A little." I look up as she lays a bandage across the broken skin.

"He hurt you, too. Didn't my grandpa care what he did to you?" I blurt out. I know nothing about him. "Was he nice? I never asked about him."

Her smile is soft. "He was lovely. Such a sensitive man. I could be hard, but Arthur was kind, and warm. Your father was so much like him."

"I would have liked him." A wistfulness fills me, because that was stolen from me. Not because of my dad taking himself out of their lives but because of Jack and the legacy of our family. So many normal, wonderful things were taken from me before I ever got to have them.

"Yes, you would have loved him, and your aunt Juliet, too," Agatha says. "There is ugliness in our family line, hard truths we don't always want to see. You have a strength I never had. You have the same strength your father and Juliet had. The same my sisters both had, and my mother when she was younger. It's just that having strength often punished those people far more than behaving did."

"You were still punished," I tell her. "You were still scared. And scarred."

"Yes." She tears up before looking down, packing up the first aid kit. "But I had everything else I could have asked for, for so many years. Such wonderful children. The respect of this whole town, wealth, security. The kindest husband ever. Some Starlings weren't that lucky. Despite his fortune bestowed upon them."

I recall names. "There were twins who were killed young. A lot of the Starlings seemed to die young. Franny, too."

"Yes, some at his hand. Others, natural deaths, because he can't stop every bad fate from unfolding. Then there were some who died at the hands of those who should have protected them. Florence Starling was murdered by her own husband because jealousy drove him mad. She's not the only one."

"That's terrible," I murmur sadly. I remember some of those stories from the diary. "Why doesn't anyone really fight this? Why don't they end it? Because of the money?"

"It's not only money," she says. "It's protection, too."

"It's all bullshit." Except it's not bullshit to most of Rosemont, or even most of my family. It's a complicated equation with only one answer: a Starling girl must be given to the monster. If not, the people will suffer. But look how my family has suffered.

"And now?" I ask, wishing she could just tell me. "Now what?"

"I don't know." She washes her skin of the ointment, dries her hands, then holds one out to help me stand. "Right now I am with my favorite grandchild, and we are talking, and we are safe, here, in this moment. So, for now, I suppose, pancakes?"

I follow her, past the white orchids. Past the gold frames on the wall and into the kitchen, where I take a seat at the island, looking around. There is a beauty, a hominess to the apartment. But it's not my home. My home feels so far away.

Will I ever get back there again? Will my mom be with me? I watch Agatha open cabinets, the fridge, pull out ingredients and bowls, set them on the island in front of me, her ring glinting.

When she glances at me, I'm surprised to see tears in her eyes. "Kit," she says, pausing, a measuring cup in one hand. "I shouldn't have—"

"I—" I stop her, unsure what to say, even though I'm the one who cut her off. "I forgive you."

"Ah," she answers with a slow nod, mixing flour and baking powder in a bowl, shoulders bent forward. "I wish I could forgive myself."

I sit at the island while Agatha makes pancakes—shockingly from scratch. If I didn't watch her make them with my own two eyes, I'd wonder if maybe she laughed and cried into the batter. They taste sweet and bitter at the same time.

CHAPTER TWENTY

It's like a dream, how this morning starts and continues into day, the way the hours fade in and out. The way there are still so many normal moments, even as I wait for tomorrow. I even help Agatha fold a load of laundry. We don't speak of Crowning Day, but the air is thick with it.

It's long after lunch—which I didn't even have the will to eat—when our neighbors start making noise, like someone's having a party. The usually quiet building seems to come alive, someone playing music with bass loud enough for me to feel in Agatha's living room.

"What's going on?" I ask. It feels weird. Like they're already celebrating even though the festival doesn't start until tomorrow.

She looks up from the diary, which she's had her nose in now for hours. "It's New Year's Eve."

"Oh," I say, feeling silly. "Right." Of course it is.

Lowering the book, she asks, "Do you want to order food? We could get sushi? Or pasta, maybe?"

I shake my head and stand from the couch. "I think . . . I think I'll go for a walk, I guess."

Before she can talk me out of it, I sling my tote over my shoulder and grab a coat. This whole building feels like it's closing in on me, and the sooner I get out of here, the better.

I turn to glance at her before I slip through the door. "Sorry. I just . . . I can't sit here."

"I understand," she replies softly, blue eyes shining even as she lowers them, returning to the diary.

People loiter in the hallway, one here, two there, three laughing and drinking champagne in the stairwell. I ease past them all, careful to avoid eye contact. I hear gossip at my back. This must be an especially big deal for them. Crowning Day's never been on New Year's Day—at least not since Franny. Did eighteenth-century people here even celebrate this holiday? Surely not if they were killing each other. My mind spins as I make my way to the lobby, past people singing karaoke in one apartment, door flung open.

I don't feel like celebrating.

I don't know what I feel like. No, that's a lie, I tell myself. If we were at home, my mom and I—

But we're not, I remind myself as I step outside and over a huge snowdrift. We're not home, not yet. And I have to figure this out. I have, what? Twenty-four hours, maybe a bit more.

I can do this, can't I? I can still save her.

My feet move of their own accord, and I find myself on the other side of downtown, moving past the funeral home. Almost robotically I swerve, turning left and climbing up the little stairs off the sidewalk. There's a graveyard.

The air is cold and thick, promising a blizzard to come.

I wear a thin layer of nervous sweat as I walk under the arched gate and into the cemetery. The farther I walk in, the older the graves get. I scan the headstones carefully—searching. Not for my dad, of course. He's not here. And these people aren't *here*, not really. It's only bodies. Dust.

I find a row of headstones—the oldest are crumbling with age. The surname is in distinctive cursive. Starling. I know some of these names, not all—only the women wrote in the diary, but I read each name aloud in whispered tones as I move past the grave markers.

There's a weighted presence here as I repeat each name like a prayer.

"Help me," I say to them, the girls and women who can't hear me. Or maybe they can—it feels like something is listening, but then again maybe it's just the cold air, haunted with regret.

The snow is falling faster with each breath, and when I leave the graveyard, the air is cold enough that it hurts to inhale. I stayed too long, and for what? Hoping for a big aha moment?

I turn to go back to the apartment, hurry down the sidewalk. Out on the streets people are cheerful—groups of friends, couples, are drinking. Despite the snow, the steakhouse has its doors flung open, jazz music floating out, a full house inside.

I shove my way into the apartment building, and there's an older couple making out by the stairs. I turn on my heel and head to the stupid elevator instead.

When I step into it, I hold my breath, waiting for it to plummet, before I remember I'm on the ground floor. There's probably a basement, but still.

After a determined jab of my finger, the mirrored doors close and the elevator heads up. I grip the rail and stare at my hazy reflection. A dark spot of blood inches its way out of my nose and runs down to my lip, and I can taste it.

"Shit," I mutter, reaching up automatically. My mittens go wet with blood just as the elevator pauses before the top floor—and the doors slide open and three chatting girls step inside, then stop as their collective eyes rest on me. Charlotte, with Molly and Daphne. Daphne, God, whose sister was murdered by Jack only last week. Daphne, whose mother hates me. Daphne, who probably hates me, too, and if she does, there's no doubt her best friends do as well.

Charlotte stares at me. "Kit? You're bleeding."

I shake my head, but it's obvious that they see it. The blood is running freely into my mouth. "Just a nosebleed," I say, even as I press against the rail for support and push myself straighter. I tip my head back, and the elevator spins, the walls feel like they're closing in on me, and I start to shake.

In a fluid rush, Charlotte moves forward, takes my elbow, floral-scented hair waving against me. "Let me help."

Molly stands, wide-eyed, glancing at Daphne, then back at me.

"You don't have to." I shrug Charlotte off. "I'll be fine," I state firmly.

"Come on. I'm taking you to my place," she says.

"Charlotte's mom used to be a nurse," Molly explains. "She'll help."

Before I can argue, Daphne nods. Our eyes meet, and I let Charlotte lead me out of the elevator and to her apartment. This floor is quieter than Agatha's, or even the foyer. I can feel the other girls behind us, their eyes on my back, can feel them silently communicating. Why did I agree to this when I could have just run upstairs to Agatha? I taste more blood pouring into the back of my throat, and a wave of vertigo hits me and I almost fall down. Oh, that's why. Because maybe I would have passed out on the way.

Charlotte's mom gasps when she sees me, and helps me sit in a chair. She's all soft pastel and smells of vanilla and rose—a plumper, taller version of her daughter. I pinch my eyes shut when she regards Charlotte proudly. My mom used to look at me that way when I took care of things. When I did the right thing. I picture her face, her smile.

Mom, Mom, I'm scared. I'm sorry. I can't figure out what to do in time.

I wait for the moment of reckoning, when Charlotte's mom will say something about me, about my family, will gush about Crowning Day, but she doesn't. All she does is suggest I tip my head forward instead, and hand me a box of tissues, smiling gently, her rose perfume hitting my bleeding nose, that's how strong it is.

"If it doesn't stop within about ten minutes, you let me know," she says.

Then she's gone, leaving us to move to Charlotte's brick-walled bedroom. I watch the girls through a lens, like I'm not here, as they pull off their outerwear, kick off their shoes.

"I'll call Pixies," Daphne tells them. "They can deliver instead, maybe?"

I realize now that they were probably going to pick up dinner. "You don't have to change plans for me," I call, even as she walks out the door, holding her phone high, trying to get a signal. Her voice drifts from the other room.

Charlotte is watching me when I hesitate and turn back. She smiles. "It's fine."

"I'm not staying," I say softly. But I make no move to leave, and she and Molly settle onto the bed, clearly continuing a conversation they began previously. I finally move over against the wall, take a seat on the rug near a pile of colorful floor pillows.

Molly lies on her stomach, chewing on a pen, while Charlotte sits cross-legged next her, pointing at a piece of paper in front of them with a perfectly manicured finger. "What about this?"

"Nuh-uh." Molly shakes her head, scrutinizing her artwork, her sleek hair pulled up into a ballerina bun, silver shadow on her lids. "I think that would read better as a tattoo."

Charlotte makes a face as she thinks. She's so not the tattoo type. I can faintly tell by that expression, from my position on the floor. Why am I sitting here? Why haven't I left yet? Maybe I'm starving for interaction, for kindness. To be a part of something, to belong. Or I'm in shock. Because every time I look at the clock on my phone, I count down in my head. It's almost time. It's almost time. In the morning I'll wake up, and it will be the first day of the festival.

Molly's still drawing, sketching fast. She tells Charlotte, "For your dress I was thinking more a border. Or something along the bodice." Her eyes are lit up. I love watching artists work. Love watching my mom draw. Loved watching my dad type away. It's a drug, seeing someone adore something so much.

Daphne appears at the doorway with a bag of chips and four bottles of juice in varying shades. She hands out the green and berry-red to the girls on the bed. "They said it will take over an hour to deliver. So, snacks," she explains, and she offers one of the remaining drinks to me. I hesitantly take the orange-hued one and expect her to leave me, go join her friends on the bed, or just get as far from me as possible.

But she doesn't. She sits next to me on the rug and opens the bag of chips, while Charlotte insists that we all start resolutions soon. Daphne tips the bag my way, and, surprised, I reach inside and grab a handful. How normal it is right now—four girls snacking and laughing. Daphne, who just lost something so profound, lights up when Molly tips the sketch pad toward her to show her a color-block gown in neon brilliance. There are other designs as well—all stunning.

When I softly offer my admiration for her designs, Molly hesitates. She explains, "These are the prom dresses I mentioned before. It's part of my senior project."

I smile, and the two girls continue critiquing the designs. Daphne opens her bottle of juice, takes a long swig of the pink stuff. I should say something to her, because she sat next to me, and the other girls are distracted. What do I say without bringing up Crowning Day? I don't want to talk about it. I don't want them to celebrate while I sacrifice myself tomorrow. But they will, won't they? I peek over at Charlotte's closet doors—closed—wondering if her Crowning Day dress is inside.

"Daphne, I—" I begin.

"I know it's not your fault, okay?" she interrupts, keeping her voice low. Molly and Charlotte are giggling over something, Molly choking on her green juice a little. This moment is private, should be private.

"I'm sorry," I say, but I want to tell her, *I know.* I maybe don't know exactly, but I know grief, I know loss, how it lays itself over your skin, and never lifts.

"Your dad was one of my favorite authors," she says, changing the subject. "You know, if you ever want to talk about things."

It hurts. But I know she hurts, too, and so I quietly confess, "He was writing his next book."

She flinches. "Shit. Was it for Jewels?"

I twine my finger around a thread in my holey jeans. Miserably I watch it fray. "Yeah. I have the first couple of chapters. That's all he wrote. Before."

"I wanted to, too." She pushes at the highlighted hairs around her face that have escaped her neat ponytail. "Right after Corinne. I wanted to be with her. I know that sounds bad. And I keep forgetting she's dead—it's only been a week. I keep wondering if it gets easier."

"I don't know," I answer honestly. "It hasn't yet. Not for me. But I hope it will one day, for us both."

That's all we say. That's all we need to say.

She picks up the bag of chips and keeps on eating. Molly and Charlotte laugh on the bed. I stare out the window, lean back against the brick wall. I think about resolutions and hope, but those seem like pointless things to dream about now.

The snow is coming down hard against the glass. I shiver, even though I'm warm and dry. I'm glad I came home when I did, but I wonder, what is Sabelle doing right now.

My phone rings and I jump in surprise, peek at the name. Agatha. She's probably wondering where I am.

I accept the call. "Sorry," I say instead of hello. "I'll be back soon. I just stopped—"

"Kit—" Her voice is high, excited, but the connection is bad. "I figured it out!"

"Figured what out?" I ask, straightening. The three girls go silent, staring at me.

"The key!" she says. "Where are you? I'll show you—come home now!"

I jump to my feet, my heart jumping along with me. "I'm just down—"

A smooth voice cuts in and says, "Oh, no, Kit. Goodbye."

"Jack," I whisper. Molly flinches. Charlotte stares at me wordlessly. Daphne acts immediately, grabbing my hand, tugging me forward.

"Let's go," she starts. "I'll—"

"No." I pull my hand from her. My voice is steel. "I won't let you get involved. I'll be fine."

They watch me run from the room, the blood at my nose crusted over. A wad of tissues still clumped in my fist. I dart to the stairs, pushing past partygoers in tinseled hats. When I get to the fifth floor, I race down the hall. But the door to Agatha's apartment is ajar.

I know it even as I push inside, that she's gone.

"Agatha?" I call, just in case, as I run through each room. But she's gone. Taken by Jack. It shouldn't scare me as badly as it does, maybe. How many days, nights, mornings has she spent with him? But she knew something. And he knew she knew.

I grab the car keys and run downstairs and out of the building, into the snowy night. In the private lot behind the building I climb into Agatha's car, put it in drive, head straight to the woods. The snow is coming down fast, and the streets of Rosemont are eerie and dark, but the windows of the apartments and houses I pass are lit up, with people celebrating inside.

I pull off the paved road and drive into the woods as far as I can go, almost slamming into a tree before I pound my foot on the brake. *Please, let him not be too pissed at her. Last time she irritated him, people died. What will he do this time?*

I jump out of the car, and I run, jumping over the private-property chain where it sags in a low spot, my heart pumping with exertion, with fear of what I'll find deeper in the woods. Agatha, in danger.

"Kit." Sabelle is pulling me faster, toward the river. What has she seen? I'm too terrified to ask.

Then the sound of splashing water. As I get closer to the river, I can see a head of pale hair going under, arms flailing. Another form, a familiar one, shoving Agatha under the icy water.

Jack, drowning my grandma.

270

"Stop!" I cry, throwing myself forward, down the sloping bank. It feels like I'm running in slow motion, the snow holding me back like sand. I stumble the last few steps, and at the edge of the river, I yell, "Jack, stop!"

He turns to me, handsome face twisted. Eyes pinned to mine. He releases his hands, and Agatha's body bobs to the surface. Limp.

I stare at my grandmother's blank face, gazing up at the falling snow and the glittering black sky beyond it. I scream.

CHAPTER TWENTY-ONE

"No, no, no," I moan, *running into the water, past Jack, to the* body. I heave her up into my arms, not caring about the cold of my submerged legs. Her cheek is pressed against my heart. "Why?" I cry.

He doesn't answer.

With some superhuman strength I didn't know I had, I drag Agatha up onto the bank, her feet dangling in the water. I press my cold lips onto her wet mouth, try to give her CPR.

I pump on her chest, trying to remember how to do compressions, wondering if I've got it all wrong. I wait for color to return to her face, for her slow smile, for her hands to wrap around me.

But nothing. I keep trying, but no matter how long, how hard, how frantic, there's no response. I fall over her body, shaking. It's only in the quiet space between sobs that I realize Jack is gone. I look around and find a pair of eyes shining in the shadows. Sabelle materializes from the darkness, becoming solid.

Suddenly her arms are around me, her lips at my neck, her voice saying, "Kit, Kit. I'm sorry. I couldn't help her."

"Agatha—" I trail off, looking down at her body, her wet hair, the beads of icy river water on her skin. Sabelle reaches out and gently closes her eyes.

We gaze down at her silently. Sabelle lays her hand atop mine, mine on Agatha's. Under my fingers, the ring. I move to see it better.

"That was her ring," Sabelle whispers. She adds begrudgingly, "Franny's."

Something connects in my next breath.

A flash of the photo album I looked through. The portraits on the wall. In the journal—Franny's granddaughter got her ring. This ring was passed on and on and on.

Could it be more than an heirloom?

I thought the key was something obvious, but maybe there's more to it.

I pull the ring off Agatha's hand and slide it onto my finger.

This time it fits my finger perfectly—as if it were made for me. It's mine now.

I look closer, pull at the giant black stone, searching for a seam, a hinge, a button. Maybe it pops open like a locket, and there's a tiny key inside. I saw an antique sewing kit built into a bracelet once, miniature scissors and all inside. But the ring is solid.

Even as I accept that, Sabelle shakes her head. "The stone, twist it."

My hand trembles as I try to turn the stone itself, and, with enough pressure, it starts to move. Sabelle inhales sharply, and I look up to see the air to our right shimmering. An invisible wall has slowly peeled itself away, and an empty doorframe forms above us. It glitches in and out of focus as I stare at it in disbelief, as I stand and run my fingers against its solid form.

It's a doorway.

"His lair," Sabelle whispers.

I look beyond, within it, and can barely breathe. My mom is sitting on a large stone, with her back to us, crouched over something. I rush through the door, Sabelle at my heels.

"Mom!" I throw my arms around her from behind and crush her to me. Then I turn her so that we face each other, and it's her, her eyes and the blue shadows beneath them, the hollowness of her cheeks. I embrace her again, tighter. She's alive. And I found her before Crowning Day. I forget everything, how freezing cold and wet my feet and legs and hands are, how frightened I've been. Agatha. I grasp my mom and breathe.

"Kit?" Her voice is surprised, and she wraps me up in a hug. "Did you have a bad dream?"

I pull away, look at her, at the scene around us. He's done something. She's no longer sitting on a stone but on a barstool in a kitchen identical to Agatha's. The room is dark—like there are no lights on in the apartment, or the building, or all of Rosemont. It's a twisted version of the apartment—there are dirty dishes in the sink, and a rat cuts across the counter, running along the wall, and I fight the urge to jump up onto the empty stool. It's a trick, an illusion. I touch my mom's thin cheek, fingers quivering. "Is it really you?" I ask, knowing well how Jack can disguise himself.

It can't be him, though. This is her; I know it in my bones and in my heart. I take her cold hands in mine and rub them gently.

My mom gets a funny expression, confusion crossing her face, her eyes glassy. "Yeah. I . . . Did I drink last night? I can't remember." She leans into the backrest of the stool, placing a hand to her temple. "My head hurts bad."

"What do you remember?" I press.

"We had dinner at the restaurant and went to bed."

Her last memory is the night of the restaurant? "Then what?" I ask.

That same strange look of bafflement. She shakes her head, sets her pen down, her fingers black- and blue-splotched, stained with ink. I glance at her drawing, and swallow hard. It is full of shadows. Roots hang from the top of the page, what looks like claws, like spiders, like ghosts, crawling along it. I don't care that it's too abstract for me to know for sure. It looks like a nightmare I remember having.

"I guess I came to the kitchen, and maybe had some wine and passed out? I'm sorry, baby. I don't mean to worry you. I'm okay. I just feel a little off. Where's Agatha, by the way? I thought we were going to breakfast this morning, but I don't think we did?"

"He's getting close." Sabelle pulls at my sleeve. "Let's go."

My body is already starting to ache. She's right. I close my eyes tight in one breath and reopen them, saying carefully, "Mom. Agatha had to go out. She won't be back, and I want to go. We need to go now."

"Go? Where?"

"Home." I grab her hand, pulling her up. "Come on."

"Kit. I don't understand." She touches her head, looks at Sabelle. I didn't know if she'd see her, if Sabelle would let her. She slurs, "Who's this?"

I push my mom forward. "She's a friend, no time to explain. Mom, hurry! We have to get out of here before he gets back."

Yawning, my mom gives me a sleepy nod.

"She's not right." Sabelle stares at her. "She's—"

My mom smiles up at her and lets out a sound. A snore.

As I stare at her, dread fills me. "She's asleep."

What has he done to her? She's sleepwalking. Or something. Lucid, but not. Here, but not really. Her glassy eyes shine. How could I have mistaken her for awake before?

"I'm fine, Kit. But I need to pack," my mom says. She tips forward, unsteady on her feet. Sleeping standing up.

"I packed for you," I tell her, pulling her away from the fake kitchen and out the magical door. She's like a rag doll, floppy and uneven. I pull harder. "Let's go."

"I feel bad leaving without talking to Agatha," she frets as I take her hand, forcing her to run out of the fake kitchen and into the woods. She staggers, clumsy, steps heavy. "Something feels wrong about this."

"Rosemont is wrong." I can hear how scared my voice is even as my steps pound through the snow. But we're leaving. And we're never coming back. If we hurry, we can go. Get out of the woods, get out of town.

All my nerves zip with a fearful knowing as the car comes

into view. He'll be furious that I beat him. He'll kill people, maybe a lot of them. What am I doing? But how can I not run? How can I not get her to safety? Wasn't that the deal anyway? I win, and she stays safe?

"Kit?" My mom is startled as I pull her along. "What's that on your neck?"

"I fell," I lie.

I fell, I fell, but I'm picturing Sabelle. I turn to her as we reach the edge of the woods, and she pushes me forward, to the car right ahead. "Go," she urges. There's no time for goodbye. She can't come with us.

I keep going. Get my mom inside, jump in the driver's seat, and *go.* I steer away from the woods and toward safety. We drive down deadly quiet streets, snow flying up at the windshield as I speed away, as I near the road that will take us out of Rosemont, the sign straight ahead. But the car shudders, a snapping in the air, and something in me turns inside out. I'm slipping out of my skin and upside down and being squeezed back into myself. I almost throw up.

My mom's voice is confused. "That's strange. I just got déjà vu."

What happened to the car? We're standing in the woods again, just outside the lair, the air cold as needles stinging my skin. "What the fuck?"

Sabelle appears beside me. "Kit," she says. I know what she's thinking.

"No!" I yell. I know she can't leave the woods or Rosemont, but there's no logical reason why *I* can't. *I'm not bound. I'm not bound. I'm not bound.* I hysterically repeat the words over and over in my mind as we race out of the woods again, to find the car parked exactly where I left it the first time.

I restart it, my hands shaking so badly that I nearly drop the key. I won't let it be true; I can't. This time, I press the gas harder. Maybe I wasn't serious enough before; maybe now it'll work. We go as far as before, and the same thing happens, that shuddering, inside-out feeling, and we're back in the woods again. Rosemont will never let us go, will never let me go. Jack won't.

My mom stares, wide-eyed, her knuckles white, picking at her cuticles, making them bleed. She may be sleeping, but she can still see what's going on. Her confusion, her fear, is palpable.

"You have a bad headache," I tell her, keeping up a calm facade. "You're not thinking straight. Migraines can make you see things, you know."

Though she nods, her chin wobbles, and she wrings her hands even as she snores slightly and shudders. She's asleep, but this must be a nightmare for her. It's a nightmare neither of us can wake from.

The aching in my bones announces his presence before he appears, his golden, perfect self contrasting against the snowy backdrop. "Oh, Kit. You sneaky thing." His face is hard.

"Please," I beg. "What did you do to her?"

"She's confused. She has been asleep this whole time. An enchantment. She won't remember a thing."

Though she's standing right at my side, she doesn't seem to hear anything he says. Her eyes are closed now; she sleeps upright. Her eyelids are veined with blue, but other than the hollows under her eyes, other than the cold thinness of her, she is still okay. All this time she's been asleep, hibernating under the river. I shake her gently.

"She will not wake." His voice is mild. "Not yet."

Tears run down my face. "When will she?"

Jack comes behind me, sets his hands on my shoulders. I turn to look up at him, holding my breath. "Perhaps she won't," he says.

I stand there, frightened into silence. He studies me a moment, and then takes her elbow gently, sending her on through to the lair just behind him. She disappears into the darkness, and my breath skips as I reach after her, but he is there, blocking me from reentering the lair. "No," he says. "Not yet."

He takes my hand, lifts it, and I only now feel how numb my fingers are. He brings the one with the black ring to his mouth, slips it inside the wet cavern between his lips, and gently bites at the ring, tugging it off, sucking it from my finger.

"Naughty, sneaking in there."

"All this time if I'd had the ring—" Then I remember. The pain is swift, brutal, and needle-sharp. Agatha was going to tell me, wasn't she? This was the secret. She found out how to get into the lair. She knew what the key was. "Why Agatha?"

He sighs, turning away, walking about with his hands clasped behind his back. Behind him, I can only just glimpse my mom, seated in that fake kitchen that exists within the lair. "I didn't want to do it, yet she was pushing back so much, my love. She was trying to be smart."

"What do you mean?" My heart pounds.

"She's been resisting me for a while. She began to argue with me, trying to get you out of the contract, to get me to send you and your mother home. I had to punish her for it. Sacrifice a few lives, to show her what was at stake here. But it wasn't enough. She kept pushing."

I let out a breath. Inside, my heart wrenches. It was real. She gave me the diary. She was going to tell me about the key. She did care. But now she's gone, and it's too late to save her.

"She would not let it alone. I'd had enough, and so she's gone now." He waves the memory of her away with a hand, as though she's nothing.

"And my mom? Our deal?" I manage to ask, keeping my voice level. I stare over his shoulder at her. Sitting at the island, shadows closing in around her. Kicking her feet vacantly. Pen moving in circles. She's humming, but it sounds like she's in pain.

"She will be free to go. You have my word, on my honor."

"Thank you," I let out a sob, a breath. "Thank you—"

"*After* your Crowning," he reminds me. "That was the deal, no? You find her beforehand—lucky you, mere hours to spare!—and she goes free. You should be proud of yourself." He gives me a smile, like he's proud of me, too. "You have saved her life."

"But not my own," I whisper. I will be his bride. Just as Sabelle foretold. My fear, more than my sense, finds a voice. "Are you going to hurt me?"

"Of course not." Jack lifts my hand, eyes wounded. It takes all my willpower not to yank away from his touch. "I just have to teach you not to defy me. See how you lean from me? Even your body is doing it right now."

"I'm done defying you," I say, relaxing my tight limbs. I force myself into submission. I press into his chest a little closer even though everything hurts, even though my mind spins. I have to figure this out.

Fear trickles through me and makes me still. What will it be like? How much will tomorrow hurt? I flutter my fingers to my neck, to where he clawed me.

"It will be different, when we are wed," he promises. "You will have me as well. You will have my heart, and I will have yours." Sharpening, his voice becomes a warning, "There will be no others. No others to have your heart as I do."

I can't do it, I scream inside. But my mom . . .

"Kit," he whispers, moving aside the neck of my sweater to graze his lips along my collarbone.

I push back the revulsion and force myself to wrap my arms around his back, and I hold him. That's what he wants. "Yes?"

"I will meet you here, tomorrow evening." His fingers stroke my hair, like I'm his pet. "Do you know what to do?"

"I think so." I nod, but I'm uncertain. "I just have to walk into the river?"

"The people will accompany you; they do so love to see a spectacle, those bloody cannibals," he says, and then laughs cruelly. "Then yes, you simply walk in when it's time. You will find me here, waiting. Look pretty for me, won't you? Wear your flowers like you're supposed to."

"You said 'when it's time,'" I say, trying to imagine how I go into the river. Dread fills me. "What time will that be?"

"Sometime after the sun has set. But you will know when I call for you."

"Okay." My smile is empty. I take his hand and lie, "Wonderful."

"So bright, so bright," he murmurs, kissing me gently on each cheek, each palm, the back of each hand, on my lips. "So beautiful. So much like her."

I kiss him back, his hands tucked into my coat, wrapped around me. He runs a hand along my ribs, down to my hip, and in the darkness, my mouth tastes like dirt. Then everything goes black.

CHAPTER TWENTY-TWO

I open my eyes to find myself sitting in the driver's seat of Agatha's car, keys in my hand.

I look up. Sabelle is standing at the border of the woods. She's staring at me, waiting for me. I get out of the car and go to her.

"There's no point looking at me like that." My sigh is heavy, resigned.

"Like what?" Her voice is sharp.

"Like you're disappointed I need to make sure my mom's safe." Even to myself, I sound rejected. Hopeless.

"You said you'd try to kill him. You're the only one who can hurt him. I know it," Sabelle insists. "It must be a Starling!"

"But how?" I cry. "And why a Starling?"

Her eyes are wide, knowing. Her voice softens and she shakes her head, black locks swinging gently. "I don't know. But I don't want him to hurt you."

"Yeah," I say, nodding. But that's the whole point.

She bites her lip, such a human gesture. Finally she speaks. "I wish I could do more. I'm only sorry I couldn't save you."

The tension threads itself between us, knots into a shape I can't name. My chest rises and falls as I stare back at her, at our fingers laced together. When she touches her mouth to mine, I startle. Why didn't I expect it, after last time? I let out a sigh and sink into her. In this moment, there is her. It is only us. I have no thoughts. I am only connected to this being, this creature, only this kiss, and nothing else, not cold, not fear, not grief, not trauma. I shut out everything else. There is only Sabelle. Only this moment, her mouth greedy on mine.

But something inside stops me short. Gently I pull away, understanding what is bothering me. Not about her specifically. It could be anyone.

When I kiss her, the aching in me doesn't hurt so bad, like I'm sharing it with her, but isn't it mine to feel? To handle? To somehow heal?

I can't just go kissing my pain away, falling for every beautiful being that looks my way. First it was Bear and now it's her. The thought of being alone is suddenly terrifying, which is exactly what makes me realize that it's what I need to do.

When I open my mouth to say it, Sabelle is staring at me, her liquid gaze unblinking.

"I want to." My words are thick. I shake my head. "But we shouldn't."

After a moment she tips her head in understanding.

I don't want to tell her goodbye. But I know what my future is: I'll be Jack's, for the rest of my life. I can't kill him.

"Was, is, will always be," Agatha said.

"I just want my mom to be okay," I say. "Nothing else matters."

"I understand," she says. Then she vanishes into the shadows of the trees and leaves me.

Hours later, I wake up in the empty apartment, the space Agatha left behind echoing. I sit up and blink, my head aching, my eyes swollen. Outside, people are celebrating. There is singing, music, some happy shouting. It feels different even from the New Year's celebration. Sharper. Hungrier. When I stumble off the couch where I fell asleep, I peer out the window and see that the downtown streets are packed with people—the festival is well under way. I glance at the clock, which says it's almost noon. From where I'm standing no one can see me, and I watch them, strangely disconnected from what it all means.

Families walk together, clustering up, chatting. There is a man painting children's faces on the far corner, someone selling trinkets across from him. Dread leaks in when I realize that every girl is wearing a white dress, their hair done up and adorned with the dead flowers. While the rest of the people are dressed in puffy jackets and boots for warmth against the chill, none of the girls seem to mind the cold, or at least they put on a show that they don't. They dance around, tipsy with joy. They walk, arms hooked in each other's. Near one shop, two girls stop to braid each other's hair, then adjust their crowns. The snow sparkles like diamonds.

In my dream universe, I'm back home and it is a Monday morning. I don't feel like going to school but I do anyway, and my friends make it worth it, Brenna and Leo and me laughing our way down the halls. When I get home, there are lemon bars my aunt Juliet dropped off for me, and Agatha is coming by later for dinner, when my mom will make pasta. Right now, she's barefoot, drawing, one leg bent under the other, ink on her cheek. My dad is in his office, keyboard clacking, in his flow. He calls me in, asks me about a scene. His blue eyes are warm, full of joy. He smiles.

I wipe my tears away, shake my head. How to get through this? How can I actually win?

It's around four when there's a knock on the door. I open it to find Charlotte, eyes bright. "Kit? Can I come in?"

I fight the urge to close the door in her face—it's not her fault. But why is she here? I slowly swing the door open wider. "Yeah."

She steps inside, smoothing her dress. A pretty white lace that nips in at her waist, sweetheart neckline, tea-length skirt. My eyes go to the crown of dried flowers on her head. Death.

"Shouldn't you be celebrating?" I croak.

If she hears the resentment in my voice, she ignores it. She doesn't ask me about last night—the call I got from Agatha, how I rushed out of her apartment. Instead, eagerly, she says, "Where is your grandma?"

"She's . . . gone," is all I say. I'll have to tell people, won't I? But I can't stand to share it now. "She won't be here today," I add.

Surprise crosses her face and disappears. "Well, then I'll bring you down!" she says. "I'd be honored. Mrs. Starling should have known that you should be at Starling House by now. People are getting restless."

"Starling House," I repeat dully. "Why?"

"To get ready. Where's your dress?" She glances around the room, impatiently searching.

"The bedroom," I whisper, pointing through my confusion.

Without a word Charlotte moves past me and down the hall to collect it. I stand there, frozen. I'm not ready, I'm not ready, I'm—

"Okay, I have it!" she calls, reappearing, garment bag flung over her arm. "Anything else?"

"Why are we going to Starling House?" I ask, barely managing to grab my bag from where it was puddled on the coffee table. Then she tugs me through the door.

"It's tradition! All the brides have!" she says, turning back with a big smile. Something in her expression isn't right. Something about it makes me want to take a step away from her. To go back inside and lock the door against her.

"I—" I swallow, pausing in the hallway. "I forgot something. I'll be down in a minute," I say instead.

Her smile hardens. "Kit," she says patiently. "Please. This is your duty. Just like fixing the roses will be."

I remember then that her mother owns the perfumery.

"Charlotte, the roses—"

"You don't understand," she cuts me off, agitated, her cheeks flushed. "They're already losing money, and who knows how long until the roses grow back—if they even do. All the inventory—what do you think happens if they can't fill orders? People will lose their jobs."

"It's not my fault," I say. "*He* let them die."

The revelation doesn't seem to surprise her, though. "If he

let the roses die, that means something," she answers matter-of-factly. "Don't you know the history of our town?"

"Yeah, um." I shift, fidgeting. I can't believe she's acting like this is all so *normal*. "It doesn't mean anything like that winter will happen again."

"Of course it won't." Charlotte softens the intensity in her delicate face, and she leans in to kiss my cheek, fingers cupping my elbow. "We'll never forget all that your family has done for us. All that *you're* doing for us. You're going to make it better. But we need to go now. You don't want to be a late bride!" Her bright laugh cuts through the air. Her hand on my arm tightens.

"I thought you were my friend," I say, anger rising. She never was, though.

Charlotte's eyes glitter. "I am. And I'm so proud of you. You're doing such an important thing. You'll take care of us all. I know you will." She drops her hand and adjusts her crown, then steps back to let me take the stairs first. I glance at the elevator, and she says sweetly, "I know you don't like elevators. I've been watching you."

My stomach twists. I need to get away from her. "I don't need your help," I say, taking my dress into my arms.

Her face is surprised as she yelps, "Oh! But—"

"I don't *want* it," I cut her off, determined.

Increasing the distance between us, I step hurriedly down the stairs, hand tight on the railing, suddenly afraid that if I try to prolong the moment any longer, she'll push me. I can feel her behind me as I descend, and when I reach the bottom, as the entryway comes into view, I finally let out a breath of relief.

Without looking back, I turn and cross the foyer and push through the door, heart pounding. The cold hits me when I step outside, and the crowd quiets. It takes everything in me not to turn around and run back up to the apartment—if Charlotte weren't right behind me, I might. Surrounding me, all around, are the people of Rosemont. I stare out at the sea of them, big smiling faces. Old, young, families and single people, business owners and schoolchildren. Again, it's the girls who stand out. Girls, like Charlotte, wearing white dresses and dead flowers in their hair. Their lips painted red, their eyes wide and almost fevered with excitement. Some of them, only a few, look somber. Scared for me? I scan the group for Daphne and her family, for Molly, even. But I don't see them.

A tiny old lady motions me down the steps with a curled finger. Her eyes are powdery gray and kind. "You'll be beautiful, just like the brides before you," she says sweetly.

I manage to nod even though it sends my heart through my stomach.

"Tell your grandmother that Nora said hello," she adds as she pats my cheek. I smile as I lie that I will.

There are whispers. I can hear people wondering why Agatha isn't by my side, but nobody asks me outright. My heart aches. But there's no time to grieve. Someone else gently tugs at my elbow, pulling me forward. The door opens at my back, Charlotte coming out behind me. I ignore her, stepping down, and the throng of people part to let me through.

Somewhere someone is playing instruments—strings? A quartet? I march forward thinking of the *Titanic* musicians playing people to their watery deaths. Shivers run through me.

I didn't even grab a coat. My breath clouds the air as I glance down at myself. I'm wearing the clothes I slept in. Everyone is dressed for the weather except for me and the girls in white dresses, though the girls don't seem cold. Some run on ahead, holding hands, giggling. Some stay in step with me, looking proud to be walking with the bride. Me. Others trail behind, and I can hear their friendly chattering, occasionally cut through with fearful whispering.

Are they afraid for me? Or just afraid I won't make everything better again?

The dull thud of reality hits me as Starling House appears ahead. Any hope I had springs away, quick, a running rabbit, chased by a monster. Time is running out, and I am going to get ready for Crowning Day, alone. If Agatha were here, she'd help me into my silk dress and kiss my forehead. But she's not. I don't care what Charlotte says, I am not letting her in to help me.

"Go on." Someone pats my shoulder encouragingly. "Go get dressed. We'll wait."

I turn around. There's a food truck near the park. The people scatter, dispersing again, some headed toward it. Some mill around, talking to each other. Others linger to watch me approach the house.

I should probably be scared to go inside, but it feels like a stay of execution to open the door, walk in, close it behind me. Lock it. I stand there and breathe for a long minute. Trying not to think, to force myself to move. Just as I step forward, Sabelle appears, materializing from a shadowy corner of the room. I'm still not used to seeing her do that, but I'm more surprised by how she's here right now.

"What are you doing here?" I ask. "How are you out of the woods?"

Her liquid eyes observe me quietly, taking everything in. "He sent me to you. To attend you," she answers.

"What?" I blink. "Why?" I can only guess it's his sick idea of amusement. He knows who and what she is to me. Something.

"What does it matter?" She takes my hands and squeezes. Despite the boundaries I've placed between us, there is nothing uncomfortable about the gesture. "I'm here."

Throat thick with gratitude, I say, "What do I do? What did others do?"

"I don't know." Sabelle's face is solemn. "But someone has prepared a bath for you upstairs."

I cast my eyes to the ceiling. Then I move to the grand staircase and wait for her to follow.

"No." Shaking her head, she says, "I'll wait down here."

I go up the stairs, and to the bathroom, where I'm hit with the scent of roses and herbs. The tub is full, the water still steaming.

I hang the garment bag on a hook on the wall, the bottom of it brushing the floor. I pull off my clothes, then slip into the giant claw-foot tub. The last time I came here, the room was empty of almost everything, but someone has set jars of bath salts and bubbles on the ledge. I use them, shave and scrub my skin pink, suds up my hair twice over.

When I'm clean and dry, I brush my teeth with the toothbrush and toothpaste someone set out. There's a toiletry bag as well, makeup inside. My mind whirls as I apply a little of everything, then fix my attention to my hair, damp and waving around my face. I pull it into a messy updo, grabbing a handful of bobby pins to secure it. When I'm done, I stare at myself in the mirror. I didn't think I'd look this good, when I feel so bad. I can't find any fault other than the dull fear in my eyes. And I can't put the next step off any longer. Then it will feel real.

I take the dress and leave the bathroom. I walk down the hall to the blue room, my dad's bedroom. I channel his adventurous spirit even as I take the new dress out of the bag, my mind racing, trying to figure out how to get out of this before I bind myself to Jack forever. My mom will be safe. But is there any way I can save myself?

Numbly I pull the dress on. Sabelle will have to do up all those damn buttons in the back. I can't reach.

I run my fingers along the cool silk. The dress tugs at my body, at my skin, and I am cold and warm all at once. There's a tight pressure on my ribs, making it hard to take a deep breath, like I've been caged.

I glance down, and my breath is strangled. I'm not wearing the white dress Agatha gave me. The dress affixed to my body is black, the color of night. *Married in black, wish yourself back,* I read once. He's changed me. Why?

I leave my father's room and go to the green room to look at myself in a full-length mirror, and gasp when I see what he's done.

It's Franny's gown, from the museum display. I whirl around, and behind me the dress form is bare, just the placard remains hanging around the top of it. My stomach turns because he's put me in Franny's dress, but it's Sabelle's premonition that resounds in my mind, pushing aside the nausea. She said it would be a black dress, and she was right.

She also said we would drive away, my mom and me. *But how, but how, but how, but how?*

I stare at myself in the mirror—finger the black skirt. I'm wearing a velvet-and-jeweled choker around my throat. I imagine him under the river, pleased with himself. My mom sleepstanding, or maybe he's let her lie down and rest. I hold tight the picture of her in my heart and mind and turn from the mirror. As I leave the room, I look down at my feet and see that I'm wearing a pair of embroidered shoes.

Think, I tell myself. *Keep moving. But* think.

I walk down the servants' staircase this time, not even mindfully, just floating, and enter the kitchen, smelling food before I realize what it is. A platter of cheese and fruits and small pastries that looks catered rests on the large worktable. A silver tea set is laid out. I swallow the lump in my throat. It smells like Agatha. She definitely had this planned ahead of time, probably hired someone to organize it all. Or maybe they did it for free, for the honor of helping Starlings. She would have been here to sit with me, together. If she weren't dead. I stare down at the food, but I can't eat a thing.

I pass through the kitchen to go look for Sabelle, and stop at the doorway to the portrait room. I stand silently watching as she peeks through the bookcase, trails her hand along the settee. She stops, frozen, when she sees me.

I pull at the low top of the gown awkwardly. "He changed the dress."

Her full mouth draws together, and I glance up at Franny's painting.

Sabelle follows my eyes and, disgusted, says, "Her."

"Did you know her when she lived at this house?" I ask curiously.

"They'd already bound us all by then. But I can smell her in this place."

"Oh." I blink, surprised by the idea that Sabelle can sense someone so long dead.

"This house is full of secrets," Sabelle says, staring at the faded rug for a long, long minute in a way that makes me feel wary.

"What do you mean?" I ask her.

"Oh. There's been death here," she says breezily as she turns from the room.

I shiver, dragging my eyes away from the rug and the stain that I know is hiding beneath.

Sabelle takes my hand and tugs me into the hallway. "I won't leave you until I have to," she says.

I let out a sob then—it just falls out of me—and her hands are in my hair, trying to lift the loose strands out of my eyes. I shake her off. There is no tearful goodbye. She knows I can't do that.

"My crown?" I murmur. Shouldn't it have been here, waiting for me? "He mentioned the flowers; he'll want me to have the crown. Will someone bring it?"

Sabelle shakes her head. "I don't know."

When my gut twists violently and I double over, I still can't cry.

He is calling me with pain. Crown or no, I can't wait any longer. Outside, the energy of the crowd is heightening, cheery shouts and sharp laughter, music growing louder as the sky darkens. They are tired of waiting for me, I think. They've been celebrating all day, drinking and dancing. It's time.

Just as I get into the foyer, I notice my bag where I left it, remember the dagger inside of it. I reach in and grab it, blade shining. I turn it over in my hands. When I look up, Sabelle is nodding.

"Good," she says. "Keep it with you. Just in case."

Even as I nod, internally I'm sighing. I'm not sure why I even grabbed it. She knows about when I tried to stab him. But she looks so insistent, I can't stand to disappoint her. I lift my skirts, and she cocks one eyebrow as I tuck the dagger into the garter on my right thigh.

"The minute I go out there, people are going to swarm me again. Please, stay?"

"I cannot." She rubs her thumb along my wrist. "But I'll be with you, watching."

Wordlessly I stare as she steps backward and disappears into the shadows of the room. Gone. There is a gaping hole in the atmosphere with her gone. I'm afraid, and there's no one to take my fear away. Instead I must face it alone.

I take a deep breath. It's time. The sun is dying as I step from the museum, the crowd gathered outside to meet me.

To carry me to my fate.

CHAPTER TWENTY-THREE

There are whispers about the color of my dress. I spy Vivienne St. James in the crowd, her mouth pinched as she stares at my gown.

The crowd parts, and everyone quiets as Miles walks up. He meets me, his eyes large and full of sadness.

"Your grandma didn't pick up your crown," he says. Then he leans forward and murmurs, "Belinda didn't come. She didn't want to watch."

It's apparent that he'd rather not be here, either. I don't blame her, or Sabelle.

Miles holds out the crown of white flowers, and I lower my eyes, hiding my view of the people peering on, watching while he places it on my head. It occurs to me in this moment that this was the order Agatha had me place days ago. How did he feel making it, knowing what it meant? His hands are shaking. He's afraid for me.

Purity. Honor. Innocence. The flowers are beautiful and smell wonderful, but the weight of them is almost unbearable. I've never worn anything heavier—it feels unnatural. More than flowers could possibly weigh.

I hold myself steady. I have to get through this. I have to stay calm.

Miles hovers for a moment, eyes searching mine fearfully.

"Thank you." My reply is raspy.

As the townspeople watch, Miles kisses me on my forehead, almost like how a dad would kiss a bride, and something in me hurts.

I squeeze his hands and let him go. I can't be angry at him for making the crown. I stand as he steps away and others appear, soft thank-yous, more kisses, a pat on the cheek, promises of tokens to come, to get into my good graces—into Jack's. Someone shoves a sugared doughnut into my hand. Someone asks me to sign their forearm with a Sharpie. The crowd is a haze of faces and voices, little children who watch me wordlessly, their round cheeks painted with roses and starling birds. The air smells of ice and deep-fried foods—from the vendors all the way from downtown, and those who've set up stands in the park—and of the flowers perfuming my hair.

Another twist of pain in my belly and I gasp, bend from the stabbing sensation. It's time to go. The excitement in the people seems to grow as they realize what's happening to me. They know he's calling me.

When I straighten, sweat beads my forehead despite the chilly air. I hear myself say, "I'm ready."

I walk, and the people follow me like a pack, through the

neighborhood and on. They are beginning to sing softly, humming a melody I know by now—the river song—their voices growing louder and merrier.

I continue on to the woods, people pressing in on me, until the shoveled sidewalk turns to snowy ground. The trees are dark and seem taller, somehow. There's not a breath of air today, not a sound to be heard apart from the singing. I try to block it out even as the voices grow louder.

"The monster loves a bride bound in roses."

A horrible thought pops into my mind: *Rosemont is a mouth and it's going to swallow me whole. No.* I shake the image away even as I keep walking into the forest, black skirts brushing the snow, which climbs up the satin heeled slippers Jack magicked onto my feet, to soak my stockings, reaching past my ankles. Try as I might to numb myself now, my body won't cooperate. I am both cold and terrified as I walk in the heavy brocade dress, dyed black as night. Franny's dress.

I veer away from the area where Agatha lies, and I pause, searching for a familiar face in the group of people. Over the many heads I see the guide from Starling House, and I move forward, pushing through, to pull her to me. The people stop along with me. The woman's eyes go big as I tug her closer. I don't remember her name.

"Please, find Sheriff Thompson," I say to her in a low voice. "Tell him Agatha's body is up ahead, through the woods to the left, just near the bank."

"She's—"

"Dead," I finish for her, and release my grip on her arm.

She says nothing, a look of shock clouding her eyes, but finally she nods in agreement. At her side stands a girl, white dress on like the rest of Rosemont's maidens, wreath atop her tight curls. She can't be more than twelve or thirteen. She looks at me in fear, and I smile for her, to show her I'm not afraid.

I hold my head high and march forward to meet my monster at the river, the sky turning lavender, then as blue as a bruise, then indigo, all in one breath, it seems.

The people sing the whole way, the song swelling like a wound.

I stop about twenty feet from the river's edge, and the song dies. I can feel the people watching me, waiting for me to move, smiles on their faces. I turn back to see groups of girls in white dresses huddle together, shivering—*now* they seem cold. A woman passes out blankets for them but doesn't give me one.

"We honor you," one man tells me. I nod resolutely and walk closer to the river, stepping over twigs and soggy leaves clumped together beneath the snow, my gait careful. I pause once at the edge and look back at them all, watching me. Words hang in my throat, unsaid.

My mind clears, and I move down the slope to the edge of the river, bracing myself against tree trunks along the way in the snow. Everything is too quiet, the animals, the people, the wind. Everything is holding its breath.

I search the dark spaces between trees for a glint, a pair of eyes, burning silver and lilac and black, but I can't find her.

Another wave of pain twists my stomach, making me gasp. He is growing impatient.

I stop at the river's edge, breathe in a huge breath and slowly exhale. This is it. I put one snowy shoe into the water, wait for the icy pain of it to soak up my stocking, but the river is bathwater warm. Still, every cell of my body is aching. I put the other foot in, except I remain dry—as though there's a coating on my body that the water cannot penetrate. I am glazed in protection.

The water hits my knees.

Did other brides feel this alone?

I touch the crown of flowers, and in some way I feel closer to the Starling girls that came before me, like they're with me, leading me in. Assuring me that it will be okay.

The water climbs up to my waist, and somehow the river feels as though it's becoming an ocean, bottomless. My breath clouds the air.

There are low murmurs from the bank, the people encouraging me. He was right; they love the spectacle.

With every step the water covers me another few inches. Down, down, down, into his magic. There's a part of me, a horrible thing, water slipping around my throbbing bones, that's whispering, *Yes, yes. It's in your blood, to be his.* The water hugging my thighs, my hips, my waist, my neck, the choker around it, the jewels hanging off it bobbing on the surface. I hold my mom's face in my mind as I go on. Her hazel eyes big, and sad, worried for me. Her laugh, quick and generous. Her hands, moving gracefully as she draws. Her kiss on my temple. Her arms wrapped around me, when she had to tell me about my dad.

For her, anything. So long as she is safe.

My body is shaking and my breath clouds in the air when I whisper, "I'm here. Bear."

I say his name, like that boy part of him that pretended to love me will take pity on me. That he'll take my hand, pull me down, and take some of my fear.

Keep going, a voice calls. His.

Something brushes my ankle, gently, and I am afraid to do what he wants. Instinct forces me back a step, and it's only then that I realize my mistake. I hesitated, and as that thought occurs, something wraps around my leg, hard, and jerks me down, and I'm no longer dry and warm, but freezing. Water spills into my mouth, stealing my breath. I kick against the river's hold, my heart battering my chest, yet there's nothing but darkness. I struggle, sputter to the surface. Hazy faces of the people stare at me, in alarm, in disbelief. Nobody moves to save me, and I'm pulled under again.

The water itself is yanking me down. Drowning me. But he is there; I can feel him. He is the river, the one behind this.

Shut your eyes. It'll be so easy. So quick . . . A voice floats through the water. Faces emerge. Flashes of girls. Corpses. Flesh peeling back from bone, long hair floating in the water, delicate fingers reaching for me, and all of them, all wear dead flowers upon their heads. The Starling brides, or versions of them, their ghosts, have come to take me to him. I can hear their voices, low, buzzing, singing.

Our blood is the promise. The promise. We give to him forever.
Forever.
Forever.

All at once I know that I *need* to fight for my life, and I kick hard. My foot connects with something that feels like bone.

He only pulls more fiercely, and I go under. It hits me then that I'm going to drown. I'm going to freeze to death in this river. And the people are going to let me.

Flowers float around me as I struggle against the force pulling me down as I lurch up toward the surface. The desire to live presses me to fight, to flail harder, to wake up. As I break through the water, I gulp down a wild breath of air, and ice drives needles into my skin. Then something pulls my ankles violently. Icy water rushes into my mouth and nose, burning my lungs. This time my body won't move the way I need it to, and the pain pours through me, into my lungs. I'm aflame now.

Then nothing but the river, swallowing me. Turning me inside out.

His hard laugh echoing through the water.

My face is wet, is my first realization. Something is trickling on my forehead, something cold.

Then I feel a hand, gentle, brushing it away, warm fingers trailing down to my jaw, tucking my hair back around my ear. I lean into the hand, exhausted, in pain, reveling in the familiar touch and scent. Something sharp and clean yet wild, like pine needles, like the river.

My eyes shoot open, and I recoil.

Bear's eyes twinkle. "Hello, love. You slept for hours."

I'm lying in a bed, and he's holding me, wearing Bear's face now, Bear's body. *I'm not your love.* I think it but I don't dare say it. Not yet. Not until I know she's safe.

Instead I clear my burning throat and say, "Hello." My voice is scratchy.

I have to wonder, why did he come as Bear? To ease my nerves? Why would he care?

"I thought you were going to drown me," I tell him, trembling. I didn't realize just how scared I was until now.

"Oh that." His smile is malicious, unnatural on Bear's face. He wears a golden crown on that tousled, brownish-gold hair. "You were afraid to come in. You almost waded out, didn't you? I told you, you only had to walk in and I'd deliver you here, safe and warm."

"I'm sorry." I sit up. Squeeze my hands into my damp dress. I would have stayed dry, if I hadn't fought, I know.

"Welcome to my home. Or should I say, welcome back." He sweeps his arms out, and shadows cross his face. There are thick earth walls all around us. There's no sign of the faux kitchen. It was replaced with this . . . place. This *lair.* Below us, wet earth; above us, more ground, roots hanging; water dripping, forming icicles as sharp as knitting needles. A gigantic mirror leaning against one earthen wall. An ornate wooden bed, piled with snowy white blankets spattered with mud. A stack of gold coins is on the ground in the corner, an old-fashioned sword beside it, and hung on one chair is an antique buttoned jacket so threadbare that it looks like I could blow it to dust with half a breath. The scent of smoke and sulfur and cold earth envelops everything, even me.

It's freezing here, and although there's a fireplace, it is unlit.

There's no wind like above ground, but there's something so unbearably uncomfortable about this place it makes my teeth chatter. I shouldn't be here. No human should.

"You are beautiful," he says, helping me to stand. "The gown suits you."

He wears a fine shirt and trousers, fitted to his body, tailored by magic. He looks perfect.

As he looks at me, amused, he waves his hand, and the air flickers, heats. I look down, stroking the suddenly dry fabric of the dress, my dry hair, the soggy flowers in my crown perked up, lush. I thank him, and he tips his head, pleased, not only by my gratitude but by my appearance.

His expression is proud, satisfied. A cat that ate the cream.

"My mom?" I ask, desperate to see her. To know she's all right.

"Waiting back at the apartment for you, the real apartment," he assures me. "Safe and sound, as promised. I can be kind, Kit, my love."

But can you? I doubt it.

"How do I know you're telling the truth?" I ask, daring to question him. "Can you prove it?"

His eyes dig into mine. Half-amused, half-irritated. "The ring." He slides it onto my finger. "Turn the stone and think of your mother."

I do, pressing my need into the tiny rotation. Before me, a doorframe appears, and through the opening, I see Agatha's apartment, my mom asleep on the pink couch, throw tossed over her.

Relief surges through me at the sight of her, chest rising up and down, the flutter of her fingers.

"She will wake, soon," he promises. "Moments, even."

"Thank you, Jack." I purposefully don't call him "Bear."

He inclines his head, nodding. "We will say our vows here, and then you will be mine."

I bow my head and say, "Yes."

"Shall we dine first?"

"Whatever you like," I say, grateful for my mother's safety, and he flashes an indulgent smile. I answered correctly.

He wraps his arms around me, and the air changes. I choke out a gasp, looking up. He has strung roses from the dirt-packed ceiling, which might be pretty if they weren't rotting. If I reached my hand up, I could brush my fingertips against the decaying petals. His idea of romance, I suppose.

I keep my tone light. "Isn't that a little cliché?"

He throws back his head and laughs. It's Bear laughing, his dimple showing. "I'm happy to see you still have some fire. I thought the roses would please you. I only wish they were as perfect as before."

"But you'll fix them now?" I ask.

"I shall, since you've pleased me so," he says. He looks above us and reaches for a flower, pulls it from the earth, and it crumbles to dust between his fingers. "They may yet bloom as new by dawn," he adds with a bright smile.

"Thank you," I answer, trying not to sound so hollow. I almost wish there were witnesses; the horrible aloneness of this moment is crushing me. Bear's eyes are too warm. I force mine to stay open, to not look away from him, from the betrayal I can never un-see.

He lowers his arms and cages my waist with his hands. "Are you ready? Before we are bound with our words and hearts, I want to explain something."

I will never be ready. I blink back the fear and try to smile. It was bad enough last time when he was Jack. I can't imagine what it will be like, having Bear hurt me.

Nervously I nod, digging my hands into my skirts just to keep them from trembling. "Okay," I say. "I'm listening."

His mouth tugs up into a smile.

"Your hand," he murmurs, and holds his own out for me. An invitation.

I lace my fingers into his, dread filling my chest.

As petrified as I am, though, I'd rather lose myself. Rather turn myself into what Jack wants. Rather die than have him kill another. The struggle to escape last night now seems like such a pathetic attempt. Where exactly did I think I was going, and how did I think I'd face myself if I succeeded?

Jack takes my other hand, palm up, and without lifting his eyes from mine, presses his mouth there, gently, almost gentlemanly. I stare at his curls, bent over the blue veins of my wrist, his lips on my skin.

I manage to shake my head as he touches the black ring on my finger. I stare at it, the way it glints in the candlelit lair.

"It was for her," he explains, turning my hand over, stroking the ring with one finger. "She would turn it as she stood, and find a way to me, whenever she needed. You are welcome to use it whenever you like, now. No one else figured out what it was, and so I shall let you have the use of it. You simply must imagine where you want to go, and you will be there. The intention, obviously, is to use it for me. Please do not abuse it."

"I won't," I say, looking away from his eyes. "Thank you."

"You're welcome, Kit." Such a tender voice, such warmth. Such lies. Jack goes on, "Now that you're mine. Almost mine. We have not quite finished. There will be words said, blood shed, but not yet." At my quizzical look, he softly adds, "First a kiss, my love. A true one."

Then his lips are on mine, his hands tight around my waist. A million thoughts in my head in a moment, or maybe time stills. Maybe it stops altogether. He waits for me to move toward him. Maybe that's why I do.

I kiss him fiercely, pressing everything into him. Taking, taking, giving as his tongue swirls with mine in a dark dance. I devour him, imagining how he loved Franny, how he may have killed her. Imagining people starving and feasting upon each other. Sabelle's hands on my face, my dad, my mom, Agatha. I think about all the Starling girls and women, bent over the diary, writing their secrets and fears, denying them, swallowing them down and birthing them anew in a river of blood. The words in the tiles on the floor of the flower shop. *Our blood is the promise.* Blood. It hits me then. It's a promise *I* never made.

With a gasp, steadying myself, I pull away, the words echoing: *We give him forever.*

Give.

Could it be that simple?

Could it be that easy?

Didn't Juliet say so herself? *I think it's not so much that he's all that powerful or the contract is all that ironclad. I think sometimes we let him do it.*

We've let him. Well, *I* won't let him. I won't give him anything.

I stare up at his face, at the dying roses above us, everything finally connecting in a way that makes perfect sense. I'm a Starling; the blood of Franny Black Starling runs through my veins. She could do things. Our blood is the answer—but it's not just the blood. It's our will. Starlings have the potential for magic. Don't we?

"Stop," I say, chest heaving, breaking out of his arms.

He raises his brow as he watches me casually move over to the bed. I need to put space between us, but I make it look like I'm frazzled over the kiss.

"Where are you going, my love?" His voice is amused.

"I'm not your love." I finally say it, my body shaking.

His smile fades, though his tone remains mild. "Be careful, Kit. I do not wish to quarrel with you. We need to finish the ceremony."

"I'm not going to make a vow to you."

I glance down at Franny's ring glittering on my finger, the sudden courage in me growing. There's more there, too, that drives my bravery. Memories. The click-clack of my dad typing on his computer on Saturday mornings, my mom making pancakes on the sizzling griddle, slick with butter. Our old Lab Lulu in my dad's lap, and her fur under my little hand. Tulips sagging in the slim brass vase my parents got for their wedding. Laughing so hard with Brenna that we peed our pants in my backyard last summer. Underdogs on my swing over the years, with strong, warm hands pushing me toward the sky. As if I were a real bird.

As if I were a real bird. As if I could fly away from my destiny.

And I think I can.

His laugh is sharp. He takes a step nearer the bed, and I retreat.

"Consider it a spell instead." My voice rings clear now. I slide my hand under my skirts and lift the dagger from the garter. "Consider it the undoing of one."

"Where did you get that?" His face drains of color as he stares at the blade I raise. "That is her dagger."

Yes, it was. But it's mine now.

Franny's blood began this nightmare of a legacy, and mine will end it.

All those years that nobody questioned this rotten contract. If I don't, I have nothing.

I take the sharp edge of the dagger and push it against my arm, just beneath the lace of my gown. My skin burns as I pierce it, and I wince as crimson blooms from the wound. "This is Franny's blood that runs through me," I say.

His face twists. He's enraged, but as he lunges forward, he stumbles to his knees.

"It is Celine's, and Sylvie's. It is Maria's blood and Aurora's." My voice doesn't waver as I continue, speaking the name of each Starling girl who sacrificed her life, as many as I can remember.

With each name I call, he goes paler, and his form begins to flicker in and out of focus, from Bear to Jack to a beast to another beast to nothing and back again. I don't know what

I'm doing exactly, or how I'm doing it, but it's working. I go on as the blood drips down my arm. I speak each lost girl's name, and my heart breaks as I think of each, wandering into the river with a wreath of flowers on her head. And the monster before me is immobile as my strength and resolve grow. As I end the promise Franny made, and turn it into something new.

"It is Alice's. June's. Amy's. It is Agatha's blood," I say, lifting my chin, tears raining down my cheeks. Bear tries to climb to his feet, to get to me, but he can't. I stare into his pained face, flickering. In and out, in and out. This time I step forward, closer to him.

I'm not afraid anymore, or maybe I am, but it doesn't matter.

"It is Juliet's blood," I scream. "It is Starling blood. It is mine! And I didn't promise to give it to you."

As I stand before him, looking down, I say, "As the final Starling, I end the contract you made with my blood. I don't give you my body, or my pain, or my heart. You won't have any one of us ever again. I won't *let* you!"

There's a ripping apart, a fracture in the air, a scream torn from a throat, maybe mine. With the last of my words, then with one terrible cry, I plunge the knife into his chest as hard as I can. Blood dribbles from Bear's mouth, the blade to the hilt in his body, the link between us destroyed. He drops to the ground, and I sink down next to him, the roses hanging overhead. They crumble to dust, falling, settling on my skin.

I look at him, but he is barely here, turning grotesque before me. A half image of fur and teeth and bone, a skull flashing in and out, a hazy nightmare. But his amber eyes still shine.

"You remind me so much of her." He chokes on his own blood, dripping blackish red. He reaches for my hand.

I let him take it, I don't know why.

We stare into each other's eyes. For one brief second, he is still Bear.

I watch him transform, his perfect hand turning to nothing in mine, a shimmer of darkness drifting from me on the air, floating away like smoke. It dissipates before it even reaches the dirt walls. I close my eyes a second, exhaling like I never have before.

He's gone.

As the thought floats into my awareness, the earth around me begins to quake, and dirt rains down from above. Fear freezes me for a moment as I realize. The lair is collapsing. I'll be trapped. I'll die here, underground, or the water will rush in and I really will drown this time.

My mouth is closed. It's the river that is screaming.

CHAPTER TWENTY-FOUR

As the earth pours down on me, I remember—the ring. Covered in blood and dirt, it's still on my hand. I twist the stone a quarter turn and think of Agatha's apartment and my mom, praying the magic of the ring still works. I hear my mom's voice.

The last thing I know is her hands tugging me against her chest and the feeling of being safe. Then, nothing.

When I come to, my mother is still holding me.

"Kit!" she cries, pulling me closer to her. "How did you get here? What are you wearing? And you're bleeding! You're hurt—"

"Mom." I can only sob, gripping her to me so hard that I think I might hurt her. When I finally let go, I wipe my face. Then I fling the crown off my head and begin to tell her everything—about Agatha and Rosemont. And as I do, recognition flickers in her eyes.

When I say the name "Sabelle," she appears. Stepping from the shadows. Coming to my side. I find myself without words as I look at her face, then glance at my mom. She stares at Sabelle, hard, first in shock at *how* she appeared, just like *that*. Then with her forehead wrinkling, like she recognizes her.

"This is my . . . friend," I finally say. The word fits well, actually.

My mom buries her face into her palms. "I remember," she breathes. "I had that nightmare . . ." She starts, looking back up, wide-eyed. "I had a nightmare of you, a beast hurting you in some cold, dark place."

I swallow. And I keep listening.

"I got up then, and made a cup of tea, but when I'd finished, I heard something in Agatha's room. I went in to check on her, and there was someone in there with her, standing behind her. He had his hands around her throat, and she was crying. They both looked at me then. That's the last thing I remember."

She pulls me to her again and hugs me harder than before. I tell her everything that happened, and we cry ourselves out. I don't know how the body doesn't run out of tears. Especially when we talk about how I'm still afraid I'll lose her. That she'll take herself away from me, like he did. More tears, and her hands on my face. "You don't have to put on a brave face anymore, Kit. You don't have to save me or hide things from me. I'm the parent, and I'm not going to leave you."

"I know."

"We'll be okay. The pain over Dad may not ever get smaller, but it will get easier in some ways. I think it would be good if we both talked to someone. What do you say to therapy?"

I consider it, the benefits. "I say, 'Okay. I'm in.'"

"Although—" she adds. "We probably should keep the whole Rosemont/monster thing to ourselves."

I laugh with her. It hurts, but life goes on, even after death, even after trauma.

I can't believe it's over. The legacy ends with me. I turn the ring's stone, just to check, and it won't budge anymore. There's no magic left, because there's nothing of Jack left. The bond is destroyed.

My mom gives me another big hug and then stands. "Let's get going, love. Okay?"

"More than okay," I answer. Then I hesitate. "It will be fine, right?" I ask my mom uncertainly. "Agatha—"

"Shh. I'll have it taken care of. But first, let's wash this dirt and blood off us." She looks meaningfully at me, at Sabelle, who is leaning against the wall. My mom squeezes my hand once and disappears into the hallway, leaving us alone.

When the shower starts, Sabelle comes to stand before me, pulling me from the couch. But she drops her hands as soon as I rise.

"It's over," she says.

"Can you go somewhere else?" I ask, searching her eyes, knowing as I say it that even if she could, she wouldn't. "You can leave Rosemont now that Jack's gone, can't you?"

"I believe so," she says, thoughtful quirk to her mouth. "But I belong here."

"There are other places . . ." I remember what Agatha once told me. "Other places for ones like you. And I thought you hated Rosemont."

"I hate what it has become," she says without hesitation. "I'm going to undo that, though."

The fire in her gaze spurs me to take her hands back in mine, serious. "Whatever you're going to do, please just make sure people don't get hurt. They've been through enough. There are still good people here, friends, who will be glad I won, that I'm leaving them behind."

Her eyes burn, but she nods. "I won't purposefully hurt anyone. But I can tell that the others are waking up."

I gulp. Just picturing them, pushing through the ground. "The whole town will be in danger," I say, making sure I understand. "Instead of Jack they'll have a dozen more—"

"Hundred," she interrupts. "At least. *Hundreds* more."

I gape at her, and she glances at me, holding back a half-tipped smile.

"It's not funny," I say, irritated. "You don't have to worry about the ones like you."

"Nor do you," she counters. "You did what you set out to do—kill him and release your mother and leave—and you'll be far away before they awaken enough to know they can leave the woods."

"What if—" I start.

But she shushes me. "It is no longer your concern, especially if people choose not to leave once they know. I cannot control what may happen."

"Yeah." Some people won't leave, I know that. No matter what.

We are quiet for a moment, and the time loosens. I'm going to miss this sharp-eyed monster girl. Her skin, her eyes, her tangled inky hair, that blue, blue dress, her visions, her sarcasm, the fire that consumed her. But she's right. She belongs here, and I don't.

I press her hand to my heart in appreciation. "Thank you. You saved me."

"We saved each other," she corrects me.

"You gave me the dagger."

"But you used it," she laughs, and she looks so beautiful that it almost hurts. "I hoped it would help you. Though, perhaps any knife would have done the same. The dagger wasn't magic. It was all you."

"Not really. I don't know how I was able to do it," I say, still in wonder.

"Don't you?" she asks, her head cocked. "The dagger was only a tool. You put something of yourself into what you did. I told you it had to be a Starling, though I was speculating. It probably didn't have to be blood. Bone, even hair might have done. But it was *yours*."

It takes me a moment to speak. She's right. I do know. "It was also deciding I wouldn't allow him to do this anymore. The intent."

"Those things are magic, then. Aren't they? In their own way?" She tips my chin up. Kisses me once on the cheek, chastely. Like a friend. Takes both my hands and squeezes. "Perhaps you'll see me again one day."

"Where?" My mouth tugs into half a smile. "In my dreams?"

"No." Sabelle's eyes are luminous. "In the shadows."

Then she slips her hands out of mine, blurs away into a dark corner of the room, and is gone.

My heart cracks a line as I stand alone in the living room, breathing this all in, exhaling it out.

I don't bother showering, as filthy as I am. Any motel shower along the way will do, but I do slip out of the dress, and leave it on the floor of the guest room. Someone will find it someday. Maybe add it back to the museum, if they even want to keep it now that Starlings won't be here. I throw on a grotty old T-shirt and sweats, grab some granola bars and shove them into my bag because I can't remember the last thing I ate. While my mom gets dressed, I dial Miles from Agatha's quiet kitchen, tell him, briefly, that I'm leaving town, and ask him to meet me at the shop. When I hang up, I stand there and look around. I miss Agatha. She liked to play poker. She was a collector, like me. She had great taste and she could lie without batting an eyelash. She cried alone. She had so many secrets. She also had many losses. People will mourn her, or pretend to. I'll miss her. She tried to save me, in the end.

I say a prayer for her and say goodbye. And then I turn into a thief. I'm never going to return to Rosemont, so this is my only chance. Without thought or reason, I take some of Agatha's books, the linen photo album along with my dad's letter, that creepy framed eyeball, her pearl necklace, one of her tea tins. I nestle the items among my things. It's all I have left of her, and of Rosemont. Except for the memories.

Except for the scar.

I'm running my fingertips along the healing wound on my neck when my mom appears in the hallway, dragging her big suitcase behind her to meet me where I stand. Her hair is wet, slicked back into a bun, her eyes tired. But she's here and I am here, and we are leaving.

"Ready?" she says, taking my hand.

"One stop, okay? Someone is expecting me. It will be quick."

"Okay." She kisses me on the cheek, hugs me hard. "Anything for you."

"Thanks, Mom," I say. I'd do anything for you, too.

*The streets are littered with dried wreaths, with greasy food wrap-*pers, stale popcorn. Somewhere someone is still playing music, though the dancers are all tucked away in bed now. But it's early. Rosemont is mostly asleep; the ones awake are still drunk from yesterday, or giddy with fatigue. They will dance and sing, kiss and laugh. They will celebrate without realizing what happened last night. Most of them anyway. Then they will celebrate tomorrow. They might wonder where I am at some point, but they'll assume I'm with Jack, still. Because who knows the full truth? Only me, my mom. And Sabelle.

Before I leave, I will warn two others about what is now loose in the woods, and they can warn the rest of the people.

My mom parks in front of the florist shop, and we hold hands walking in. The sun is barely streaking the horizon; the air is cold and fresh. It will be a beautiful day in Rosemont. But I won't wait to see it. We step through the unlocked door. They're waiting for me, Miles and Belinda, looks of surprise on their faces, but to their credit they don't question why I'm not still with Jack.

They greet my mom with kindness.

"Thank you for helping Kit while I was gone," she says. "I'm glad she had friends to look after her."

"We've been glad to know her," Belinda says with a warm smile. Silence settles around the room. A waiting silence.

I take a slow, deep breath then, and tell them the truth about what happened in the lair, a condensed, safer version of it. Jack is over and gone. The legacy has ended with me. There will be no more Crownings. But also, Jack will no longer protect the town.

They don't say anything for a long minute, as they take it all in.

Belinda chews her lip. "I almost can't believe it. We won't have to worry about Jack. I've been terrified of him since I was a little girl."

"He protected us," Miles says warily. "Or at least *did* until lately. I don't know how to feel about that protection being gone."

"I know. I don't think it's going to be safe here anymore," I say, voicing my fear. At my side, my mom takes my hand, gently squeezing, but remaining quiet.

"So, maybe we should leave," Belinda says, and by her half smile it seems like a joke. But then her face clears, the longer she stares at Miles. "I mean it. Maybe we *should* leave."

He nods slowly. "I . . . I've wanted to leave, even before the roses started dying. But there just never seemed like a good enough reason." His laugh is without humor. "Even with every-thing that happened here."

"Maybe—" I start, and cut myself off, wondering about things like contracts and binding and if somehow the people in this town were bound to stay here as well. But it doesn't seem helpful to tell them that. Instead I say, "I think you should pack your essentials and get the hell out of here. Like, tomorrow. Today, even."

They glance at each other.

"I mean it," I insist.

"I understand," Miles says. "We'll move on to the next adventure, right, B?"

She nods, with a grin. "I'm ready whenever you are."

He looks to me, his eyes shiny with tears, his smile fond and bittersweet. "I'm glad you stopped before you left."

"It felt wrong to just leave." I reach into my pocket and pull out my phone number. "I don't know if you guys want this . . . but I hope you'll be in touch."

"Yes, we will," Miles says as we all drift toward the door. "We'll stay in touch. But we'll miss you, Kit."

"I'll miss you, too," I say, my voice thick with emotion.

They hug me then with smiles, enfolding me in their kindred warmth. Belinda hands over a bag of cookies, her nails painted fire-engine red.

"They're from yesterday. I didn't have time to make any fresh, before I came here," she apologizes.

"Thank you." I hesitate, taking the bag, peering inside. I pull one out and take a bite. They're chocolate chip, but not the kind Bear brought over that day. They're different. I know he carefully manufactured every experience we had together, to trap me, to entice me, to disarm me.

"I have something for you, too." Miles smiles. "Flowers, of course."

I try not to wince. "Not roses, I hope."

He shakes his head, handing me a huge bouquet of dark purples, and soft lavenders, and white and green, wrapped carefully to survive the trip home. Not a rose in sight.

"Oh, how lovely," my mom says with a smile. Miles gives her a smile in return, silently accepting the praise with a nod of gratitude.

I blink away the tears, hesitating at the door. "I'm still worried for you both. For everyone."

"Us?" Belinda laughs lightly. "We'll be fine. We shall take the world by storm. As for you, kiddo, Starlings have done enough for Rosemont, including worry." Her eyes are firm as she looks at my mom, then back at me. "Both of you go on ahead and leave."

And we are. We're finally leaving.

I listen to the shop bell ring one last time as I step over the word near the door: "forever."

I catch my mom's smile as she puts the car in drive. We roll through the perfect downtown, past all its charming shops.

"Can you drive past the park?" I ask. As much as I want to get the hell out of Rosemont, I have one more thing I want to see. "To the right."

She gives me a questioning look but nods, turning at the end of the block.

We pass the park, and Sabelle is standing in front of the roses. As we drive by, I see that she's lighting the roses on fire. They were already dead, but she turns and she's smiling as they burn furiously. I lift my hand once, our eyes locked, and if this were a movie, my mom and I would pass her in slow motion, giving Sabelle and me extra seconds to silently say goodbye. *This is the last time I see you. This is the last time you see me. This is the last time.*

But the time moves normally, and Sabelle's smile burns bright, like the fire. She watches the car until my mom turns onto the main road. This time, we keep going. Resting my head against the seat, I hold the image of Sabelle's face as she set the roses on fire, the ghosts of them curling up into the bright sky, as blue as forget-me-nots.

I turn on the radio, and it actually comes in okay, as if Jack's very presence somehow was the thing interfering with the technology. I pull out my phone to check, and I smile when I see that I'm no longer roaming. Pentatonix sings "Hallelujah," which happens to be one of my favorites. It was my dad's, too. It's January second. A fresh year. A fresh start.

I don't know what it will look like, our new version of life, without him, with all this behind us. We don't know a lot. But now I know what I come from, who I am, and what I'm made of.

I watch the landscape fly by. My mind and heart grant me the image of my dad, faded, just on the other side of some veil. I almost feel the brush of his warm hand on my shoulder.

I reach into my bag, for the pages in there, and I rest my fingertips on them.

We went into the sapphire water with our pockets stuffed full of jewels, the story begins.

I can't presume to know exactly how he would have continued the story. But I don't need to know. I have my own story to write. I'm ready to let this one go. It wasn't my fault or my mom's or his, even. Especially not his. He loved me, he always will. He's not in pain any longer.

Just as we pass the Rosemont sign signaling our exit, my mom twines her hand into mine. I smile into her eyes and look down again.

The black stone ring glints on my finger. It fits me perfectly. I think I'll wear it forever.

ACKNOWLEDGMENTS

I count myself beyond lucky to have such an amazing editor. Krista Marino, thank you for your brilliant mind, for the way you pushed me to connect all those small points (and the big ones), and for politely ignoring how nerdy and nervous I was in those early days we started working together. It's been a dream making this story the story it was always meant to be—with your guidance.

Lydia Gregovic, you were a gem to work with. Thank you for your thoughtful insight and everything else! I cannot wait to read your book next year!

My wonderful agent, Juliana, what can I even say? Thank you for taking a chance on me, for knowing *Starlings* was special, even all those drafts ago. I am so grateful we did this together and I can't wait to see what we do next.

Thank you to everyone at Delacorte Press and RHCB who had a hand in working on this book: Tamar Schwartz, Colleen

Fellingham, Shameiza Ally, Michelle Crowe, Trisha Previte, Kelly McGauley, Barbara Marcus, Beverly Horowitz, Judith Haut, Mary McCue, and the RHCB Publicity & Marketing team.

Colin Verdi, the talented cover artist . . . I love everything you did here. Thank you!

An enormous heap of gratitude to my Book Besties: Cathie Armstrong, for all the agent research, Bianca Schwarz and Kelly Cain for reading early drafts and being so very encouraging, and Jamie McLachlan, who read multiple versions and gave me excellent feedback. I love you all.

Thank you to my Sixers and *especially* the core of us who've met almost every week since WWTS. I've loved our Wednesday night chats, from tuna salad to tears to Vampire Diaries to blue aliens. Jennie, I adore you; thanks for letting me tell you about my dreams. Amanda, you are so warm and I can't wait to hold your book in my hands. Anna, your stories are hilarious and I still think you should write a rom-com! Rachel, what can I say? You are an absolute rock star for helping me with that damn puzzle, and for being the best cheerleader. Lex, it's been lovely getting to know you.

Thank you to early beta readers and friends I love to pieces—Theresa, Lindsay. Melly, you haven't read (yet) but I so appreciate your support. Thanks to Madeline, and I meant what I said about you making this into a movie. Autumn, I can't wait to hug you one day and thank you in person for your unwavering support, guidance, and love for my stories, especially this one.

Thank you to friends who may not have been critique partners for this book, but who were encouraging along the way, cheering me on in DMs and sending hearts to my stories, always showing up in a way that means so much to me. I can't name you all, but a ton of you are writing friends from Writing with the Soul by the amazing Adrienne Young, and if you think I'm talking about you, you're correct.

Thank you to Pang for your thoughtful insight! And to Anastasia Hedrick for helping me with the whole geothermal pocket thing because I failed science miserably.

To my fellow #Tenacious23s—we did it! We are doing it! Huge thanks for support and congratulations on your own books coming out this year. And to the writers out there who are waiting for their own stories to be born, I'm sending you some of my own stubbornness and a lot of good vibes! Keep writing.

To some of my favorite authors, it means the world to me that you took the time out to read *Starlings* and had such kind things to say. Thank you. Thank you.

Thank you to the booksellers, librarians, and teachers, the Bookstagram community, and more. Your love of literature is such important work, and you truly inspire me.

Thank you to my beloved family, near and far. Especially my parents, and Melanie, the best sister in the world.

My love, who is my anchor in this world. I am so glad we have had lifetimes together.

And my children, my little monsters, my darling babies, my heart split in three. I hope you're proud of your mama, who wrote this book during many long hours at the computer while you ate mac 'n' cheese and watched silly shows and were so loud and rambunctious I had to wear headphones most of the time to get anything done. Thank you for bringing so much life to my life, so much color and feeling I often think I could burst into a million pieces. When you are very, very old and I am gone, I hope you will remember certain things about your mother. Like there were always fresh flowers on our table. Like I always had music playing. Like I wrote books that mattered to me, and hopefully to others. That I didn't give up. I hope you never do either. Dreams aren't always easy. But they are always, always worth reaching for.

ABOUT THE AUTHOR

Amanda Linsmeier has been a book nerd for as long as she can remember, and it is that great love of reading that led her to write her own stories. She lives in a small blue house surrounded by trees and cornfields, with her husband, their three wonderfully wild children, and, somehow, five pets.

amandalinsmeier.com